ANDY DAVIDSON

THE BOATMAN'S DAUGHTER

Andy Davidson holds an MFA in fiction from the University of Mississippi. His debut novel, *In the Valley of the Sun*, was nominated for the 2017 Bram Stoker Award for Superior Achievement in a First Novel, *This Is Horror*'s 2017 Novel of the Year, and the 2018 Edinburgh International Book Festival's First Book Award. Born and raised in Arkansas, he now makes his home in Georgia with his wife and a bunch of cats.

ALSO BY ANDY DAVIDSON
In the Valley of the Sun

THE BOATMAN'S DAUGHTER

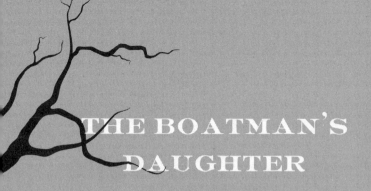

THE BOATMAN'S DAUGHTER

ANDY DAVIDSON

MCD × FSG ORIGINALS

FARRAR, STRAUS AND GIROUX   NEW YORK

MCD × FSG Originals
Farrar, Straus and Giroux
120 Broadway, New York 10271

Branch illustration (detail) by iStock.com/stevezmina1

Library of Congress Cataloging-in-Publication Data
Names: Davidson, Andy, 1978– author.
Title: The boatman's daughter : a novel / Andy Davidson.
Description: First edition. | New York : Farrar, Straus and Giroux, 2020. |
   Identifiers: LCCN 2019025806 | ISBN 9780374538552 (paperback)
Subjects: GSAFD: Horror fiction.
Classification: LCC PS3604.A9459 B63 2020 | DDC 813/.6—dc23
LC record available at https://lccn.loc.gov/2019025806

Designed by Abby Kagan

Our books may be purchased in bulk for promotional, educational,
or business use. Please contact your local bookseller or the Macmillan
Corporate and Premium Sales Department at 1-800-221-7945, extension 5442,
or by e-mail at MacmillanSpecialMarkets@macmillan.com.

www.fsgoriginals.com • www.fsgbooks.com
Follow us on Twitter, Facebook, and Instagram at @fsgoriginals

1 3 5 7 9 10 8 6 4 2

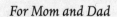
For Mom and Dad

. . . what's past is prologue . . .

—*The Tempest*

THE BOATMAN'S
DAUGHTER

✦

Now, Myshka, I will tell you the truth. Let my voice bury my words deep inside you. Before the sun sets, I will tell you secrets you have longed to know. For I was a girl once, too, and like you, I have known sorrows so great there are no words to account for them.

I

✦

In a Certain Kingdom,

in a Certain Land

◆

It was after midnight when the boatman and his daughter brought the witch out of Sabbath House and back onto the river. Old Iskra sat astride the johnboat's center plank, wearing a head scarf and a man's baggy britches damp with blood, their iron reek lost to the night-fragrant honeysuckle that bowered the banks of the Prosper. In her lap: a bread bowl, wide and deep and packed with dried eucalyptus sprigs and clods of red earth broken around a small, still form covered by a white pillowcase. The pillowcase, like the old woman's clothes, stained red.

They angled off-river at the mouth of a bayou and were soon enclosed by the teeming wall of night. Cries of owls, a roar of bullfrogs, the wet slopping of beaver among the stobs. Miranda Crabtree faced into the wind, lighting Hiram's way with the Eveready spot mounted on the bow. The spotlight shined on branches closing in, cypress skirts scraping like dry, bony fingers along the johnboat's hull. Spiders in the trees, their webs gleaming silver. A cottonmouth moccasin churning in the shallows. Miranda held up arms to guard her ears and cheeks from the branches, thinking of Alice down the rabbit hole, one small door opening upon another, and another, each door smaller than the last.

"Push through!" the old witch cried.

Branches screeching over metal, they did, the boatman breaking off fistfuls of dead cypress limbs until the boat slipped free onto the wide stage of a lake. Here, Hiram cut the motor and they drifted in a stump field, a preternatural silence descending over frog and cricket and owl, as if the little boat had somehow passed into the inner, sacred temple of the night itself.

To the west, purple lightning rolled thunderless in the cage of the sky.

In the water were the twisted, eerie shapes of deadfalls. They broke the surface like coffins bobbing in flooded graves.

"What is this place?" Miranda asked, angling her light all around.

But no one answered.

Ahead, a wide muddy bank stretched before a stand of trees, tall and close, and when the boat had nosed to a stop in the silt, the old witch got up with a pop of bones, stepped over the side, and staggered off along the path of the light, bowl in her arms. Her shadow long and reaching.

Hiram brought up a shotgun and a smaller flashlight from behind the stern seat. Miranda knew the double-barrel to be her grandfather's, the only gun Hiram had ever owned. She had never seen him fire it. They were bowhunters, the Crabtrees. Always had been.

"She needs me to go with her," he said. "You stay put."

"But—"

He stepped out of the boat into the mud and came around to the bow, where Miranda could see his face in the light. Long and narrow, sadness in his very bones, it seemed, the first touches of gray at his temples. Drops of moisture swirled thick in the light between them.

"Stay," he said. "The light will guide us back."

He took her chin in hand and brushed her cheek with his knuckles and told her he loved her. This frightened Miranda, for these were not words Hiram Crabtree often said. They struck her now like a kind of incantation against something, some evil he had yet to fathom. He kissed the back of her hand, beard rough against her skin. He said he would be back. He promised. "Leave that light shining," he said, and then he left her, following the witch's humped form into the trees. Their deep tracks welling up with water, as if the land itself were erasing them.

The spring night grew hushed save for the the far-off mutter of the coming storm, which had been threatening since twilight, black clouds like a fleet of warships making ready to cannonade the land with fire, water, wind, and ice.

Hours before, when Hiram woke her, Miranda had been dreaming of stumbling through woods and brambles onto a path that brought her out of the trees and into a clearing, where the land sloped up to a hilltop draped in flowering kudzu, little white blossoms aglow in the moonlight. Cradled in her arms, a black bullhead catfish she had only just pulled slick and dead from the bayou. Atop the hill: the witch's cabin on stilts, one yellow flame burning in a window. Miranda went up the crooked, red-mud path, up the wide board steps of the porch, and into the cabin, where the old witch stood waiting. She dropped the fish in the old woman's bread bowl and the witch took her filleting knife from her apron and slit the fish's belly. Miranda put her thumbs in the fish's gills to lift it and the innards slopped out in a purple heap. The old witch slung the guts into her boxwood stove, where they hissed and popped in the fire, and the dead fish heaved in Miranda's hands, came alive, began to scream. It screamed with the voice of a child.

Then Hiram's hand on her shoulder, shaking her.

Now, in the johnboat, she was waiting. Chin in hand, elbow on her knee, just as she had sat waiting earlier that night on the porch steps of Sabbath House. They had fetched the witch from her cabin on the bayou, and from there upriver to that ugly, paintlorn manse.

The front door of the plantation house stood open to let in the cool, blustery air. Last fall's leaves skittered over the boards like giant palmetto bugs as, inside, the witch went about her ancient trade behind a shut bedroom door. Across the gravel lane, Hiram stood in the bald, root-gnarled yard of a low shotgun house, talking softly to a man who was not quite five feet tall. The little man listened intently, head down, hands in his pockets. Windows of the other five shacks that stood beneath the trees were lit, a few men smoking anxiously between the clapboard dwellings, just beyond the reach of their own bare-bulb porch lights. Vague, grown-up shapes to Miranda.

Within the manse, a woman screamed, freezing every soul who heard.

Another scream: the wail of something deep and true torn loose, lost to the dark.

Hiram and the dwarf went charging past Miranda into the foyer, only to halt in shock at the foot of the stairs. Miranda pushed between them and saw an old man, all legs and elbows in black suit pants and a bloody white shirt, stagger out of the bedroom to sit like a broken toy at the top of the stairs. He clutched in his hands an object, something Miranda could not see, forearms red with blood up to his cuffs, which were rolled at the elbows. Miranda felt her father's hand on her shoulder, and when she looked up she saw Hiram's face gone pale as chalk. The little man to her right was stout and strong, but she glimpsed it on his face, too: horror.

The witch came solemnly out of the bedroom. Carrying the bread bowl. She passed the old man on the stairs, whose eyes never strayed from whatever faraway place they had fixed.

Blood dripping on the boards between his scuffed wing tip shoes.

Hiram pushed Miranda toward the front door, and she glimpsed, off the foyer in the downstairs parlor, a man sitting on an antique sofa. He was young, slim, handsome, a lit cigarette between full lips and a glass of amber liquid in hand. He wore a gun, a badge.

He winked a cornflower-blue eye as Miranda scooted past.

Now, in the johnboat. Waiting still, picking at a scab on her bare knee.

Thunder boomed, closer.

Straight ahead, a white whooping crane stepped out of the trees into the Eveready's beam. It stood in the mud and seemed to glow, stark and bright and otherworldly against the black of the swamp. Miranda watched it, and it watched her. The spotlight's beam like a tether between two worlds, Miranda's and the bird's. Something preternatural crept up her spine, raised gooseflesh on her arms.

A slow, rolling rumble that wasn't thunder came out of the trees, and the crane launched itself into the dark.

The water in Hiram's bootprints rippled, and Miranda felt the aluminum boat shudder.

The distant trees swayed in their tops, though the air was heavy and still.

Miranda's heart pounding in her chest.

Then, deep within the woods: a gunshot.

It cracked the night in two.

A second shot followed, reverberating huge and canyon-like.

Miranda drew a single breath, then leaped from the boat. The mud yanked her down, but she struggled up and ran for the trees, forgetting that the Eveready at the bow shone only so far. In the woods, darkness reared up and closed her between its palms. She skidded to a halt.

Called for Hiram. Listened.

Called again.

Heart racing, blood pounding, shore and spotlight at her back, she ran.

Lightning flashed at close intervals, lit the trees bright as day.

She ran on, calling out until Hiram's name was no longer a word, just a raw, ragged sound. She struck a tree, bounced, came up hard against another, and there she hung against the rough bark, gasping.

More lightning, and in that staccato flash, the land sloped down to a maze of saw palms wrapped in shreds of mist. Beyond the maze, the undergrowth rose up in a tangled, briar-thick wall, impenetrable. Great thorny vines, woven tight as a bird's nest.

Shining deep within that nest, like a string she had followed from boat to forest, was the faint orange beam of a flashlight. Fixed and slanting across the ground. All but swallowed by the darkness.

Miranda staggered into the saw palm maze, blades nicking her bare arms and legs. She felt the wisp of orb weavers against her cheeks, webs enshrouding her as they broke against her, as if nature were clothing her in itself, preparing her for some arcane ritual. When the fronds grew too close, she went down on hands and knees and crawled in the moist earth, and the light ahead grew stronger, closer. When she finally reached the undergrowth, she saw a kind of tunnel through it, just large enough for a fox or a boar—or a girl. She pressed her belly to the ground and worked elbows and hips and legs to worm through the thick tangle, aware a sound was coming out of her, some primal grunt that made her think she might vomit up the whole of her insides and there, in the sticky pink folds of stomach, would be a pile of stones, the source of this grunting, clacking noise. Finally, she came out where Hiram's flashlight lay bereft in a clump of moss and pale, fleshy toadstools.

"Daddy," she was gasping, "Daddy."

The glass of the lens and the blue plastic housing crawled with bugs.

Covered in mud and spider silk and tiny rivulets of blood, the squished remnants of a green-backed orb weaver stuck like a barrette in her dark hair, Miranda took up the light and got to her feet. She called again for Hiram, sweeping the beam over bare, bone-white trees, like great spears hurled down into the earth. Clumps of marshy reeds rising out of black pools that sheened in the light like oil. Narrow, mossy strips of earth among the pools.

And something else, too, glimpsed in the lightning, just beyond the trees.

Miranda went carefully alongside one of the pools that branched into a stream, black and thick. Moss along the bank festooned with brown toadstools and odd, star-shaped plants she had never seen the like of in all her trips hunting, fishing, trapping with Hiram. Sticks and clumps of bark were lodged in the stream and blackened, and at what appeared to be the widest, deepest point, her light caught the shape of something large and half submerged on its side. Brown feathers speckled black. An owl.

The stream opened out into a kind of moat that circled

a great wide clearing, and at the center of the clearing was the thing she had glimpsed in the lightning. A shape, huge and dark and shrouded in mist. Peering up at it, Miranda saw what looked like a head, two great horns, and two long ragged limbs ending in crooked fingers. She almost cried out, even took a step back. Then realized, in the rapid shutter of the lightning, that it was only a shelf of rock, atop it a tree, thick and twisted and dead, its trunk canting out at an angle that should have sent it tumbling from the ledge into the muck below.

A bark-skinned log bridged the black moat that encircled the rock. Miranda crossed it, balancing as she went. Sweat soaked through her shirt, her underwear. The earth beyond the moat was spongy, soft, rich. She felt it sinking underfoot with every step. She went through clumps of reeds and grass and played her light up at the rock as she came into its shadow and saw a long branch reaching like an arm from the tree, and from this arm a thick vine dropped straight down like a plumb line into a mound of freshly turned black earth, at its center a hole, deep and dark. The opening big and wide as a tractor wheel.

Among a stand of thin brown reeds at the base of the mound: the old witch's bread bowl, drawn in blood, overturned. A pillowcase in the dirt.

Miranda heard a snap in the dark, a squelch from near the rock.

Eyes were on her, she could feel them.

Bugs crawled over Hiram's light.

Her voice small and swallowed by the night: "Daddy?"

She played the light over the distant rock, its cold surface shining back, a tangle of fat roots and vines like a fall of wet hair. Her beam caught something in the mud, a glint of brass. She went to it, bent, and plucked up the red wax casing of a shotgun shell. She touched it to her nose, smelled the acrid scent of gunpowder still fresh on it. She knocked bugs from the light and cast about for Hiram's blood, a second shell, some track or sign.

Nothing.

She pushed the shell into the pocket of her shorts.

A rustling, in the clump of grass near her feet.

Miranda swung the light.

Something round and red and raw lay in the moss, not far from the upended bowl. At first Miranda didn't recognize it. Slicked with gore, more like a skinned rabbit than a baby. Its flesh a lifeless gray. She played the beam over arms and legs. They were mottled, rough and scaled, a long white worm of umbilicus twisted beneath it. Leaves clinging to a head of dark hair.

Its belly heaved. Its mouth opened.

For an instant, she did not move. Then she ran to it, dropped on her knees beside it.

Below its chin, a wide slit bubbled fresh bright blood like a second mouth as the baby gulped and sucked air.

She saw the pillowcase among the reeds and stooped for it, not looking where she was stepping. She splashed into a shallow pool of black liquid, thick and warm. It flooded her shoe, soaked her sock. Miranda gasped as her foot began to tingle, then to burn. Working quickly, ignoring her foot, she turned the pillowcase inside out and used a clean edge to press the wound at the baby's throat. But now it seemed it was not a wound at all, for the blood wiped free and the flesh there, beneath the jaw, was whole.

Had she imagined it? Some trick of shadow and gore?

She wiped her hand on her shorts, snakes of adrenaline still in her fingers as she worked her thumb into the baby's old-man palm and the digits parted. Between each digit was a thin membrane of skin, purple veins alight in the glow of Hiram's flashlight.

Webbed—

A sudden rustle from the reeds where she'd found the pillowcase.

A whiplike blur, pink tissue and fang.

She felt the sound: a tenpenny nail punching flesh.

Shocked, she fell back on her haunches. Barely caught a glimpse of it, fat and long, the color of mud. A cottonmouth, corkscrewing away.

. . . snake-bit, oh, oh, Daddy, no . . .

. . . she grabbed the flashlight, shined it on her left forearm, saw the wound welling blood, the flesh already puffing . . .

. . . stay calm, keep your heart rate down, the boat, the baby . . .

One last clamor of thunder and the rain began to fall. Big fat drops, cold and stunning.

Oh, oh no, Daddy, I'm sorry . . .

Miranda staggered to her feet, picking up the baby in her right arm, holding the flashlight with her left, right foot gone numb from the sludge that slicked it, and set off back in the direction she had come.

At the tunnel she fell to her knees, heart racing, sluicing venom, head fuzzy.

The flashlight went tumbling. Lost.

Crawling now, pushing through, slow, so slow, the numbness in her left arm reaching her shoulder, the tingling in her foot inching higher, into calf and thigh, her whole body assaulted, long thorns snagging her shirt and hair, and all the while the baby's heart hammering against her own, a fish odor wafting up.

Upright again, lurching—

Left arm tight against her side, stumbling, sharp fronds slicing, right leg numb from the hip down now, oily black sludge burning skin—

She fell.

She lay on her back and the rain pelted her face, ran beneath her in tiny rivers.

The fingers of her left hand swollen thick as corks.

The baby lay at her small, girl's breast. Alive but weak.

You are going to die tonight, Miranda Crabtree thought, staring up at the dark boughs of the trees, where the lightning made jagged shapes and turned the trees into devils come to minister. *This is your death.*

She had a sudden urge to taste the black licorice they kept in jars to sell. Catfish bait, the old-timers who came to the mercantile called it.

Oh, Daddy, where are you, I am sorry, Daddy, so sorry I was not clever . . .

The rain was hard and cold and numbing.

Then, from the dark recesses of the trees behind her, a terrible rumble, the boughs overhead thrashing. From the forest all around a cracking, a *rending*, as trees tore free from the earth and hurled themselves to the ground, and a wind blasted the cold rain sideways so that it seemed the breath of a huge thing was blowing over Miranda, and with the wind came a bright piney scent of fresh resin that stung her nostrils, and yes, something massive, something dark and horned and snarling and impossible, emerging now from the trees—

Not real, it's not real

—to lift her up in its terrible, rough-bark hand, entwining vines around arm and waist and leg, setting her afoot and nudging her over wet ground, stomach turning, hair wet against her scalp, and a fever burning in her arm and head.

Feeling had returned to her leg, she realized, the burning from the black sludge subsided, so she staggered off, soaked through, the baby against her breast chilled and silent.

Eventually there was a light, a pinhole in the darkness, and at first she thought it was the light to bring her over to another land, to the place her mother, Cora Crabtree, had gone long ago, when Miranda was only four. But it was not. She looked around and saw she stood mired in the muddy shore, where her footprints, like Hiram's, like the old witch's, were filled with water and led back to the place where the johnboat was lodged in the mud, Eveready spot still shining from the bow.

To guide us back.

But she saw no boatman in the lightning, no witch in its glare, and her left arm was hot and hard like a length of stovewood despite the cold, cold rain. She spoke her father's name. A whimper. Tears. Retching. Vomit. She collapsed in the mud, lay over on her back and let the baby rest atop her, right hand cupped around its weakly pulsing fontanel.

Out of the dark, into the weak beam of the boat light, a stooped shape came, small and hunched and peering down. Smooth chin and black eyes glittering within a head scarf. In one hand, Hiram Crabtree's shotgun, in the other an empty, bloody bread bowl.

Thunder, the whole world booming.

I'm only eleven, Miranda thought, fading. *I don't want to die—*

She felt the baby's weight against her, its faint warmth a promise.

She closed her eyes. Darkness took her.

The storm poured down ruin upon the land. Indeed, it was a storm the people of Nash County, Arkansas, would remember for years to come. It raged like a thing alive. On the outskirts of the defunct sawmill town of Mylan, the painted women of the Pink Motel stood watching the rain like forgotten sentries from their open doorways, the night's business washed away. They smoked cigarettes and hugged themselves as hailstones broke like bullets against the weed-split parking lot. The older women turned away, shut their doors, drew curtains. The young remained watchful, restless, eyes fixed, perhaps, on the position of some faraway star they had long looked to, now obscured by the storm. Miles south, where the land became a warren of gravel roads twisting back upon themselves, where the sandy banks of the Prosper gave way to stumps and sloughs, bottom dwellers came out onto the porches of shanties, long-limbed men in overalls and rail-thin women in cotton shifts. Children not clothed at all. They watched the rain pour from the eaves of their tin roofs to wear away the mud below and saw in this the promise of their own slow annihilation, their fates tied inextricably to the land they or some long-lost forebear had claimed.

And finally, along the river's edge, the congregants of Sabbath House, numbering no more than a dozen souls, this clutch of ragged youth sheltering not from the raging heavens but from the terror that was their mad, lost preacher Billy Cotton, who even now sat soaked in the blood of his dead wife and child in the old manse across the lane. Their numbers ever dwindling since the madness had first bloomed in the old man years past, they huddled in the little row of shotgun houses as the wind howled and pine branches cracked and fell to lodge like unexploded bombs in the earth. They prayed, some of them. Others wept. Come the morning, surely they would all be gone.

Inside the manse, the old preacher sat unmoving on the stairs, even as a great oak bent and crashed into the western wall, shattering glass and stoving in the copper-sheeted roof. Billy Cotton's mouth was dry, his tongue like sandpaper. His heart ticked steady as a clock. The object in his bloody hands—what the boatman's curious daughter had not seen—was a pearl-inlaid straight razor, closed. Outside, the wind roared like a great cyclone come to funnel the old preacher up and away, and now as the water began to strike him he looked up through the hole at the sky above and saw lightning crack like God's own judgment of his sins. And so he stood and went down the steps with his razor in hand, down the gravel lane and out onto the rickety dock that jutted over the stagnant water that flowed off the Prosper, where the boatman had brought the witch to deliver his child, and the child had been a monster, an abomination Cotton had held aloft by the ankle to show it to the twisted, pain-ravaged face of its mother, who would have loved it had she lived, because how could she not, this woman he had once given his heart to, whose pity and voice had moved mountains, and so the razor flashed in the gleaming light from the bedside lamp, and the old witch watched him draw it sharply, quickly. And did nothing, because she knew, as he did, that it was monstrous, this thing, this child that was not a child. And now, here, at the end of the dock, he closed up the razor that had been his since the days of his youth in a Galveston orphanage and hurled it into the water and fell to his knees and began to weep, great racking sobs, and soon he lay prostrate, bereft, a wailing banshee slicked in blood and rain, and after a while he curled up on his side and slept there on the boards, and soon the storm abated, and the air grew fresh and cool, and the dark rose up in a chorus of frog song.

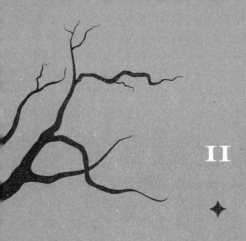

II

✦

First Run

UPRIVER

Cook hunkered at the bottom of the ramp, let his fingers play in the slow-moving Texas water. Downstream, just beyond where the river became Arkansas, a train traversed a trestle bridge, tearing through the last lingering rag of night. He could almost read the graffiti on the boxcars. The sound of it put him in mind of an old song, something about a baby in a suitcase, thrown from a train, the woman who raised it. In forty-nine years of life, Cook had never ridden a train, and the woman who had raised him was long dead. He scratched his beard. Put his fingers back in the moving water, liked the feel of it flowing on, the river indifferent to his presence. The world needed nothing of him to keep on spinning.

He checked his watch: 5:12 a.m.

The train had been gone only a few minutes when he heard, downriver, the Crabtree girl's boat.

He trudged back up the short ramp, over corrugated and broken concrete, to where his Shovelhead was parked.

The road leading into the clearing was old gravel, long dis-
used and grown over with Bahia grass. On a patch of ground
where the grass was worn were the long-ashed bones of a
fire. The woods beyond the clearing dark yet, the only light
a blue mercury-vapor lamp shining at the edge of the trees.
Cook took two longnecks from his saddlebag and popped
each with a bottle opener on his key chain. Down the ramp,
he saw her, rounding the bend in her Alumacraft, the trestle
long and dark above. Cook lifted a hand, and she raised her
own. She pointed at the old flat barge tethered along the
bank, just up from the ramp. He walked down to it, through
shin-high weeds, toes of his boots getting damp with dew.

The barge had been there as long as Cook could remember, rotting but never sinking. Parts strewn across the deck
as if the vessel were mid-repairs when abandoned: a rusted
inboard engine, gaskets, water pump and solenoid, all beyond good use.

The girl tied the Alumacraft to a starboard cleat.

Cook waited, holding the beers in one hand behind his
back, as if they were flowers.

She bent to pick up her blue Igloo cooler and was about to
board the barge when she saw his hand, hidden. She tensed.
He held out the beers, waggled the bottles. She gave him a
look and set her Igloo onto the barge and came aboard.

They sat cross-legged against the wheelhouse with its
busted windows and graffitied walls, drinking, listening to
the slow current of the Prosper, the distant whir of Whitman Dam four miles upriver. Beyond the dam the lake, and
beyond the lake a hundred more miles of greenish brown
water running south from northeast Texas like a scar on

the land, cut eons ago when fossils were fish and the whole of the country was a Jurassic sea where great behemoths swam. Now, birdsong in the maples and oaks and beeches, the day coming alive.

Cook stole glances at the girl in the graying light. Her profile was sharp and long, like the rest of her, scattershot freckles across nose and cheeks, a few acne scars like slash marks across her chin. Her jaw was hard and set. Dark hair pulled back, tidy but unwashed. Her eyes a murky gray-green. She had cut things out of herself to survive on the river, as a man cuts free a hook barbed deep in his flesh. There were words for what she did not lack: grit, mettle. What it took to carve up an animal, to cut through bone and strip skin and scoop viscera with bare hands, to wipe away sweat and leave behind a streak of blood. She did not lack these things.

She'd see it coming, surely.

The end.

Perhaps already had.

She caught him watching her. Fidgeted, then finished her beer in three long swallows and tossed the bottle over her shoulder, through the broken wheelhouse window. The bottle clipped a shard of glass and the sound of it breaking was loud and jarring. She got up, dusting the loose seat of her jeans, and made a business of ignoring Cook. Stepped back into her boat, checked her fuel. Picked up a metal can and tipped it into the motor's tank.

He drained his bottle, tossed it into the weeds along the shore, and tromped off the barge and up the ramp, back to the Shovelhead, where he fetched his bedroll with the money wrapped inside. By the time he returned, she was on the deck of the barge again, hands on the small of her back, stretching and staring at the distant silhouette of the railroad trestle. Cook took a knee by her cooler. He untied his roll and spread it on the deck. Tossed her the cash in a rolled lunch sack that lay at the bedroll's center like the meat of a nut. Her lips moved silently as she counted it. Cook peeled the duct tape from around the Igloo's lid and took out the dope and laid it all in a row on the roll: eight pint canning jars, stuffed full and sealed. These he rolled in a serape, then rolled the serape into the sleeping bag.

When he was done, the girl dropped the paper sack into the Igloo and closed it and made to pick up the cooler.

"Wait," Cook said. He reached out, took her wrist gently. She jerked back, studied him.

Searching, he knew, for some clue she had overlooked these last seven years, since the very first run. Any truth that could hurt or trap her. Cost her something she was not willing to pay. He held up his hands, palms out, an apology.

She just stood there, looking at him. Suspicious as a cat.

"I've got something else for you," he said.

Wanting to add: *It's all been leading here, ever night since the first, when you were fourteen and came piloting that big boat alone.*

He reached to the small of his back and brought out a pistol from his waistband.

She froze.

He flipped it, held it out flat on his palm like an offering between them.

"Smith and Wesson snub-nose," he said. "Good close up, if it comes to it."

She stared at him, unreadable as stone.

"Take it," he said. "Learn to use it. Bring it next time. Keep it out of sight, but you bring it, hear?"

"Why?" she said, making no move to take the gun.

He set the revolver down on the barge between them and cinched each end of his bedroll with a rawhide cord. "Because," he said quietly. "Maybe one day the man says do this one particular thing for the preacher and I say no, it ain't the kind of thing I do. I truck in dope, that's all. A man trucks in innocence—" He swallowed. Shook his head. "They put you under for things like that. If I'd known they'd ask me to, maybe I never would have . . ."

He lapsed, staring off into the river, which flowed quietly on, implacable.

"Gets you thinking," he said, more to himself now than her. "What are you willing to do? Where's the end of it?"

A muscle in her jaw ticked. She looked away.

Cook stood and shouldered his roll. He left the pistol on the rusted metal deck of the barge. "They'll ask you to make another run," he said. "Maybe one more, maybe two, I don't know. It's the last one you best worry about, savvy?"

The dawn had almost fully broken around them.

Her answer was barely audible, but Cook heard it. He always heard her, no matter how low she spoke, and she was in the habit of speaking very low.

"Crabtrees don't use guns," she said. She took the Igloo and hopped from the barge into her boat, leaving the pistol on the deck.

So he picked it up and did something that he had not done in all the time he had known her. He called her by name, and just speaking the word was enough to turn her head, if only for a moment, but it was a moment that would hang between them forever, so long as one of them lived. The morning mist curling up from the river like wood shavings. "Miranda," he called, and when she turned, he tossed her the gun.

She caught it, a reflex. Held it in both hands.

He thought about what he might say next. He wanted to tell her what knowing her had meant, how every few months he grew restless not seeing her and did not know why. That she was a mystery and a magic in his life. But words like these had never come easy to Cook, so instead he just said, "Tell that dwarf to watch out for himself. We was friends. I reckon he'll understand."

A shadow of something—doubt, fear—crossed her face. But it was gone, just as quickly as it came, and after it had passed she tossed the gun carelessly in the bottom of her boat. She whipped the Alumacraft around and aimed it back downriver, sparing him no look, no farewell, not even a wave. As if putting distance between them as quickly as possible might erase this new, mysterious line just drawn. A border to be crossed, and she, retreating from it.

Least she took the gun, Cook thought. *That's something.*

He walked back up the ramp and stood at the top, listening, until the sound of her motor had faded.

He had just kicked the Shovelhead to life—it snarled and spat—when a wave of loss so profound washed over him that he slumped on the seat. He looked one last time at the muddy river, where the only mystery left in his life had just disappeared, she, perhaps, fully ignorant of the empty wake her passing had left in his heart.

He rode his bike out of the woods and down the long, straight gravel road, which ran parallel to the train tracks for a time, a field of grain sorghum stretching away on the left in the amber light of morning.

Maybe I will buy myself a big silver Airstream and a truck to haul it, and I will head west. Way out west—

Ahead, where gravel met asphalt, a white Bronco was turned crosswise, and two men clad in T-shirts and denim stood outside it. One—short, pale-skinned, bald—looked down the road at Cook through a pair of binoculars. The other—huge and hulking—held a scoped rifle. Cook slowed, had just enough time to register what he was seeing, then caught the puff of smoke from the barrel. He never heard the shot, but he felt the impact in his chest, like a metal fist driving him backward, separating him from his bike, his daydreams, his tether to the world. He hit the gravel on his back and the bike skidded into the long grass.

Lying in the dirt, the taste of blood rising in his throat, he could not feel his body. He heard the pop of gravel under tire, heard doors slam.

A voice said, "Dope's no good. Got glass all in it."

He saw a giant dark shape blot out the golden sky. In its hand a blade, long and curved and wicked. A scythe.

"More where that came from," the giant said, and raised his blade.

Cook shut his eyes.

SABBATH HOUSE

The dwarf John Avery leaned against a piling at the end
of Sabbath Dock, head downcast, boots angled sideways
in the weary posture of a man turning life over between
his soles. He wore a pair of unwashed jeans and a wrinkled
plaid shirt, the tail of which was half untucked. A bird's nest
of hair held at bay with a crocheted sweatband of brown
and green. Hollows beneath his eyes and the stink of old pot
about him.

He stood waiting, watching the narrow waterway
ahead, a row of toothpick trees where white cranes perched
to catch the rising sun. Behind him, a ragged line of sweetgum and pine, and beyond these: the great wreck of Sabbath House, laid bare in the dawn. Squares of cardboard in
the still-broken western windows; shutters missing slats;
peeling white porch columns strangled by saw briars. The
roof a hodgepodge of tin nailed down over copper where
the storm, ten years past, had torn half of it free. All man-

ner of leaks inside, Avery knew. Cracking plaster and water stains and furring strips like ribs exposed. The weight of that house fell like a yoke across the dwarf's shoulders. Shoulders that had borne far more burdens than nature had given them width or strength to bear.

And yet. Here he was.

At a quarter past seven, a small engine droned up the inlet that flowed off the Prosper River. Miranda Crabtree's boat emerged out of the mist between a marshy strip of land and a stand of cedars. Tall and sinewy at the tiller, she wore a threadbare gray sweatshirt and dirt-pocked jeans rolled at the calves. The sleeves of the sweatshirt were torn off and her arms were hard and lean. Avery felt a familiar stirring at the sight of her, some feeling deep in his breast he'd never named for fear of speaking it aloud, either to the Crabtree girl in a moment of weakness, or in dreams, where he lay in bed beside his wife, who loved him far more than he deserved.

The boat's engine cut out. Miranda tossed a rope and caught the lowest rung of a crudely nailed ladder at the end of the dock. Avery tied the rope off to a piling. She handed up the paper sack from the Igloo and waited. He counted the cash, produced a much thinner fold of bills from his own shirt pocket. This she did not count but stuffed into her hip pocket. She passed the empty Igloo up the ladder. "You look like hell," she said.

"Handsome Charlie wants to talk," Avery said and hooked a thumb over his shoulder.

She looked up the gravel lane from the dock, to where a white Plymouth cruiser was parked in the shade of a blood-red crepe myrtle, blue bubble light on the roof. A fat man in a hat filled the passenger's seat, blob-like, a thin line of cigarette smoke curling through the cracked window.

"Why?"

Avery shrugged. "He doesn't tell me anything."

"Cook's gone squirrelly."

"Squirrelly how?"

She shrugged. "Squirrelly. Says tell you watch out for yourself. Says you'll know what it means."

Avery's mouth tightened. "Well," he said, after a moment. He cut his eyes to the Plymouth. "He wants to talk."

Miranda looked from the Plymouth to the inlet, the river beyond. Avery watched the muscle in her jaw work.

Behind the dark glass of the Plymouth's passenger window, the cherry of the fat man's cigarette flared.

"He knows where to find me," she finally said.

"He won't like that."

But Avery's voice was lost in the cough of the motor and she was gone, quick as she had come, wake rolling back beneath the dock.

When she was out of sight, he walked the sack of money up to the Plymouth, dragging the empty Igloo over the gravel. The passenger's window cranked low, revealing the immense dark shape of Constable Charlie Riddle, two chins and a black satin eye patch beneath a badged fedora, the brim extrawide, neck fat beneath his shorn hairline like two rolls of quarters. Riddle took the sack from Avery and thumbed the bills, lips moving around his cigarette as he counted softly to himself.

Riddle's deputy, Robert Alvin, sat behind the wheel, rail-thin and fanning at flies.

"She said—"

Riddle held up a hand, still counting. Satisfied, he opened the Plymouth's glove box and shoved the sack in among paper napkins, a spare set of handcuffs, a citation pad. A single pair of white cotton panties dropped out like a bird fleeing a cage.

"She said if you want to see her, you know where to find her."

Riddle tucked the garment back in, had to slam the box twice before the latch caught.

"Teia and I are leaving tomorrow," Avery said. "First light. We're taking Grace, we're walking out. We're done, Charlie."

"Walking out," Riddle laughed. "Just stick out your thumbs when you hit the highway and fly, eh? Where y'all headed?"

"Anywhere but here."

"Well." Riddle flicked ash out the window. "Just remember, John-boy, you can light out with nothing in your pockets or you can light out with pockets full. Which you rather?"

Avery thought of Grace. "How long?" he said.

"Another day, two tops."

"Cook may have split on us. You can't ferry dope if there's no one to take delivery."

"Who says they ain't? Maybe I made me some new friends."

"You never had a friend in your life, Charlie."

Riddle smiled, shrugged. "Figger of speech."

"You owe me three grand for the last six months. I know you've got it. You've been helping yourself to my share ever run. Last two, I got nothing at all. I have to pay the Crabtree girl, I have to gas up the generators to keep the grow lights burning, I have to buy fucking epoxy to patch the pipes when the goddamn toilets won't flush—"

"How much you say I owe?"

"Three thousand."

"See, that's funny, I thought it was two. Or was it one?"

Avery said nothing.

"Don't be sore, John. Just make sure the last of that dope's in jars and ready to go by tonight. Then you head on back over to yon shack and crawl in bed with that long-legged wife, right next to that pretty baby, and just drift on off to dreamland for a spell. I wrap this whole thing up, you'll get everything you're owed, you and the missus. I promise. And that'll be the end of Billy and Lena Cotton's grand experiment here on the Prosper, once and for all. How's that sound?"

Avery looked to the heavy iron gates of the compound at the end of the lane. They stood open. Across the gravel county road, surrounded by chain-link, was the low, window-less brick building that had once been Holy Day Church. In back of the church, a red steel broadcast tower, at the pinnacle of which was a wooden cross lashed to the metal with rope. Nailed to the cross, in a grim parody of the cru-cifixion: the long-rotted corpse of a white whooping crane, its six-foot wingspan all bone save for a few last shreds of flesh and feather. Gourdlike skull and scissor bill turned up toward heaven, eyes empty hollows. Avery didn't know who had put it there, or why, but he felt no particular horror at the sight of it anymore, only the weariness of time and failure. "It sounds too good to be true," he said.

The fat constable smiled, flicked his cigarette past the dwarf into the lane. "Get some shut-eye," he said. He tipped his hat, cranked up his window.

Avery stepped back as the car rumbled away.

Sabbath House cast its horned shadow over an unkempt lawn thick with yellow-blooming dandelions as Avery made his way up the lane that bisected the property, dragging the Igloo behind him. Past the paint-flecked shotgun houses on his right, bare gray board showing through like exposed bone, the porches of three fallen away with rot. All dank and empty now, save the one nearest the gates, where Avery's wife and infant daughter slept on through the morning heat. Here, the porch was swept clean and the two-seater swing that hung from eyebolts in the haint-blue ceiling was free of widow webs and wasp nests.

The greenhouse—*his* greenhouse, John Avery's and no one else's—stood on an open patch of ground across the lane, about fifty yards east of Sabbath House. It was iron-framed, Victorian, like so much else on the vast, wooded property: a resurrected ruin. Who had built it, some rich plantation wife? Possessed of an urge to grow something that was hers and hers alone? It had stirred him, this wreck, when he'd first laid eyes on it at nineteen, himself a new addition to the Cottons' upstart ministry. The brick foundation crumbling, panes missing in the gables. These, Avery had covered with blue plastic. The glass he had blacked out with aerosol paint, every inch of it. Purpose conjured from neglect. A forgotten thing remade. The dwarf's own story told in glass and paint and steel and the careful cultivation of new life.

He pulled a cinder block out of the weeds, stood on it, and unlocked the padlocked door with a single key that he wore around his neck on a length of knotted rawhide.

Inside, the plants grew three and four abreast in old tractor tires and wooden boxes and plastic five-gallon buckets. Those nearest the front were low and dense and pruned, while those at the back stretched six, seven feet high. Fluorescent lights hung on chains above them, backed by tin pie plates that made them look like flying saucers. He could hear the sound of the generator out back, chugging away, the lights above always burning. Avery shoved the empty Igloo against the wall and climbed onto a step stool and stood at a workbench scattered with cured buds and stray papers. He took up a bud and mashed it between his fingers and rolled it, tacking and licking the paper.

We were a whole community of fools, he thought. *Me, not the least among them.*

He sat on the gravel floor of the greenhouse, beneath the tallest trees, and smoked.

Later, weary, thickheaded and high, the sun climbing behind the trees, he crossed the lane to the last shotgun house. He tromped up the porch steps and went in through a ragged screen door, into the living room, where there was a couch with a busted spring and a ratty wingback chair, beside it an end table and an orange glass lamp with a dented shade. Through the kitchen, where the empty icebox stood open, a vaguely sour smell emanating from inside, palmetto bugs fleeing over peeling linoleum before him, and into the bedroom, which was small and cramped, a mattress sagging in an iron frame. Knotholes in the walls through which daylight peered. He climbed into bed beside Teia and lay atop the covers in his clothes. The baby lay beneath the single sheet, molded to the curve of her mother's belly, mother and daughter both naked in the humid morn. In the window, a box fan blasted warm air. Teia lay between Avery and the baby, she a foot taller than his four-seven, her dark skin damp with sweat. "I love you," she murmured, voice thick with waking.

"I love you," he said.

Her eyes didn't open. "What time is it?"

"Early. Go back to sleep." He squeezed her hand.

Avery soon fell asleep and dreamed of a menacing figure in black, limping to and fro in a slanting room high above the ones he loved.

SIGNS AND WONDERS

Far behind Sabbath House, deeper in the blue pine woods than any congregant had ever been, on a slight rise at the center of a clearing, stood the burned-out shell of a forgotten stone chapel, its buttresses holding fast to the earth like the wings of a crippled dragon. Here, in a cold black crypt beneath the church, the old dying preacher Billy Cotton dreamed of a girl, darting among the woods, a child of twelve in a white dress soiled with river mud. A faerie creature. Cotton chased after her, and the trees grew thick and tangled and great rotten trunks surged up from the moist floor, roots and spiderwebs and shaggy leprous birches. A clearing at the base of a hill, where the child stopped, waiting. Holding out her hand. He took it. The moon shone on kudzu vine growing up the rise. A dark old shack at the summit. From beneath a stilted porch, carried by the wind, the oily reek of fish.

"Your hour's near," the girl said, her fingers twined in Cotton's, so soft, so warm.

He came awake.

It took a moment to remember where he was. Curled fetal and naked on stone between two coffins made of opal glass, each on a concrete pedestal three feet off the floor. The one to his left was empty. The other, sealed for a decade, held the dry husk of Billy Cotton's wife, her remains wrapped in folds of gold and purple silk. A small bronze placard at her feet, engraved:

LENA BOWEN COTTON
1936–1968
Mother of Many, Servant of God

A kerosene lamp burned low on the floor, Cotton's dark suit coat and pants and white shirt and red suspenders folded neatly beside it. He sat up, and just this simple motion lit the warrens of his bowels and groin afire. By the time he stood, he was slicked with sweat, pain like a dull coring knife working at the base of his tailbone. He slipped on his pants with no small effort and, shirtless, took up the lamp and followed the flame out of the crypt to the iron door at the end of the tunnel, which opened heavily onto the morning.

Birds sang as he stood bleary-eyed, beard shabby and uneven, bald pate spotted. Old white scars of expiation crisscrossing his belly, layer upon layer. Inflicted in the days and weeks and months after his Lena had died, most made with a sliver of broken glass right here in this dank place, where he had prayed over her corpse for forty days and forty nights, begging God's forgiveness for the pain he had caused her. Forty days on bended knee, forty nights on cold stone.

This morning, Cotton stood on the threshold of the crypt and felt the urge to piss but couldn't because the cancer in his prostate had *metastasized*—the word used by the doctor who had examined him three months past, the same doctor Cotton and Charlie Riddle had bribed to cut loose babies and cure diseases, back when they'd started running whores out at the Pink Motel. An old sawbones with a penchant for whiskey, he'd come to the manse and snapped on a rubber glove, then presented Cotton with the findings over a stiff drink. He left a pamphlet, half a dozen pill bottles. Cotton took the pills for a few weeks, but not for a while now. He had decided: he would not die in some chemical fog; rather, he would endure all the petty indignities and pains until he could make his exit on his own terms. Those terms in execution now.

Cock in hand, straining, popping sweat.

God damn *it*—

And that was when he saw it, in a slant of morning sunlight, among the crabgrass: a dove. Pure white, unblemished, save the head, which was all but severed from the trunk. Stuck in the body, like a piece of candy into a plastic Easter egg: the pearl-inlaid handle of a straight razor.

The old preacher tucked his thin, gray penis back in his trousers. He stepped over the threshold and into the light and bent to pick up the bird. The head lolled. Ants crawled out of its neck. He brushed at them and saw that the razor actually *grew* out of the bird, like some kind of—

cancerous

—tumor.

Cotton pulled the razor free. A wet, tearing sound. He dropped the bird. The razor's mechanism was rusted, caked with river mud and algae. He pried open the blade and the sun gleamed along a sliver of steel yet sharp. It might have been any razor, except it wasn't. Cotton knew this blade. He had carried it in a boot when he was young, then later in a hatband, and, finally, as a grown man, in his pocket. He had carried it almost forty years, until the night his Lena died, when he'd used it on that, that *thing*—

He felt a presence, a cold breath at his neck that stirred the hairs. Slowly, he turned.

She emerged from the long dark throat of the tunnel, blurred, then resolving into a delicate frame clad in a white dress long and flowing and trimmed in pearls, light tulle across bare, pale shoulders. She was elfin, golden hair pulled back in a graceful bun. A gossamer veil covered her face. A red-leather Bible clasped at her breast like a bouquet of roses. She did not smile. She did not move. She simply stared. A breeze blew through the hollow and chilled the sweat on Cotton's bare back, but it did not stir a single fold of Lena Cotton's wedding dress.

"Lee?" the preacher said.

She made no answer, stepping from the shadows of the crypt to stop the blood in his veins. A cruel smile stretching her mouth as she remembered, perhaps, a long-ago night when he threw her across the bed and forced himself, enraged, engorged, upon her. Or the last night of her life, nine months later, when Cotton bade her watch as he held aloft her boy, took out his razor—

Her eyes shifted downward, to the pearl-inlaid handle. Her features melting like wax. She opened her mouth behind her veil and roared the mad electric shriek of an insect horde. It fell on the old preacher like a wall and claimed his skull with its horrid frequency, canceling all consciousness in an instant and leaving in its place a single image: the baby's throat, opening beneath the blade, Cotton's other hand closed around a tiny, reptilian ankle. The weight of the child—no more than a bag of onions—lessening as the blood pattered on the frayed Oriental rug. A sick squirming in the old preacher's gut at the forced vision of it now, that grotesque issue of his good seed sprouted in her faithless womb—

He fell against the doorframe. "No, Lena—"

Cotton slid down the wall, felt his heart slowing in his chest.

"Monstrous—" he gasped, though his breath had all but left him.

Lena took a step toward him, hem of her gown ragged and moldering.

Her voice in his head now, a slow rasp: *I . . . was . . . robbed . . .*

Another step closer, fingers dry and flaking like autumn leaves where they clasped the Bible to her chest. Reaching for him, for his heart.

So much . . . you robbed me of . . .

Her jaw distended, opened. Inside: a boiling black mass of nature, beetles and ants and flies. Swarming-crawling-sailing-hatching out of Lena Cotton's face. Pouring out from behind her veil in a black mass, spilling down her white dress. Not his wife's face behind the veil but a thing of green and blue iridescence now, hand a reaching claw.

Paralyzed, trembling, the old preacher willed his own hand to move, even as hers closed about his face, enveloping him in the stink of moldering earth.

You took him . . . Billy . . . you took them both . . .

Slowly, he turned the razor's open blade against his thigh, and it cut as if just set to the strop, parting fabric, parting flesh. A sting, a sudden well of blood.

Then clarity.

Gasping, Cotton fell backward into the dewy grass.

Pain in his hips and groin, springing hot.

When his breath had returned, he struggled up on his elbows, then folded the blade and put it in his pocket. Pressed the heel of his hand against his bleeding leg and hauled himself up by the crypt door. Sweat-slicked, he limped over to the old stone bench and sat. He picked up the dove from the grass. Grunting in pain as he shifted. He fitted the dove back together, then looked into the maw of the crypt, where the sunlight penetrated only so far before a black curtain fell.

What killed you, Lee? Cotton thought. *The horror of what came out of you, or what I did to it? Or was it an accumulation of horrors, borne all the long years you lay your head upon this hollow breast?* For the boy was not the first child he had taken from Lena Bowen Cotton.

He remembered his dream, the girl in the woods.

Sent away when I was filled with fury and hate— No, he thought. *No more of that. That evil has passed. All my evil is passing away, yes. Passing away, Lena.*

"I'm bringing her home," he called suddenly, into the

darkness. A new calm or clarity, pushing away all fear. "Avery's man Cook, he wouldn't bring her. Wouldn't do what needed doing. But Charlie Riddle, he's set things in motion. By morning, she'll be here. As for the other one . . ." He touched the razor in his pocket. "It was never meant to be."

No answer came from the crypt. Perhaps she was gone. Perhaps she had never been there and he was finally, truly mad.

"We'll be together, Lee, you'll see."

His voice echoed flatly down the tunnel.

"What was it you used to say to those kids, in the pulpit? 'A promise unbreakable.' That's what I'm making you."

Somewhere in the woods, a mourning dove cooed, and its mate answered.

"At long last," the preacher said. "We'll be a family. You, me, our little lost dove."

Signs and wonders, this summer morning.

There, in the sunlight, sweat drying on his back, Billy Cotton sat cradling the torn bird in his lap and wept.

LITTLEFISH

Meanwhile, across the Prosper, hidden deep in the green folds of the old witch's island, the boy Littlefish slept and dreamed. High above the ground in his lookout, rough pine bark at his back, a small picture book with a cracked spine spread over his stomach. In his dream, he walked down a wide dirt path shaded by the large, reaching arms of oak trees, and at the end of this path was a gate, and beyond the gate a road, and beyond the road a brick building set back on a little hill, low and square, no windows, only a metal door painted fading yellow. A red steel tower topped by a wooden cross rose above this building like the steeple of a church. The boy saw the vague shapes of houses, fuzzy, as if rain had washed them out like chalk on a rock, and another structure, too, a great glass building where plants and vines grew wild all around it. From the woods came the sudden yammer of cicadas. The day began to darken. A man stood before the yellow door, tall and thin and dressed in a black hat and black coat, and he held in his hand a blade, long and curved, and in the sky the moon was overtaking the sun, and purple clouds came billowing out of the dark, full of lightning and terror, as the world slid askew. The boy knew he had to go to this man, to this building, though he did not want to. He had taken a single step when a blue spear of lightning flew earthward and struck the red tower, sent snakes of electricity writhing along the steel. They lashed the tips of nearby trees and set them afire, and the man in black came striding down the hill, swinging his blade, and the boy turned to run, breathless, as everything burned, the fire spreading faster and faster, and when he reached the river, the river was thick with snakes. Coiled along the bank, they waited for him, pink mouths open. So he turned inland, found a pine tree, began to climb, higher and higher. But the man in black was below him, climbing after him, calling out in a funny, singsong way, and the boy seized on a weak branch and the branch was not a branch but a cottonmouth snake, and he fell. Down, down, down, cracking through sap-sticky branches, into the smoke, into the fire—

Littlefish jerked awake.

He pushed his wide, webbed hands against the wooden platform beneath him, felt it there, sturdy, strong. Across the river, the tip of the red metal tower stood just visible among the treetops, its wooden cross and strange collection of bones lashed there reaching for a still-blue sky. Below, the bayou curled like a reptile sunning itself on the earth.

Safe, he thought. *Safe*.

The book slid from his stomach into his lap as he sat up. It was Sister's, or had been when she was small. On its cover was a town: streets and houses, a barbershop, police station, hospital, school. He knew these words because Sister had taught them to him, had taught him to say them with his hands. He traced a finger over the cover: *This Is Where I Live.* He sounded each word in his head, but the voice he heard was not his, for he had never heard his own voice, just as he had never seen a barbershop or a police station outside of books. The voice he heard was Sister's. It was like the platform. Strong. It would not break.

He quickly opened the book to a page where a man in a black suit and white collar stood smiling, behind him a church with a steeple.

He knew the words *church* and *steeple* from the rhyme Sister had taught him when he was little, taking his hands in hers and showing him how to fold them: *here is the church, here is the steeple, open the doors, here are the people.* Only his hands couldn't fold because of the webs between his fingers, so his church always came up empty. Secretly, he had always imagined another verse to the rhyme, every time he put his hands together: *here is the church, here is the steeple, I am not like other people.* For Sister's church was always full, six rosy people seated and ready to do whatever it was people did in a church. On this subject, his book was vague, but a church seemed to be a happy place.

Unlike the building in his dream.

He remembered when he had seen the red tower for the first time. Two years ago, when he and Sister had built his lookout. He had asked her then what it was, and she had told him, after a long quiet, that it used to be a church.

"But now it's nothing. It's a ruin."

What's a ruin? he had signed.

"A place that shouldn't exist anymore," she said.

If it used to be a church, where are the people now?

"Try not to speak while we're working up here," she said, a nail between her lips. "You'll fall."

Maybe, he thought now, *it was a church for people like me. A church that does not look like a church, for people who do not look like people.*

He rummaged in a knothole above his head, where he stowed bits of things he had found in the river: a sprig of fishing line with hooks tangled in it; a rusted tin can with a hole punched through the center; a little white ball no bigger than a plastic bobber, strange dimples on its surface. A wooden pencil box he had found along the riverbank, mired in a clump of mud and grass. A faint paper image peeling from its top: a girl in a red cloak with a basket, a wolf standing upright on crooked legs. The wolf wore a man's coat with big wide buttons and smiled, teeth sharp. Littlefish took four colored pencils out of the box. With these, he began to color on the page that was opened to the church: first the red, then the black, holding the yellow in his teeth. He pushed his tongue through his lips, switching out colors, pressing so hard against the page that he snapped the orange pigment.

For a while, he sat looking at what he had done to Sister's book, trying to comprehend the mystery of it.

Here is the church, here is the steeple—

Suddenly, like the bark of a crow, crying his name in her strange tongue, Baba's voice: "Rybka! Rybka!"

Littlefish put the box and pencils back in the knothole.

He tucked the book in the front waistband of a thin pair of dime-store jeans he had outgrown by several inches, then swung deftly over the edge of the platform to the boards he and Sister had nailed up and down the pine's trunk. Down he went, bare-chested, quick, his scaly skin very near the color and texture of the tree itself. He hit the ground running on wide bare feet, heedless of the pine needles and roots that jabbed the webs between his toes.

He came out of the trees to the rim of a small limestone gorge that carved the island in two, a channel at the bottom where duckweed and water grasses grew and there were pools deep enough for swimming. The gray shale walls were stairstepped by time and water and studded with pines that grew at odd angles, and the boy leaped nimbly among these, descending one side and ascending the other.

He ran down the slope and out of the trees and past the goat pen with its one white goat chewing cud. Past the little toolshed where he kept his pelts and skinning knives, his bow and arrows, his comic books. Past Baba's bathhouse with its spiders and forever smoky damp smell.

Past his own garden, where squash and beans and corn and okra and tomatoes and strawberries grew tall and thick and lush, as if the soil itself approved of his efforts. All manner of tin-can contraptions and bottle chimes and odd homemade bric-a-brac lodged around the perimeter to ward away rabbits and deer, though no animal had ever ventured into his rows. They had eaten their fill of the clover and the kudzu blossoms and the occasional flowers Sister had planted over the years, but never a single leaf had been harmed in Littlefish's garden.

Baba stood at the edge of the yard, short and round and impatient, brown chickens coming out from the shadows beneath the stilted porch to cluck at the old woman's feet. She scattered feed from her apron and *chick-chick-chicked* at the hens. She looked up at the gasping boy and said, "Sister."

At the bottom of the hill, he saw her, carrying a cardboard box packed with goods.

The boy set off down the red-dirt path through the kudzu.

The old woman flapped the rest of her feed to the ground and kicked a rooster from the steps.

THE LANGUAGE OF FAMILY

✦

Miranda walked out of the trees into the clearing, carrying on her shoulder a cardboard box packed with cans of beans, sauerkraut, coffee, tobacco, sacks of flour and sugar. A long hunting bow and a quiver of arrows slung on her back. The boy came running out to meet her, down the steep, kudzu-tangled slope from the cabin into the grass, where he threw his huge paddle-arms around Miranda, squeezing. She cupped the back of his head, his face at her stomach. The smell of him strong and fishy, alive and good. He smiled up at her. His teeth small and crooked. She handed him the box and watched him go nimbly up the path. She followed, using the lower limb of her bow as a walking stick.

Old Iskra sat in her rocking chair on the porch, killing flies with a wire swatter and tipping their corpses into a bent metal spoon nailed to the railing. She did this with the greatest of care. She wore a long apron over a housedress, a man's muddy boots. Her thin, silver hair tied up in a blue rag. Eyes narrow and dark. As Miranda and the boy came onto the porch, the old woman shot a jet of chewing tobacco into a metal can packed with kudzu leaves. "Bring the corn," she said to the boy.

Miranda took the box from Littlefish and went into the cabin. A large, open room, dim and musty, the only furniture a kitchen table and chairs, an old rocker by a window. A wicker basket full of broken kindling by the stone hearth of a boxwood stove. Walls of rough-cut pine. In the kitchen, she pushed through a curtain of oyster shells strung on fishing line and pulled a string to light the pantry, a musty, narrow space that smelled of cedarwood. Chickens clucked under the floorboards as she unpacked the box and set the cans with labels facing out among the jars of pickled vegetables and dried roots, weeds and wild herbs. Other jars, on higher shelves, were furred with dust, their contents plump and strange.

Back on the porch, Miranda unslung her bow and quiver and set these against the cabin wall. Littlefish was spreading ears of corn from two five-gallon buckets on the boards at Iskra's feet, the old woman sitting on the edge of her chair. "Get a sheet, get a sheet," she fussed, then hollered after him to bring Sister a knife.

The boy went into the cabin, screen door slapping behind him.

Miranda sat in the rocking chair beside Iskra's.

The old woman killed another fly, eased it into the spoon.

"Does it eat them?" Miranda asked.

Iskra's spit can shook as she reached it from the floor. "A house spirit does not eat."

"What, then?"

The old woman waved a hand, impatient. "The spirit watches over me and the boy and I offer it flies. What do I care what it does with them?" She drew a short, sturdy blade from a hidden pocket in her apron. Over the years, Miranda had seen the knife gut fish, peel potatoes, cut rope. The blade never dulled.

Littlefish returned with a paring knife and a white sheet tucked under his arm. The knife he gave to Miranda, and the sheet he spread on the planks between the two women. He upended the buckets of corn onto the sheet and gathered ears into a wide kitchen bowl, which he gave to Miranda. She touched his arm, said with her hands: Look in my quiver.

He did. Inside were three rolled comic books.

"You spoil him," Iskra said.

Sitting on the porch steps, the boy opened the first book to a storm-swept ocean, a monstrous sea beast breaching the surface. Astride its back, mouth open in a savage cry, eyes huge and white and wild, a bare-chested barbarian, plunging a sword into the creature's neck. The boy turned the page, bit his thumb, and a memory, sudden and strong, blew over Miranda like a wind: she, sitting where he sat now, every evening at dusk, a girl of eleven nursing a baby with goat's milk through a homemade nipple, cheesecloth stretched over a jelly jar. Burping him in her arms, the rough texture of his skin. That long dark summer, she had surrendered her heart completely.

"Boy," Iskra said roughly.

Miranda jerked as if the old woman had set a hook in her.

"Go hunt. We need meat. Read your funny books later."

"I'll go with him," Miranda said, setting her bowl out of her lap.

"Stay," Iskra ordered, stacking ears in the lap of her apron. Her hands gnarled. "I cannot do this by myself."

Miranda signed at Littlefish: I'll be here when you get back.

The boy tucked his comics behind his picture book in the waist of his jeans and disappeared around the side of the cabin.

"He stinks to God and back," Iskra muttered. "Having him indoors in the summer . . ."

"I like the way he smells," Miranda said.

"Every night, he comes tromping in to sleep on the floor, curls up in front of the stove like a dog."

"He isn't sleeping in his tree? What's wrong?"

Iskra shrugged, spat in her can. "Bad dreams, maybe. Ask him yourself."

After that, they worked quietly, cutting and shucking corn. Topping each ear, peeling back the husks to pluck the silks, Miranda's blade crunching through the cobs. Their chairs made a warm, wooden sound as they rocked. It was a rhythm they had fallen into over the years: in place of words some task, and out of the silent motions of that task—the shelling of fresh peas, the gutting of fish—the old woman and Miranda had fashioned the peculiar language of family.

More memories, as the day's light grew long beyond the trees below, like fragments of a fevered dream: water carried from a well, poured over hot stones in a low, rough hut; heat and steam and lantern light dancing on the beams of the bathhouse above; Miranda, snakebit and thrashing and seizing on the slatted bench above the rocks, the hard, dry taste of a stick in her mouth; the witch beside her like a preacher at a river baptism, rough hands washing wounds with a cloth wrung from a cedar bucket; and words, words Miranda did not understand. Grunts and whispers. Comings and goings. All that long night.

Her first clear memory, unbroken by delirium: waking on the floor near the boxwood stove, wrapped and sweating in a heap of buckskins. Her left arm swollen, bound in strips of cloth. Lamplight orange and oily, a lantern set in the middle of the table. She sat up, skins falling away. Felt her nakedness and drew them close. The old woman's snores came from the open door of the bedroom, big and cracking like the felling of trees. Something moved in the bread bowl on the table, made a shadow-play on the wall in the lantern light: a little hand reaching, fingers spreading, and between each digit a soft, fan-shaped membrane like a tiny sail. She stood, pulling the buckskin around her, and the room pitched. Her left arm hot, unbendable. With her right, she gripped a chair for balance.

The baby filled the oblong bowl. Its cheeks were round and ashen, its forehead lumpy, whole head a knob of misshapen clay. But the eyes that peered out from beneath that brow were focused, alert. Its webbed fingers clenched and unclenched, and Miranda, helpless not to, reached out and let it take hold of her right index finger. She felt something at its touch, a kind of transaction, a passage of some energy, from the baby to her, from her to the baby.

The witch's voice had startled her: "He is special."

Miranda turned to see the old woman standing in the bedroom doorway, wearing a thin, tea-colored housecoat.

"Not to that preacher," Miranda said.

"No. Not to him."

"The mother, is she . . . ?"

"Dead."

Miranda swallowed, looked back at the child in the bowl. "Hiram?" She felt the hot tears sliding down her cheeks. "Is he . . . ?"

Miranda heard the boards creak, and she turned, thinking she would see the old woman advancing to offer some measure of comfort, a touch, a hug, a breast to lay her cheek upon, but instead she saw only the bedroom door close as the old witch retreated, the catch loud and final, as if the past itself were being shut away.

Miranda topped the last ear of corn in her bowl and gathered more from the sheet.

Iskra sat forward on the edge of her chair. She touched the small of her back, tensing. Hand atremble.

"Baba?" Miranda said.

Iskra shook her head. "Just fucking old."

Inside a husk, clinging to one of the still-green leaves, Miranda found a fat black grub. She plucked it free, her nails caked with dirt.

"Good luck," the old woman said, taking up another ear from the bucket. "Go fishing with it and you will catch something."

Miranda eased the worm into the breast pocket of her

shirt—a western-style shirt that had belonged to Hiram, the edges of the cuffs and tail worn thin. She felt the tiny creature through the fabric, light as an acorn. She thumbed her blade against the tip of a stalk and drew the knife toward her. *Husk and cob, flesh and bone.* A rhythm to cut by, Iskra had taught her, a kind of blessing. Miranda studied the ear of corn in her hands. She had been working too hard at the silks. Her hands were damp with the juice of burst kernels, and suddenly the bright afternoon seemed less bright, and the distant woods seemed close and dangerous.

She thought, strangely, of Cook. The gun he had offered. Locked away now in her father's old tackle box.

"Things are changing, on the river?" Iskra said quietly.

And there it was, the old woman's weird, startling ability to sense Miranda's thoughts, like an invisible web woven to catch feelings, vibes, moods. *You should be used to it by now,* she thought. "Maybe," she said.

"Things are changing all over," Iskra said, working the corn between her hands, but staring out over the porch railing and down the kudzu-draped hill to the tree line.

"Changing how? What's changing?"

Iskra picked up her can from the boards and spat. She turned her dark eyes on Miranda. "The boy says he hears things, deep in the night." She nodded to where the shaggy birches cast long afternoon shadows, the woods beyond dark and dense. "Crack and boom among the trees. Like a giant roaming the woods."

Miranda swallowed, an old stirring in her chest and stomach, part nightmare, part memory. A wide muddy shore at the edge of a lake where deadfalls bobbed like coffins and a wall of thorns protected some dark place, where she had found a baby breathing that should not have been. Great footfalls in the damp and tangled night.

"I hear it, too," Iskra said, a sudden smile curling at the edges of her sunken mouth, a smile Miranda had only seen a few times in all the years she had known the old woman. Once at Sabbath House, the night Littlefish was born. The smile of a woman with secrets. A woman who was not anyone's Baba, who had never spooned Miranda cabbage soup when she was sick or baked seeded bread so warm and soft.

"Something's waking up," the witch said. "Out there."

Cicadas drummed like a current in the earth.

"The leshii," Iskra said.

Leshii. A word to Miranda like the harsh, bone-quaking chills she had awakened to, the cottonmouth's venom still in her veins. What the old woman's ancient people had called their forest spirits, though here, it was no Grandfather Hunter, no Uncle Tree, but a queen, the witch said, no true word in any tongue for such unnameable power. A name Iskra had always invoked when eleven-year-old Miranda had asked hard questions like: *What happened out there that night? What happened to my father?* Always, first, that secretive smile, the curl of a dying spider's legs, then: *You will have to ask the leshii, Myshka, should you ever see her wandering these woods.*

Miranda's answer: *I will.*

She looked out at the trees, thick with shadow and insects singing in the late-day light. Above, a set of wind chimes fashioned out of the hollow bones of birds rustled.

The metal spoon, Miranda saw, was empty. The flies were gone.

She set a half-shucked ear back in the bowl, wiped her hands on her jeans. "I'm going after him," she said. She took her quiver from beside the door and buckled the leather strap across her torso. She picked up her bow and slipped it over her head and set out along the path behind the cabin, following her brother's trail up the hill, past the bathhouse and the boy's shed, past the goat pen, and into the woods.

The old woman's smile faded. She spat over the rail.

Went on rocking. Went on cutting corn.

THE HEART

Miranda went into the trees at the top of the ridge behind the cabin and came out at the edge of the shallow gorge that cut through the island. Some dozen feet below the tree line, the gray and white striated rock curved above an emerald inlet, where tufts of sweet flag and purple-blooming spiderwort grew along the water's edge. She saw the boy's trail in the dirt: wide, loping tracks where he had crossed the gorge and gone up into the trees. She picked her way across and stood at the top of the ridge to catch her breath. Below, the inlet widened around a bend to collect in a clear deep cistern enclosed by a wall of limestone. Here, when he was six and she seventeen, she had taught the boy to swim. Nature had gifted him the webs, the scales. All he'd lacked was the courage to dive in, and Miranda had seen to that, standing in the shoulder-deep water with arms open: *I will catch you; I will keep you; I will never let you go.* Knowing, of course, one day he would stray too far from Iskra's island,

maybe chance across a hunter and his son, or a bootleg-
ger at his still. Or even some lost, turned-out congregant
from Sabbath House, living off the land. For, though the
old woman's island was a secret place, a hidden pocket in
the lining of the world, its borders were easily crossed. *And
what then?* she wondered. Would they see a boy? A monster?
Would they raise a hand, or a gun?

She passed the boy's tree, where the land sloped sharply
down to the bayou. There, across the water, she spied the
boy's flat bark, banked among the beds of water willow.

At the water's edge, she set her bow and quiver in the
grass and dug a hole in the loose dark soil with her fingers.
She took the grub from her shirt pocket, put it in the hole,
and covered it. She stood and shed her shoes and clothes.
There were four arrows in her quiver. She fired them all in
quick succession across the water, into the ground. Then
stuffed her clothes and shoes deep inside her quiver, judged
the weight of it, and threw it across, landing it safely on the
opposite bank. Finally, she slipped her bow across her torso
and dove naked into the bayou.

She came up halfway across and saw the head of something small and reptile break the surface, then vanish. She
climbed dripping onto a bank of moss. Dried herself with
her shirt, then dressed quickly and snatched up her arrows
and set off into the woods, where she made only a half-
hearted search for the boy's sign. She knew his habits, his
trails. He would go to the black oak at the center of the
meadow.

Miranda walked quietly, enjoying the woods, which were
gloomy with the day's long light. High up and far away, a

whip-poor-will gave out its lonesome call. After a while, she came out of the trees into a field of knee-high grass, where butterflies were having at the last pink blooms of summer's fleabane. At the center of the clearing: the black oak, a gnarled giant with wide, low-hanging limbs. She scanned the other trees at the edge of the clearing for the boy, didn't see him.

Movement in the oak caught her eye.

Hanging by his ankles from the lowest branch was a man, the grass stained red beneath him. The meadow rippled in a soft, warm breeze. The body spun gently at the end of the rope, and Miranda saw the face of her father, Hiram Crabtree.

She felt a falling away inside her, like a shelf of rock collapsing.

The boatman wore the same shirt, jeans, and boots he had worn the last night she had seen him alive, thighs and knees mud-smeared. His arms hung down straight. A slit beneath his jaw like a frown, his face otherwise expressionless, save the empty, stupid gaze of the dead. An arrow protruded from his chest, just above the heart. Fletching the same light gray of the arrows Miranda carried even now in her quiver—

No, she said, or thought she said, unaware that her fingers, despite her bow in one hand, were moving in sign, the way she had taught Littlefish to speak. She forgot to breathe. She grew light-headed and sat down in the grass. The sun, low behind the oak, lit Hiram's corpse in a nimbus of gold.

Littlefish, suddenly, in silhouette above her.

Miranda stared up at him blankly.

The boy was bending down, setting his bow on the ground.

You okay? he signed.

She gripped his arm and pointed over his shoulder at the tree.

Man? she managed to sign, hands quaking. See?

Littlefish glanced over his shoulder. Man? he said. Then shook his head. Doe, he said.

Doe.

She looked up. It was a deer. The boy had shot an arrow through its heart and slid a rope through the tendons of its legs to haul it up and cut its throat. Even now, it bled out on the bright green grass.

Miranda pushed up slowly from the ground. Her legs shook. "I don't—" she said, but that was all she said.

Curious, worried, Littlefish watched her.

She forced a dry-throated laugh in defiance of the hot tears that sprang into her eyes and shook her head. She went to the doe where it hung. She touched the arrow that had felled it, its shaft buried in the chest.

Miranda looked around, saw the story of his kill. He had climbed the oak and waited, and the doe had wandered into the long grass to graze; the boy had taken her with a shot that was easily fifty or sixty yards; she saw the depression in the grass, the blood trail where he had dragged her from the tree line to the oak at the center of the meadow. Miranda marveled at the distance, the precision. The boy was pure instinct. She, a gap shooter, judged her elevation by the space between the tip of her arrow at full draw and her target. Every shot Miranda made was a calculation, whereas the boy's were riddles.

She ran one hand along the flank of the deer, its fur stiff like the bristles of a paintbrush. Good shot, she said.

He broke into a smile, and his smile was brilliant and warm.

Instantly she felt better.

"You shouldn't leave it in, though." She gripped the arrow lodged in the doe's breast and tore it free. The broadhead was a razor, one of a set she had given him for his birthday last spring.

Show me how it's done, she signed.

The sky bled vermilion as the boy drew a skinning knife from his belt of squirrel and rabbit pelts and began the work of dressing. When he hesitated, she took his hand and guided the blade to the groin. He put the knife into the deer, cut down through the rib cage, and slowly the deer came open. Littlefish buried his arms to the elbows inside the animal. Out came the viscera. He dropped it in a heap, plunged back in.

Miranda watched him. He was beautiful. Her love for him frightened her.

"Baba says you're not sleeping," she said. "Want to talk about it?"

He shook his head. The deer gave a squelch as he drew his arms out.

"Why not?"

No words, he signed, hands bloody.

"Make them?"

The boy hesitated, then stuck his knife in the dead animal's flank. He brought his hands together and worked his fingers without looking at Miranda, as if talking to himself. Flies buzzed around him, crawled on the animal's hide. She caught the words *red* and *fire* and *afraid*. Finally, he threw his hands apart, let his long arms fall at his sides, and just shook his head. Then went back to the deer. Working behind the sternum at something stubborn, and when he took his hands out, his arms red, Miranda saw that he was holding something small and round, a perfect arrow-shaped wound in its center. Smiling, he held it out to her.

It was the heart.

CRABTREE LANDING

The white Plymouth was parked on the shoulder of the gravel turnaround at Crabtree Landing. Across the way, the mercantile where Miranda lived was dark. Beyond the trees and power lines, the sun was spreading like a burst yolk. Constable Charlie Riddle leaned against the front right fender of the car and held his cigarette near his mouth, his elbow tucked close against his bulk. He rubbed, absently, the silk eye patch that covered his left orbit. His fingers were thick, nicotine-yellowed, his face grizzled and jowly. Behind the wheel, his deputy—Robert Alvin, a man so thin he might have been a series of fitted pipes beneath his jeans and shirt—sat cracking roasted peanuts out of a paper bag. He held a bottled Coke between his knees and thumbed the nuts one by one down the bottle's neck. The afternoon had passed slowly, the radio squawking from time to time. Bees buzzing in clumps of yellow ragwort all around the property. Now the sun was on its way out, and the sweat crawled more slowly down Riddle's back, his khaki shirt dried with it, stains below his shoulders like ugly wings.

Fly-fly away, the fat constable thought. From here, this long, hot afternoon spent prowling around the doors and windows of a place he had avoided for the better part of a decade. From everywhere else: the town of Mylan, the county of Nash. The state of goddamned Arkansas. Let his ugly wings carry him up into the clouds like a storybook faerie, deposit him somewhere beside a clear and rocky stream, where no man knew his name. A land without preachers and churches and dwarfs. Where the food was steak and potatoes every day and the only women were the ones you paid and there was always a piano playing and the smell of horse. Riddle touched the Schofield pistol on his hip and wondered if he might yet be a law-bringer, not -breaker. Would he slip his bonds of servitude to lesser men, crackpots and midgets, dopers and fools?

By God, Charlie Riddle was in a mood. The heat and the waiting had put him there. He was hungry and cranky and felt the first misgivings of a head-buster coming on. Old feelings, too, astir in his belly. He stared at the gravestones beneath the tall spreading sweetgum by the river, both cut from cedarwood, the man's more crudely than the woman's. He stared at Cora Crabtree's name, burned into the wood. He did not like these feelings. It would be better to be far from here.

The Landing. Always at the edges of his thoughts.

He looked down at his gut, unable to see his belt buckle

below it. Then at the dense pine thicket, northwest of the store. Touched his eye patch. Recalled stumbling out of those piney woods a night long past, jelly of his eye on his cheek.

Oh yes, I am in a goddamned state.

The Landing, like Sabbath House upriver, was a stake driven through the bedrock of Charlie Riddle's life, and he, like a dog in some bottom dweller's dirt yard, was hitched to that stake by an invisible chain, his small, well-trod orbit thick with flies and the smell of his own shit. He had lost so much of himself here. His eye was drawn to the sweetgum at the corner of the store, where the graves of Hiram and Cora Crabtree lay in the switching evening shadows. *Ah, Cora.* He fanned the air as if to shoo a fly. *Goddamn you, Cora. And damn her, too. Ain't no amount of even to be got with you Crabtree bitches.*

When Riddle heard the bright pitch of an outboard from downriver, he tossed his butt in the gravel, unpinned his star from his breast, and dropped it through the Plymouth's passenger window.

Robert Alvin stirred from his peanuts.

"Stay put," Riddle said.

He walked across the grass and around the mercantile, its paint peeling to the gray board. The Landing's rear porch was built on stilts in the water, fixed like a balcony to the second story. Just beyond the overhang of the porch, a floating dock bobbed on a raft of old whitewalls jellied with frog eggs. Riddle sidestepped down the steep embankment to the water's edge. Stood amid a tangle of kudzu, breathing hard, right hand on the Schofield. The sound of the motor grew louder, and soon the johnboat appeared from around the tight horseshoe bend of the last oxbow before the Landing.

The constable lifted a hand and the girl's jaw set like concrete at the sight of him. She wore a man's shirt, the sleeves rolled above her shoulders. The front of the shirt and the thighs of her jeans were smeared with blood.

Riddle waited where he was until she drew alongside the dock and cut the motor.

He ventured through the kudzu along the bank and walked into the shadow of the porch's overhang. She ignored him, went about the business of tying off. He stepped carefully over old cinder blocks and broken glass bottles half buried in the red mud and watched, rightly, for snakes.

"How do," he said.

The girl stood at the center of the dock, between it and Riddle a few feet of lapping water.

She made no answer. Just fists at her sides.

A right sour-looking twist these days. "What's a-matter," he said, "cat got your tongue?"

The sun was gone.

Across the river, a blue heron slid out of the sky and alighted in the water's edge.

Riddle put both hands on his gun belt, hooking his thumbs around his buckle. He eyed the boat tied to the dock. A bucket of fresh-shucked corn set at the bow. In the hull: a hunk of something bloody, wrapped in a bedsheet. "What you got there, little sister?"

"Don't call me that," she said.

"You best show me," he said, and made a swirling motion with his hand as if to speed her along.

She hunkered down, dragged the haunch of meat out of the boat, and threw it on the dock. Slipped the knot of twine and spread the sheet.

He whistled, impressed with the size.

She covered it, fetched out the bucket of corn. Her arms tanned and freckled and strong.

Damn, but he still liked looking at her.

"Where's the rest of it? Some deer out there hobbling on three legs? Or you leave it for that witch? She cook it fore she eats it?"

Miranda tied the sheet and shouldered the haunch and climbed the ladder made of soldered iron that reached from the floating dock to the Landing's second-story porch. She climbed one-handed.

Riddle stood beneath the overhang, thumbs in his pockets, watching as she disappeared up the ladder. Above, boards creaked and the porch door slammed.

He picked his way back through the kudzu and climbed the embankment, stumbling once in the dark. He stood beside the house and watched the second-story windows, where no lights burned. He saw her at the nearest window, staring down from between the drapes. Taller and leaner than the child she had once been, long legs dangling off a stool behind Hiram's register. He'd come around once or twice a few years after Cora died. She couldn't have been more than seven or eight, but God, those legs, even then. And how his badge had shone in those days, oh yes.

You want my daddy?

I just come for some candy. Got me a sweet tooth.

How she'd twisted on that stool, in her little shorts, blouse knotted above her navel.

Say, little sister, I ever tell you I knew your momma?

Riddle went on around the house, hands on his belt. Robert Alvin started up the Plymouth, but Riddle raised five fingers at the deputy. He went whistling up the porch steps and opened the screen door and kicked the inner door open, splintering the frame, cracking glass. He strode into the store and looked around at the place. Shelves nearly empty, thick with dust. Cobwebs in every corner. Tins of saltines and sardines and potted meat stamped with dates likely long passed. Near the register: a wire spinner of comic books, the ones in the front all sun-faded. Shadows and motes, stale Moon Pies.

Riddle drew his Schofield from its holster. He cocked the big antique pistol and drew down on the humming bait cooler along the wall. He fired. The bullet punched through the housing and the light beneath the sliding glass panels flickered. The compressor died with a rattle.

The store was silent.

At the back, light spilled down from the hidden stairwell, and the girl's shadow angled across the floor from the top of the stairs.

"Come on down here now. Let's talk."

Her sneakers on the steps, each footfall a scuff.

Riddle flicked the light switch near the ruined door.

In its wire fixture on the ceiling, a single low-watt bulb stuttered to life.

The small musty mercantile went thick with the gamy

scent of her as she emerged, blood-smeared, from the stairs.

Riddle took long, bold strides toward her, pistol in hand.

Her spine straightened and the muscles in her arms tightened.

He reached out and threw the tall rack of funny books over as he passed.

It gave him no small thrill when she took a quick step back, then another, and came up hard against the wall between a Coke machine and a stand of potato chips.

Charlie Riddle shoved into the narrow space with her, close enough to feel her breath, fast and shallow. He raised the heavy Schofield and drew its warm barrel along her cheek. He moved it down her throat, traced the hollow of her clavicle, the curve of a breast.

"You're trespassing," she said, waver in her voice.

Riddle mashed the pistol's barrel hard into her stomach. He liked the way it made her face turn down. He felt a stirring beneath his belt, where nothing had stirred for years. Not for her, anyway. Not since the night he'd stumbled out of them woods, one eye less.

"You and me," he breathed, popping sweat, "we got business, little sister."

She swallowed.

"I declare," he said. "Hear that midget talk, you're a by-God Amazon."

The pistol climbed beneath her shirt, inching breastward.

"Me, I don't see it. Then again, this old eye ain't what it used to be." With his free hand, he lifted the patch from his face and seated it on his head, and as the pistol nudged the nipple of her left breast, Miranda Crabtree stared unflinchingly into the fleshy red cave where Charlie Riddle's eye should have been, and into that cave, she spat.

The constable's leer wilted at the corners, drawn down by the flood tide of memory, the screaming, the pain, earthworms squelching beneath him as he fell in the leaves, the little bitch running for all she was worth. His lips peeled back into a snarl. He yanked the pistol from beneath her shirt and spun it in his grip. He drove the butt into her gut and stepped back as she dropped to all fours. He holstered his firearm, wiped her spit from his orbit, and slipped his patch back in place. He smoothed his hair where the patch had mussed it, the scent of Brylcreem strong.

Easy does it, Charlie-boy, he warned himself. *Easy does it.*

He took a PayDay from a box near the register while she lay retching, heaving, gasping. He opened it and took a bite. Chewed. Spoke through a mouthful of candy: "You got two more trips upriver. One tonight, one tomorrow. Last two, and that means forever. After tomorrow, you can run wild out there in them woods drenched in blood and howl with wolves, for all I care. But you don't show at that dock tonight, I'm coming back here. And I hate coming here, girl." Riddle spat a mouthful of peanuts and caramel on the floor. He tossed the rest of the PayDay with it and dug between his teeth. He reached into his pocket and took out a quarter and snapped the coin down by the register. "For the candy."

He left.

ROODING

Beyond the remnants of the door, the world was a jagged rectangle of black. Outside, the cicadas carried on their huge, nightmare chorus. Moths fluttered at the walls. Gun smoke lingered in the air. On the floor, Miranda pushed herself up on shaking arms, made a fist, and drove her knuckles hard into the old pine planks. New pain blazed up like a fresh-logged fire. The tremors fled. She sat back against the clapboard wall, skin split across the middle and fourth knuckles of her hand. A smear of blood and grit.

Out of the night, a white crane stepped ghostlike through the smashed door. Its feathers wet and speckled with mud. It peered at Miranda with bright gold eyes, unblinking. It took one step deeper into the room, then snapped a moth from the air, dropped a turd on the floor, and went back onto the porch.

Sweat-soaked and ripe with the wild, iron reek of the

deer, Miranda picked herself up and walked outside. She scanned the yard, but the crane was gone.

Kicking broken glass from the porch, she went down the embankment to the dock and fetched her father's green metal tackle box from the boat. She took it along the grassy slope, past Hiram's old work shed, his pickup parked alongside it, three flat tires and a trash-tree threading through the engine block. Snatching a beer bottle from the weeds, she went into the trees at the edge of the property, then down to the water's edge, where the embankment rose up steeply. She jammed the bottle into the soft dirt of the embankment wall and stepped back until her heels touched lapping water. She set the tackle box down and opened it and took out Cook's Smith & Wesson. Assumed a stance by instinct, legs apart. She cracked her neck and sighted down the barrel of the gun. She cocked the hammer, didn't care for the harsh metal click. She fired. The gun bucked, deafening. The bottle blew apart. The night was hushed, shocked into silence. She fired again. A pop of dirt and glass. She fired a third time, not really aiming, and the bullet bounced and struck the water.

Miranda looked down at the gun. A thing apart from her. Outside of her.

Like Riddle's pistol, jabbing at her belly, poking at her breast.

Suddenly the air was cooler and the leaves on the trees were brittle and brown, not green, and it was not tonight, but an autumn twilight, nine years past, and she was not twenty-one but twelve going on thirteen, leggy and rawboned, about to learn that life was a series of ceaseless struggles against ceaseless currents.

Gun in hand, she felt her gorge rise. She bent, retched into the sandy bank.

Behind her, the river ran on, smooth as black glass.

She remembered odd details, fragments: how the autumn night fell like a door slammed by the wind. Climbing the bank into the trees at a place stairstepped with roots. She wore cut-offs, a T-shirt. A duffel slung across her shoulders, contents heavy, clanking. Deep in the thicket, she dropped to a knee in the moist leaves, set her flashlight on the ground, and un-slung the bag. She drew out a ten-pound length of iron and set it beside the light. Hammered a fat wooden stake into the ground. She remembered the hungry, jagged sound the iron made when scraped over the stake. Rust flaked on her palms, the muscles in her arms steady quivering. She'd rum-maged an empty coffee can from the duffel as, all at once, fat brown worms came boiling out of the earth. Hiram's voice in her head, teaching her: *They wriggle up. You pluck the big ones.*

Rooding: a summoning through pressure, violence.

When the can was full, she wiped her brow, smearing dirt on her forehead.

Charlie Riddle, silent as a wraith, stepped out from behind a tree.

The flashlight beam caught the scuffed, square toes of his cowboy boots.

He was younger and slimmer, possessed of both eyes.

He reached a stray night crawler out of the leaves.

Plopped the worm into the can and took her flashlight and stood, shining the light in her eyes.

There were words, first. She remembered that. Something about truancy, the school, and she said something back, something smart, defiant, how his fingers were always in her till. She kept her chin up, drove a knife through every word. But he took a step closer, just one step, and the light between them diminished so that the glow was confined to the space between their bodies, the dark beyond them menacing and deep. Treetops like skeleton arms above them.

She did not move. She remembered this: how she could not move.

He touched her, caressed her cheek—

She slung the can of earthworms in his face and ran, but she fell. Maybe her foot snagged the rooding stake. She couldn't be sure. She went sprawling in the leaves and Riddle fell atop her, driving the breath right out of her. He wrenched her onto her back, pinned her by the wrists. The flashlight flew from his hand, sent a bar of light across a log. She heaved and twisted, felt his knee between her thighs, forcing her legs apart. The smell of him all coconut and heat and he was saying things, things about her mother, things about Miranda, but she was not listening, only trying to breathe, and when his iron grip on her hand loosened as he fumbled at the button of his jeans, she shot her hand out and drove her thumb hard into Charlie Riddle's left eye.

She remembered the feel of it, like a moist ball of worms.

Her thumb sinking past the knuckle.

Riddle screaming, louder than she ever thought a man could scream.

And somehow she was up and staggering, trying to run, no breath to run with, stumbling down the slope to the river's edge, following it by the light of the harvest moon. Beneath the back porch overhang, balancing over the gangplank to the floating dock, and dragging the old johnboat into the water and tugging the starter. Tears streaking her face, whole body quaking, she aimed the boat upriver and goosed the throttle.

Some time later—how long, who could say?—she cut the motor and drifted, let the current spin her around.

She felt something wet and sticky in her fist.

She opened her hand.

The constable's eye, cornflower-blue, stared up at her in jellied halves.

She flung the pieces in the river, and the river carried them away.

Miranda sat in the sand, Cook's pistol between her feet, watching the current roll blackly on. She touched her stomach beneath her blood-stiff shirt, felt the bruise already forming. By morning, it would take the vague shape of Charlie Riddle's pistol grip. Days from now, she would feel it still, memory and pain become one, as they did.

After a while, she put the pistol away in Hiram's tackle box and went back to the mercantile, where she stood outside in the glow of the front porch light, staring through the broken door, into a place that had not been a refuge for a very long time. There, on the floor, like visiting spirits, she and Hiram Crabtree sat ensconced in a fort of cardboard boxes. Hiram wore his apron, lifting cans out of the boxes and kissing them with a yellow price gun. He gave Miranda the priced cans to shelve and she moved the older stock to the front and turned them with the labels facing out, as he had taught her. A Crown portable by the register played Kitty Wells, who sang about honky-tonk angels. She saw old-timers, too, long-limbed and horn-rimmed, their sun-burned necks. Among them: Hiram, a tray of fresh Colonial in his arms, sleeves rolled up, service tattoo just visible. The men asking him questions, casting lines like the fishermen they were, reeling in strange and useless facts and Hiram laughing with them, his head full of things not yet jettisoned from the time before the Landing: some bit of mathematical or musical arcana, the names of German composers, the shapes of the stars, the pictures they made. Hiram the only one of three brothers not killed in some war. Back from Korea, deaf in one ear at twenty-one. Drawn home by his father's heart attack. Miranda wondered if he ever planned to stay away, to live overseas and play guitar on the streets like some half-deaf wonder.

From the shattered bait cooler, which would cool no more thanks to Riddle's bullet, Miranda took the last half dozen Styrofoam pints of worms, stacking them in her arms. She took them out to the edge of the trees and released them, dumping each pint on the ground, leaving the worms to sort their own fates among the dirt and leaves.

She went back inside, pulling the fly-screen shut and latching it, telling herself she would fix the busted frame later. Now she only wanted to be rid of these clothes, the stink of blood. Upstairs, she went into the bathroom shared between the master bedroom and her childhood bedroom and sat on the edge of the cast-iron tub and ran the water until it was hot. She stoppered the drain to let it fill. She took off her shirt and shucked her jeans and underwear and eased into the tub, let the dirt that ringed her neck and ears loosen, float away, the muck of the day and night dissolve. Miranda put her big toe into the dripping faucet and watched the water run around it. There were calluses on her feet, her heels thick and white. Scratches on her shins. She draped a damp washcloth over her face and slunk down in the tub. Before the water in the bath had even begun to cool, she was asleep.

DIGGING

It was after eight o'clock when she wrapped herself in her father's heavy robe and went into the kitchen, where she ate a cheese sandwich standing at the sink. In the living room, from the bookshelf beside the Victrola, she took down a slim family photo album and her father's service annual and brought both with her into the master bedroom, where she lay on her side atop the covers and flipped through each from front to back. Looking for what, she did not know—a bulwark, perhaps, against the day's bad memories. Some gentle segue into a few hours of dreamless sleep before the run.

First, in the album, pictures of Crabtrees, sepia-toned pages of stern-faced men and women in suspenders and homemade dresses. She knew nothing about them save the names and dates penciled beside their photographs in the careful, elegant script of her mother's hand. They had become, in her imagination, a cast of players whose lives were hard and grief-stricken, much like hers, and somehow this gave her comfort, that others of her blood had suffered the land. She moved on, past photographs of Cora in high school, books clutched against her sweater as she stood alongside a Ford tractor, then to a wedding photo of Cora and Hiram, her father's hair long, the little church where they had married candlelit. Finally, near the end of the album, a picture of Miranda and Cora, the only one she knew to exist, taken scant months before she died: Miranda, age four, stood at the end of a pier, wearing a toddler's overalls and a western shirt, the sleeves shoved up to the elbows. In one hand she held the handle of a cane fishing pole that lay on the pier. She was not smiling, only squinting into the morning sun. Behind her, crouching, Cora in a pair of pedal pushers and Keds, hair wrapped in a red bandanna. A minnow bucket beside them. Miranda wished she could remember what she could not: the sweet scents of honeysuckle and manure, the tang of carp discarded among the rocks. Birds picking at the meat. The wet flap of minnows in the dipper net. The brush of her mother's hair against her cheek as she reached around her and showed her, patiently, how to set a hook in the wet doll's eye of her bait.

She moved on to Hiram's service annual, which held pictures of men who all looked alike, sharp and solid in pressed khakis, standing row upon row and all wearing sun-scoured expressions. Behind them parking lots of heavy equipment, airfields scattered with jeeps and jets. She came to a circle drawn faintly in pencil around the head of a fourth-row enlistee. Hiram. Young and handsome. Cora's handwriting in the margins.

Here they were, she thought, two ghosts, side by side. Much like their graves beneath the sweetgum tree. Cora's complete with coffin and bones in the shade. Hiram's yet empty, never to be filled.

She closed the service annual, and a loose photograph skated out from the back. Miranda plucked it from between the pages. She sat up on the bed.

A color image, bordered white and double-exposed.

The original picture was a scene she had no memory of or context for: Cora, in a tire swing that had once hung from the giant sweetgum, feet bare, dress pushed by the wind to her knees, caught mid-swing like some long-extinct creature in amber.

The double exposure: Cora, again, in a blue dress, standing in the living room, electric *Gone with the Wind* lamps lit behind her. Her face obscured by her other face, the one in the tire swing, a kind of bright corona around her head. Some trick of light.

Miranda had never seen this photograph before. She flipped to the back of the annual and saw where it had been stuck between two blank pages, never curated, never cared for.

She thought of her father's camera, shelved in the closet soon after Cora died. Still there now, empty as a robbed grave. As far as Miranda knew, it had never taken another photograph since the day Hiram set it there.

What did it mean, that Hiram had stuck this picture in his annual, a book commemorating a past he never spoke of?

Had this been the last true photograph of her mother?

She tucked the picture back into the annual and set it

and the album on the scuffed nightstand, next to a framed picture of Cora, young, sitting on the porch swing of a house Miranda did not know. Dark-haired, beautiful.

Miranda drew the family quilt over her knees and switched off the light. Limbs heavy, stomach aching from the bruise of Charlie Riddle's gun, she drew Hiram's robe tight around her and imagined she lay in the shallow water of her own false grave. To bury herself, perchance to sleep and wake in a thousand years, when the horrible events of that summer had long passed from memory.

She had worked the store, back then, day in, day out, keeping up appearances while search parties roamed inlets and byways. He'll come back, she told people. Hiram would come home. Later: fried chicken and stewed corn and collard greens and purple-hull peas in Pyrex bowls, brought by the wives of the old men who came for bait and cigars and tackle, until finally the days became weeks and the weeks became months, and in August the ladies came for their bowls and the old men who still came for bait and beer asked after her like kindly grandfathers. She hated them for it. Hated them for believing that Hiram Crabtree was lost or drowned, when she knew something so much worse had happened.

But what truth did she really know? Besides crying herself to sleep at night, or the grief and fear and uncertainty of what would happen when August ended and school came around and she was worn down to a dull and lusterless thing, not a girl anymore but a collection of bones shambling in the skin of a girl. And so, Hiram's grave: an end to uncertainty, to her own secret trips, searching sunup to

sundown the bottomlands beyond Iskra's island, looking for
a wide lake where deadfalls bobbed like coffins, a great rock
and tree. Instead of finding: digging, beneath the gum tree
with Hiram's old trenching shovel until the water sloshed at
her ankles and there were blisters like fisheyes on her palms
and the walls were pocked with roots and clods and worms
and there was only three feet of red clay separating Miranda
from her mother's coffin in the grave next door. The sun
spread red by the time she finished. The grave where Hiram Crabtree would never lie.

I'll dig my own grave, she thought, nearing sleep now.
*I'll dig so deep all the tears I've never shed will well up out of the
ground and flood the river.* And in that great flood, mayhap
her father's body would rise up from its true grave out in
the vast, muddy wilds of this corner of Arkansas, or some
other land she had yet to discover, and he would be hers
again.

She fell asleep.

First, she was four, and the shovel was too big for her, and
Hiram, wearing a black suit, lifted her out of the grave,
which was not a grave but a Radio Flyer. Inside, the last
of the old men in dark suits were drawn to the woodstove
like iron filings. Air strong with the sweet stink of chewing tobacco as their spit sizzled. Wives huddled in clumps
and whispers. Hiram carried Miranda to the stairwell at the
back of the room and sat her on the steps, touched her nose,
and went back to the old men. One of them rose to give
Hiram his seat. This was Billy Cotton, the preacher from

Sabbath House. He wore a black suit and black bolo tie and had a head of sweeping chestnut hair. Square jaw, sharp eyes. He did not belong here, in this memory. An interloper. Beside him: his wife, a small, pretty woman with sad eyes.

The dream—

memory

—shifted, and now Miranda was eleven, twelve, thirteen and tromping upstairs in mud-soaked clothes, face streaked orange from digging Hiram's false grave, and she walked into the living room and there, again, was the preacher, tall as the ceiling, a pillar of black. Beside him the dwarf, John Avery, whom she did not yet know.

The preacher was older, his face lined, his hair gray. The living room curtains billowed behind them, the dwarf standing at the preacher's side in jeans and a child's plaid shirt tucked in, big wide hands clasped at his waist as if in prayer, and it was night outside, her mother's lamps glowing warmly in their globes.

The preacher's eyes were large and brown and solemn. He wanted something.

He *needed* something.

Work, she thought. *They are going to offer you work. And you will take it. Because you need it. Because the boy is growing and he will need things you can't get from selling crickets and minnows to old men.*

"Your door was open, child," the preacher said.

IN THE LAND OF SPAIN

In the hour before midnight, Miranda dressed in a sleeveless T-shirt and jeans, opened the hall closet, and shouldered a leather quiver of cedar shafts fixed with target points. On the zebra-wood rack mounted above the couch in the living room, three bows hung, unstrung: the Remington she had taken hunting with Littlefish that day, Hiram's black maple Bear, and a Root recurve she had bought from a Sears catalogue when she was thirteen. She chose the Root, slipped on a leather arm guard and shooting glove, and went out onto the rear deck and climbed down to the floating dock. Standing in the shine from the naked porch bulb, she held each end of the Root and swept it over her head and all the way down to the small of her back, then back to the front of her thighs. Up, over, down. Up, over, down. She did this ten, fifteen, twenty times, and the muscles and tendons in her shoulders and chest came awake. Next, she looped a bowstring around the recurve's lower limb, slipped her foot across it, and pulled the string up and over the fiberglass until it snapped taut at the tip. Legs apart, as with Cook's pistol, she nocked an arrow from her quiver, brought the weapon up, and drew right-handed, aiming for a pillowcase stuffed with straw. It shone in the moonlight where it hung from a maple tree far back beyond the honeysuckle, in a fescue field across the river. From tip to target, at least seventy yards. She held full-draw for the space of three breaths, as Hiram had taught her, long ago, and in those three breaths she felt the light kiss of the fletching against the corner of her mouth. The arrow went out of focus at the edge of her sight and the target came into focus. The dock rocked gently beneath her. She upped her pull, back tightening. Felt the heat of the draw, the tension running all through her, the burn beneath her breast.

Her arrow struck the pillowcase dead center.

Miranda shot twice more in the next twelve seconds, and each time her arrow found its mark, above and below the first.

In the kitchen, the clock read eleven-thirty.

She put the target arrows away in the hall closet and set the Root back in its cradle above the couch. From the fridge, she took two sausage patties she had cooked a few nights back. She unwrapped them from tinfoil and ate them in three bites.

Downstairs, she pulled the broken door shut and pushed it open again, working the splintered frame. A hammer and a few boards would fix it short-term, so she started off the porch for the work shed that stood between the mercantile and the boat ramp. On the ramp, in a circle of blue fluorescent light, less than an arm's length from the water's edge, the mud-speckled crane stood like a piece of statuary, its long white wings tipped in black. It watched her, tracked her progress from store to shed, its head a white question mark. She kept walking, though it slowed her pace, this curious bird. Holding her gaze with its bright-coin eyes.

Do we hunt them?

A memory: she was small, in a life jacket on the center plank as the johnboat drifted through a columned maze of cypress. The sky above purpling with a coming storm. Hiram paddling, bending down so his face was close to hers and pointing over her shoulder, up, into the trees, where all around them the cranes were roosting, huge and white against the day. The rain began to patter among the trees. His voice a whisper: "Watch, how they spread their wings."

She, just a child, but knowing, somehow, that this was important. A moment by which others would later be measured.

"Do we hunt them?"

"We do."

"Why?"

"There is a place in the land of Spain," Hiram said, "where parents hang their children's food in trees, and the children cannot eat until they sever the strings that hold their food. They sever them," he said, "with arrows shot from bows. Do you understand?"

In the shed, she picked up two boards from a pile of scrap, along with a handful of nails and a hammer, and went back to the mercantile to fix the door.

Down at the ramp, the crane was gone.

III

✦

Second Run

IN HIS TREE, LITTLEFISH DREAMING

Littlefish hid beneath Baba's stilted porch and watched the grassy clearing far below the kudzu, where, just beyond the fence, in the moonglow, a girl stood. He had never seen a girl like this. She was not much older than he. She wore a white gown, was pale like the underside of a green leaf turned in the wind. Littlefish stood at the edge of the kudzu and watched as the man in the black suit and broad-brimmed hat slashed his way out of the forest with his blade and went at her. She was unmoving, rigid, as if planted in the ground with a stake at her back. The man in the hat swung his blade at the girl's head and Littlefish woke, mouth open in a silent scream, the only kind he knew.

The boy reached into the knothole above his head and took out a black pencil. On the boards of his platform, by moonlight, he began to draw, pressing grooves into grain.

Bad dreams are just bits of stories, Sister had said yesterday, as they dressed the deer beneath the oak. She took his knife, cut slits in the animal's forelegs and hind legs. *Just pieces, all scattered. When the pieces get mixed up, the stories don't make sense. When stories don't make sense, they scare us.* She pushed the hind hooves through the slits in the forelegs, interlocking them. *You have to fit the pieces together, make sense of it all.* Shouldering the deer like a pack, she stood, and together they walked out of the meadow and into the dusky woods, back to Baba's cabin. A boy and a woman and on the woman's back the deer he had killed.

He looked at what he'd drawn on the boards: a crude stick figure of the girl in his dream.

Who was she? Where did she fit into his story?

Littlefish bit his tongue. Pressed hard into the wood. The lead broke.

Beyond his lookout, the moon was a silver sickle slicing the sky.

THE TRADE TONIGHT

✦

Avery did not greet Miranda as she tied off the Alumacraft. He wrestled the blue Igloo to the edge of the dock and into her arms, jars inside clinking. She wedged the chest in the center of the boat, her shirt riding up, and Avery saw the pistol snugged in the waist of her jeans. He ran a hand through his unkempt mane, fingers tangling. He took a joint from his shirt pocket, lit up, and sat down hard on the edge of the dock, where he let his feet dangle. He spoke two words, like nails punched through tin: "Things change."

Miranda gave him a sharp, questioning look, and he flapped his shirttail.

She put a hand to the small of her back and drew her shirt down.

The dwarf took a hit on his joint, his eyes already far off. He coughed, deep and rattling.

"You smoke too much of that shit," Miranda said. She had cast off her line, was bending to start the motor.

"Hey," Avery croaked.

She glared at him.

"Riddle, earlier tonight, he didn't, I mean—are you . . . ?"

She cranked the boat, drowned him out.

The motor faded, and Avery stood alone, smoking.

A mournful whistle broke the deep silence. Up the lane, beneath the reaching boughs of the oaks, a tall, gangling Cotton went wandering, bending every now and then to pick up rocks, inspecting each. Some he threw away. Others he pushed into the toe of a black wing tip he carried beneath his arm. His right foot was bare.

Eventually he disappeared into the deep shadows behind the manse, though Avery could hear him still, whistling.

The Alumacraft peeled away from Sabbath House and onto the river, and here Miranda throttled up and cruised for a while, the boat's dark wake rolling in toward the banks. The great stitching clamor of the bottoms rose up like a tide and drowned the buzz of the twenty-horse Evinrude. She knew every bend and oxbow, the low points where the sandbars would ground her, the deadfalls and stumps and suckholes. She knew the nesting trees of great blue herons. As a girl, she'd stolen their feathers and fixed them to arrows shot from blinds into rabbits and deer. She was a hunter. She understood the prey she hunted. Where it lived, where it ate. What it wanted. How to get it. She took comfort in such order, such need.

Things change.

She glanced at the blue Igloo, wedged between the

center and stern seats, packed with the second batch of Avery's dope in mason jars. The chest was heavier this time. The batch bigger. She kept one hand on the tiller, reached behind her, felt Cook's gun tucked in the waist of her jeans.

Tonight, for the first time in seven years, she did not know what the river carried her to. She only felt an irrevocable sense of things in motion. The old witch's words whispered in her ear: *Something's waking up out there.*

"Shake it off," she told herself.

The boat pushed on through the darkest hour of the night.

The moon had set by the time the boat ramp beyond the railroad trestle came into view. At the top of the ramp, two men eased out of a white Bronco. Miranda throttled back. She cut the motor alongside the barge and tied off. The men, who waited at the top of the hill, did not descend. She climbed onto the barge, watching them watch her. Two silhouettes against the vapor lamp bleeding blue over ground and trees. One was tall, broad-shouldered, wearing a hooded sweatshirt with the hood pulled up, his face a dark cave. The other man was short and stocky and bald. Both stood very still.

Miranda felt a bead of sweat drip from her hairline down the nape of her neck. It ran the length of her spine, around the cold knob of gunmetal in the small of her back. Pulse racing, she had no spit. She pulled the Igloo out of the boat and stepped into the dewy grass at the base of the ramp. Raised the cooler high above her head, a question.

Crickets along the bank fell silent when the tall man boomed: "Thirty paces up the ramp, then you stop."

Arms shaking, she lowered the cooler to her waist and moved slowly, willing herself to stay calm, to hold at full draw until the tremors passed. Thirty paces and she stopped.

The tall man came down, silver wallet chain shining. He was huge, a giant. He walked with an odd, careless grace in heavy engineer's boots, thumbs hooked in the pockets of jeans. When he drew close, he pushed the hood from his head, and Miranda took an involuntary step back. His hair was shorn, his jaw square and set. The features of his face were obscured behind a mask of tattoos that rendered him a living death's-head skull, teeth inked in his cheeks, nose a blackened, ragged triangle. Cracks beneath and above his eyes and fissuring out from the corners of his mouth. A pendant lay in the hollow of his collarbone, a crow's foot on a length of rawhide.

"What's your name?" he asked. His voice was soft, almost warm.

"Does it matter?"

The giant smiled.

Miranda set the Igloo down. The jars shifted inside.

"Open it."

She squatted, conscious of the cold revolver against her skin. She opened the cooler. The giant held out a hand, and she saw that the flesh there, too, was tattooed. Thin bones along the backs of his fingers. Miranda passed one of the jars up. The giant turned it in the vague light. "Mexican dope," he said, "is for shit. Too many pesticides. Handsome

Charlie, he vouched for this. Said it was worth the trouble. That true?"

"I don't smoke it," Miranda said. "I just bring it."

The giant put the jar back and carried the cooler up the ramp. At the top, he and his partner spoke, their voices low. The smaller man wore a white T-shirt tucked into jeans tucked into cowboy boots, over the T-shirt a leather jacket. Face pitted with acne. He took the Igloo from the giant to the Bronco, where he opened the rear hatch and slid the cooler inside, then drew out a Styrofoam chest from the bed, the kind Miranda sold minnows in at the mercantile. The small man walked it back, set the chest at Miranda's feet. Clear packing tape, wrapped twice around, sealed the chest. Scrawled in black marker across the lid was one word: PREACHER.

"This our trade?" Miranda asked.

"Tell Preacher," the small man said, his voice a rasp, "it's in the mouth." He grinned as he withdrew, every tooth filed sharp, a shark's mouth.

Sweat dripped beneath her arms, down her back. She felt her shirttail ride up over the pistol as she bent to pick up the chest. Whatever was inside was large and heavy and packed in old ice, half-melted chunks shifting. Standing, she let her shirttail drop naturally and started for the bottom of the ramp, hoping the gun wasn't a lump beneath her shirt.

"Wait," the giant called.

She froze.

A dome light lit the Bronco's cab as the small man tugged at some unseen cargo in the front seat. When he kicked the door shut, his arms were full of a sleeping child, a girl, wrapped in a serape. The tops of the girl's bare feet stuck out of the blanket, jouncing with every step as the two men came down the ramp.

Miranda felt something inside her list. "What is this?" she said.

Ignoring her, the giant drew a hypodermic needle from his sweatshirt pocket, the barrel filled with clear liquid.

Miranda set the Styrofoam chest down hard, its contents sloshing.

"What *is* this?" she said again, louder, fear giving way to fury.

The giant clamped his teeth around the plastic cap of the needle and pulled it free with his mouth. He reached into the serape and drew out the girl's arm, rolled up the sleeve of her cotton pajamas, which were patterned with little pink pigs with wings. Her flesh was etched with thin white scars. In the hollow of her elbow, a nest of punctures.

Miranda yanked the .38 from the small of her back and brought it up and thumbed back the hammer. "Stop," she said, but she heard the weakness in her voice, more plea than command, and knew instantly—as she often knew at the moment of release that her arrow would spin off wildly, drop low or high—she had misjudged.

The giant spat the syringe cap into his hand, capped the needle.

He took three slow steps down the ramp toward Miranda.

How easy it should have been, to pull the trigger. Such a small space between her target and the barrel, but this was a man, a human being, no deer, no rabbit, no beer bottle in the dirt. Her finger frozen. The gun a hunk of metal, not a part of her, not a thing she could feel, and the weakness spread quickly to her center, a kind of quivering sick. Exposed, caught out. No arrow handy. She had felt the same once when she was ten, had chanced upon a boar deep in the bottoms. Huge and shaggy and fly-swarmed, possessed of curving tusks like scythes. Only Hiram's arrow, flying out of the trees, had saved her from evisceration.

The giant reached out and took the gun.

"I don't need to tell you what you've just done wrong, do I," he said.

He seized her wrist and wrenched her around, wrapped his tree-trunk arm around her throat, and his breath was warm in her ear and smelled of wintergreen gum and she clawed at his arm as he said, "I'm betting from the way you took a shooter's stance just now you know how to handle yourself. But to pull a gun is to pull a trigger, and you didn't pull it, Does-It-Matter." He tightened his arm around her throat.

Miranda felt her windpipe closing.

He spoke, red tongue flapping in the hole of a skull's mouth. "That girl, she's nobody. Every soul we burned to get her, they were nobodies, too. Good dope for her. *That's* the trade tonight. Tomorrow night, maybe we'll trade something else. In the meantime, you think about this: what's the worst thing a man ever did to you?"

The world was sliding away, purple spots firing behind her eyes.

"You think we'll be nicer?"

She sagged in the big man's grip. He let her go and tossed the gun in the grass.

Miranda dropped to her knees, sucking air.

The needle slid into the girl's arm, hit the vein in the hollow of her elbow, and the giant depressed the plunger. When the liquid was pushed into her, the girl rolled her head against the small man's chest, as if she had been rocked asleep. He carried the child past Miranda, down the ramp, and lay the girl in the bottom of the Alumacraft. He arranged the serape over her.

Miranda had not even caught her breath by the time they cranked the Bronco, and when they were gone, she fell on her back and lay staring up at the sky, dawn's faint glow to the east. She picked up Cook's gun from the grass and set it atop the chest, all but falling into the boat with the sleeping child. With a shaking hand, she closed the gun in Hiram's tackle box and sat on the stern seat, the girl a lump in the bottom of the boat. Miranda sat trembling, staring at nothing, until the crickets resumed their song in the reeds along the bank.

IT'S IN THE MOUTH

On the return, she cut the motor and drifted off the river into a cypress grove where the shallow water was thick with duckweed, clumps of little white flowers blooming in hollow stumps. Cypress trees stretching tall and cathedral-like into the morning mist. The world graying up. As if bewitched, the girl slept on beneath the brightly colored blanket. Miranda put her a few years older than Littlefish. Her face was sallow, her frame small. A streak of soot across her forehead. Her hair was short, cut close to the scalp. She smelled like smoke and something else, something sick. Miranda moved to the center seat and lifted the edge of the serape. She pushed up the girl's sleeve. At the elbow, the needle marks, like fairy footprints, the most recent still pearled with blood. Below these, all the way down to the wrist, a faded latticework of scars.

The ice in the Styrofoam chest shifted.

Miranda covered the child and drew the cooler between

her feet. She took Hiram's Old Timer pocketknife from his tackle box. She slit the tape and opened the lid, which came free with a shriek.

No.

NO.

Cook's head peered up from inside a clear plastic bag printed with a blue polar bear and tied at the top with a twist-tie. His eyes had rolled up in his skull. His beard was matted red. An inch or so of blood had settled in the bottom of the bag. It beaded and sluiced in the folds of the plastic.

She gripped the gunwale, stared down at her sneakers, the cuffs of her jeans rolled above the ankles. Every detail of her skin—the veins beneath the surface carrying blood to her toes; the mole above her ankle and the mosquito perched beside it sucking life; her knuckles scabbed over where she had punched the mercantile's floor hours earlier—all in stark contrast to the white foam box, where death bobbed like an oversized cork.

Somewhere close, an owl hooted in a tree.

Miranda forced herself to look at Cook's head.

She saw something, a tight bundle of plastic, rubber-banded. Wedging his mouth open.

She closed the lid, the humid morning crawling wetly inside her shirt. For the longest time, she sat unmoving. Staring at PREACHER on the lid of the chest.

At some point—she wasn't sure when, or for how long—the chatter of a motor rose over birdsong from the river. Not a welcomed sound, but she was strangely grateful for it, grateful to look away and fix her attention on anything but the cooler.

Back out beyond the trees, the boat passed on.

The girl stirred. The blanket fell away as she rolled onto her side and curled fetal and moaned and opened her mouth. A spasm rolled up from her belly, and Miranda had just realized what was happening when it happened. The girl vomited into the bottom of the boat. Bile and some colorless gob, oatmeal or baby food. Brief and sour-smelling. Her eyes were open, and she was shivering. A crescent of vomit on her cheek.

Miranda slipped over the center seat to where the girl lay. She reached to wipe the vomit from her cheek, and the girl flinched and drew into a tight ball.

"It's okay," Miranda said. She reached out again.

Touched the girl's cheek.

Later, she could only think of it as a sudden breach, as a fish breaks the glassy surface of the water in the late evening purple: the entrance of a bold, beautiful presence, large and all-encompassing. It leaped up between them when Miranda's fingers touched the girl's skin and the girl's eyes flicked toward her, met hers, sharing an awareness— of what, Miranda did not know. In an instant, time had collapsed and all the rest of her days shuttered forward to the end, and they were melancholy and not without grief. A waking vision of herself, her age unknowable. She wore jeans and sneakers and one of Hiram's old shirts, as she so often did, was drifting to sleep beneath the spreading boughs of an oak, its knuckled bark scored by lightning. Bow and quiver at her side, quiver empty. And with this, an undercurrent of warmth, of goodness, a heartbeat strong and steady. Familiar.

Miranda fell back, gasping.

The girl locked eyes a moment longer, then was swept away by a drugged blankness, her eyes rolling up as she continued to shake.

Miranda felt weak, old snakebite on her arm buzzing, nerves alight.

She felt a tear slip down her cheek. She wiped it, then covered the child and cranked the motor. She eased out of the trees and back onto the river.

CHOICES

Later, Miranda took an old Zero bar from Hiram's tackle box and held it out across the length of the boat, keeping one hand on the tiller. The girl's eyes remained fixed on the blue morning sky, had been for the last mile of the river, open but glazed, empty. After a moment, Miranda split the wrapper and ate the candy herself. The wind had tugged the serape from the girl's chest. Small as she was in her child's pajamas, she was not without the first hints of adolescence.

They rounded the last bend before Sabbath House, and the high, crumbling stone wall of the property rose from the water's edge. The wall disappeared into the trees. Ahead, Miranda could see the inlet.

Without knowing she was going to do it, she cut the motor and drifted. Listened to the silence of the morning, a few birdcalls, mist on the water burning away as the sun crested the trees. She looked at the girl, felt a sudden terror seize her heart. In a single morning, she had lost control of everything, the way ahead no longer hers. She felt the boat tugged sideways by the current. The bank ahead awash in golden light.

In the water weeds there, just this side of the inlet, standing perfectly still, a white whooping crane with black-tipped wings watched the Alumacraft spin. Miranda met its gaze, knowing it was the same bird she had seen at the Landing the night before. Again, it stood upon a thresh-old: the inlet to Sabbath House. *There are places we belong*, it seemed to say. *Places we don't.*

Places, perhaps, yet to be discovered.

She thought of Charlie Riddle, Billy Cotton, men who would take possession of this child, a girl dirty and drugged and not much younger than Miranda herself when she had gone to work for them. She remembered the preacher and John Avery in her living room, laying out their plan, asking their favors, assuring her of the money she would make. All part of God's plan for the greater good of His kingdom, Cotton said, and she, telling him she had no use for gods and their kingdoms. Suspecting, from the old man's sly smile, that he didn't, either. But cash, she said, just fourteen years old, *that* she could use. To keep a roof over her head and the electricity turned on to cool the bait. To keep an old witch in tobacco and a secret baby healthy. Outside, in the heat, waiting by the car, one-eyed Charlie Riddle, grown fatter. Chewing a toothpick, waving at flies. Miranda at the window, one hand parting her mother's homemade curtain. "Just keep that man away from me," she said.

The preacher's promise: "He won't bother you again."

If all these years had taught Miranda anything, it was

this: Sabbath House had no use for innocence. Here, the early blush of womanhood would befoul like clear water after the first fish is gutted. And there was something unusual about this child, some truth—perhaps beautiful, perhaps terrible—Miranda had yet to grasp. If the old preacher wanted her, it was for no good reason at all.

The crane watched as the Alumacraft drifted on past the inlet, where, beyond the cypress breaks, unseen to her and her to them, the dwarf and the constable waited.

Miranda ripped the engine and throttled up. She looked back over her shoulder and the crane was gone.

The Landing lay one mile south.

You need a plan, she thought.

The boat sped on.

WHAT THE GIRL SAW, ON
THE PROSPER

✦

Her mind muddled, river dizzying as it rushed past. Heart pounding, too, for there was something large and black and horrible chasing them. She saw it in the distant blue sky, behind the woman at the boat's tiller, a black cloud with tendrils coiling earthward, a monstrous hole with teeth, come to gnash them, swallow them, spit them out in pieces.

She had seen it before, not so long ago, above the trailers in the field where the rooms were red and the sad women worked behind shut doors. A monster in need of banishment by the light of something sweet and soft and good. The women in those dark red rooms had none of that, and so they had not seen it coiling for them. Waiting to devour.

But she had.

Over the giant's shoulder as he carried her away, kicking, crying, trailers burning and the women screaming. Visions jolting through her like currents: flames on a river, a wicked curved blade, the giant's face painted in blood. A dark specter of pain and suffering, spreading over the tree-tops of a wide, green land.

Then the man with the sharp teeth jammed the needle into her arm, and after that: nothing. Until—

The woman.

The woman in the boat had touched her—*Miranda, Miranda is her name*—and the girl had seen the woman's life as God must see the earth, a transparent jewel suspended in darkness. The whole cast of characters, the whole long history of everything rooted in the wet soil of the swamps, a terrible long night that had become a nexus in time for this woman, an island at the center of her ocean, a bread bowl and two shotgun blasts in the dark and a father lost and a girl, searching, searching, always searching, her heart a hollowed-out place where secrets could be hidden and found.

One of those secrets: a boy.

Strange and magical and *good*.

A facet of the jewel, a glimmer of bright green in all that darkness.

Behind them, though, that coiling cloud. Following, until finally it peeled away to glide wraithlike over the moss-thick trees and swamps, to disappear into the folds of time and wait, biding its own to strike.

The girl shut her eyes, drifted off in an empty fog.

FAITH

Leaning against the weathered dock rail, sleeves rolled past his meaty elbows, Charlie Riddle flipped a quarter in a dull, lazy way. When the boat motor had faded, he held up the coin between his thumb and index finger. "I win," he said to Avery, who stood at the end of the dock, bleary-eyed. Riddle pushed the coin into his pocket and jingled it with his keys. "Told you she'd do it. Motored right on by. It's what killed this place to begin with, you ask me. Women turning soft. Women get soft, they'll pull the pin on the whole damn thing. Trace it all back to that, I swear."

"That's how you see it?"

"It is."

"I don't guess it matters now."

Riddle looked at Avery as if considering something, then tipped his sweat-stained fedora back on thinning hair and took the quarter out of his pocket and flipped it at the dwarf and Avery caught it against his chest.

"You keep that, John. Consider it the first of all that back pay. Days to come, you might need a little faith in your pocket. Bout what it's worth around here." Riddle winked, lumbered off for his car beneath the crepe myrtles.

Avery closed his fist around the quarter in his hand. He looked out at the inlet, the river beyond. The drone of the girl's motor fading.

He put the quarter in his pocket.

ARRANGEMENTS

At the Landing, Miranda lifted the girl out of the boat. The serape fell into the river, where it was carried off to snag in the brambles on the far bank. The girl slumped like a broken reed against the gas pump at the center of the dock. Miranda snapped her fingers in front of the child's half-lidded eyes, got a sluggish reaction. She looked out at the river. Beyond the boat ramp, the pine thickets, and through the pines the road. Up the road: Sabbath House.

Riddle would be coming. Quickly.

Miranda ran out the plank that served as the gangway between the port side of the dock and the kudzu-draped bank beneath the porch overhang. She bent, lifted the girl's arms around her neck, and gathered her up. She was scrawny, light. "Don't you puke on me," Miranda said, going carefully across the plank. She climbed the embankment and went around to the front.

Boards, nailed over the door. She had forgotten.

A string of profanity yanked out of her like a starter cord.

She felt the girl's arms tighten around her shoulders. A small, warm hand brushed her neck, and Miranda thought she felt a sudden breeze sweep over her, envelop her. She was momentarily dazzled by the flash of sunlight between leaves, as if she lay on her back looking up into the lower branches of the oak she had seen earlier in her vision, but as sudden as the sensation came it was gone, and once again she was standing on the Landing's porch with a drugged girl in her arms. Her heartbeat had quickened, was slowing. She took deep, deliberate breaths.

Miranda set the child down against the wall by the bagged-ice freezer, went out to the shed for a hammer, and came back and pried the boards loose. The door swung open, hung there from a single hinge, busted. She carried the girl across the threshold and teetered up the narrow, hidden stairs.

She put the girl in her childhood bed, atop the covers. Miranda had not slept in this room in over five years. The unfinished chest of drawers and bureau still held a smattering of girlhood: a teddy bear, a porcelain clown holding a bunch of balloons, her only game trophy, a four-pound white perch, hanging above the iron-framed bed.

Time against her, she went through the kitchen onto the second-story deck and down the soldered ladder to the dock. She removed the Styrofoam chest from the boat and brought it over the gangplank onto the bank. There, she sat back against the craggy earth and opened the cooler.

Like a large melon in the water: Cook's head.

She shut her eyes.

He was not your friend, she told herself. *He thought he was, but he was not.*

She opened her eyes and stared at the head until it was not a head, just a thing in a bag, and then she opened Hiram's knife and slit the bag and reached with a shaking hand into Cook's mouth. First his lips, then his tongue brushed her knuckles, cold and rubbery. The roll of plastic she pulled out was about the size and shape of a rabbit's-foot key chain, maybe a little smaller. She unsnapped the rubber band and unfolded the plastic, and at the center of the bundle was a small ampule of clear liquid.

Miranda held it up to the light. Shook it. Remembered the barrel of the big man's syringe.

She put it in back in the plastic and put the plastic and the rubber band in her pocket. She reached into the chest and lifted out the bag containing Cook's head and set this carefully in the kudzu. Then she emptied the melted ice into the river and set Cook's head back inside, retied the bag with the twist-tie, and carried the cooler up the embankment. From the freezer on the front porch, Miranda pried a single six-pound bag of ice and broke it against the boards. She dumped the ice over the head and set the lid back in place. She put the chest inside the ice bin and slammed the door shut.

Upstairs, the girl had rolled over in her sleep. Was sucking her thumb.

Miranda gathered her up in the top spread and carried her downstairs into the mercantile, behind the counter. She set her in a bundle on the floor, then pressed a beadboard panel beneath the register. The panel slid in and to the right on tracks, revealing a large hidden compartment, big enough to accommodate several good-sized moonshine crates. Over the years, Miranda had stored her earnings here, bundles of cash wrapped in Saran wrap from a big spool on the empty meat counter. She tucked the girl into the space, near a jar of black licorice, and no sooner had she closed the panel than she heard a car turn onto Crabtree Road.

She ran upstairs and snatched the Root from above the couch. From the closet she fetched a black leather quiver full of three-edged broadheads. She fastened the quiver around her torso and drew one arrow as she descended the stairs. Stepping through the broken front door, she stood in the long morning shade of the porch and set her arrow loosely at the nock point, just as the white Plymouth came rumbling out of the trees and up the drive to park slantwise in the tire-trampled earth. Miranda took a wide shooter's stance.

The dust settled. Riddle's lanky deputy, Robert Alvin, opened the driver's door and stood behind it, one boot cocked on the frame of the car, one elbow atop the window. He tipped his felt hat with his free hand. His right stayed out of sight, behind the door.

Charlie Riddle heaved out of the passenger's seat. Came grunting around the hood and leaned against it, the car nosing groundwise beneath his weight. He wore a black tie, the tongue of which fell six inches above his gut. He saw Miranda's bow and arrow and scratched the grizzled waddle beneath his chin. He was grinning.

No one spoke.

The morning sky a wash of blue, no clouds in sight.

Miranda went to full draw, sighted her broadhead on the fat man's badge. The motion was instant, practiced, calm.

Riddle did not flinch in the slightest. He simply took a pack of Marlboros from his shirt pocket and tapped one out and lit it with a thumb-struck match. "No call to be unfriendly," he said, after a long drag.

Miranda's arrow diminished to a sharp, focused point before her eyes.

"I had a bet with that midget," Riddle said. "Told him you'd do just what you done. Cruise on by. I know you, girl. Ways that midget only wished he did."

"You don't know much," Miranda said. Her shooting arm shook, slightly.

"Hard to hold it?"

"Easier if I let it go."

Riddle laughed.

Miranda said, "Tell Avery I'll see the preacher directly. We'll talk about the girl."

"You take the cake. I told you last night, John ain't got no say-so in this."

"You ain't got half the say-so you think, Charlie Riddle."

"Mercy sakes, Robert Alvin. You ever hear this girl talk so much? Don't recollect I ever heard her say so many words in her whole life, you?"

"Nope," Robert Alvin said.

"Talking like she ain't part of this family no more."

"What about Cook?" Miranda said. "He was family."

"Weren't mine."

Sweat dripped in Miranda's eye.

"Come on, now," Riddle said. "Where's that little gal?"

Robert Alvin spoke: "We'll take her and be on about our business, Miranda, we swear."

Riddle fixed the thin man with a stare. "Robert Alvin, you are a sore upon my ass."

"Got nothing for you," she said.

The fat man's humor darkened. He put his hand to the butt of his pistol.

Miranda drew the arrow a little tighter. The bow creaked. "I'll talk to Avery," she said.

Riddle shook his head, spat his cigarette, and unhurriedly drew his pistol.

Miranda's bolt slashed air and shattered the Plymouth's headlight, inches from the constable's knee. Her second arrow was nocked and ready before the first had finished quivering in the metal.

Robert Alvin rose slowly from where he'd ducked behind the driver's door.

"The dock," Miranda said from behind full-draw. "I'll talk with Avery first. Then I'll talk with the preacher."

Riddle, who had not moved an inch, smiled. "Little sister, I think I'll let you." He holstered the Schofield and backed toward the passenger's door. "And good luck to you." He folded his bulk back into the car, and Robert Alvin cranked the engine and backed away, arrow still lodged in the headlamp, a great wounded beast she had no need to track, for she knew its lair.

When the car was out of sight, its dusty wake billowing, Miranda lowered her bow.

She went and got the hammer and nailed the boards over the goddamn door again.

BILLY COTTON

✦

Half an hour later, she met Avery at Sabbath Dock, and there she showed him what was in the Styrofoam chest. Miranda watched his face when the lid came off. A grimace that turned to shock, his color draining. Seconds passed into a long quiet. There was something fragile, almost tender, in the way the dwarf regarded what was there. Something inside John Avery teetered on the edge of a precipice.

He led her into the dense pine thicket behind Sabbath House, where the land began to rise from the river, Miranda carrying the cooler. They walked until the trees thinned and they came to a high place Miranda had never been before, where the grass and spiny thistle grew almost as tall as the dwarf. In half shadow atop the hill were the stone ruins of a very old church. Only its facade remained. Little pines grew between cracks in the spires, a slatted window high above the broken doors. In back, tombstones studded the ground. Beyond the tree line, the stone wall that encircled the vast acreage of the property stood eight feet high.

At the base of the church, set into a hollow at the bottom of the hill where a wall of jasmine had all but claimed it, was the granite maw of an iron-shut crypt.

It was here, seated on a stone bench before the crypt's gate, that they found the mad preacher, Billy Cotton.

Out of a lined, white-whiskered face his eyes shone bright and hungry. He sat with head cocked at the sky as if tuning in some heavenly frequency. He straightened and turned as they rounded the corner of the hollow, moving one hand over the black leather Bible that lay on the bench beside him. His feet were bare, toes curled in the dewy grass. A pair of wing tips tucked beneath the bench. Rocks and bits of twig and burr inside them.

When he spoke, his voice was deep, resonant. "Hello, Miranda," he said.

She set the chest in the grass before him.

"'Preacher,'" he read. "For me?" He made a show of sitting forward eagerly on the edge of the bench.

He opened the lid and peered into the cooler. He grunted. Lifted the bag and twirled the twist-tie free and took out Cook's head. The preacher peered up through the stump of the neck as if inspecting some broken artifact unearthed. His fingernails were long and sharp, little crescents of dirt beneath them.

Liar, Miranda thought. *Fake*.

John Avery set his eyes on the highest spire of the church.

Cotton sat back on the bench, let the head rest on his lap, twining his hands in its hair so that it seemed engaged in some parody of an obscene act. Lifting his own head to the sky, which did not diminish the effect. "Good old Cook. I never knew him. John knew him, though, didn't you, John?"

Avery's eyes, hard, angry, shifted from the church to the preacher. "He was my friend."

"He was," Cotton said. He tossed the head back into the cooler. It made a wet *plop*. "This is a love offering from Charlie Riddle."

Avery clenched his fists. "Riddle ordered this?"

"Charlie's ways ain't the sweetest."

"You *let* him do this?"

"See to your friend, brother."

A vein throbbed in John Avery's temple. His eyes darted to a rock in the grass. Big enough to crack the preacher's skull.

Miranda spoke his name, softly. He closed his eyes and expelled a great, shuddering breath. His fists unclenched. Without a word, he picked up the Styrofoam lid and set it back in place and took the cooler by its molded handle and dragged it away from Cotton, through the grass, the head sloshing inside. He stood with his back to the preacher and Miranda, and there, among the purple stalks, he lit an old joint from his shirt pocket and smoked.

Miranda took the plastic-wrapped vial of liquid from her jeans and tossed it at Cotton's bare feet.

"What's that?" he said, bright eyes fixed on her. His smile was quick, ingratiating.

A mask, she thought.

"It was in the mouth," she said.

"And the rest?"

"Who is she?"

"The girl?" He laughed. "Why, she's my child."

Down below, Avery turned.

Miranda, whose arms and limbs had flooded with adrenaline the moment she saw the old preacher seated on the bench, felt suddenly empty, as if the fight had all drained out of her at once. Shock, confusion, even horror: all manifested in the nigh-imperceptible tightening of her jaw.

Avery drew close enough to hear.

"She was our miracle," Cotton said, voice dropping low, though still measured in a kind of preacher's cadence. A man humbled, brought low by great trials and tribulations. "We tried for so long, we had begun to lose hope. Then, one winter, on a cold, cold night, God saw fit to change our fortunes." He stared at the vial between his toes for a moment, then bent to pick it up, grunting as he did, and this seemed, to Miranda, the first break in his performance. A grimace of pain as he moved. He sat up, breathed in, breathed out. Said softly: "I sent her away when she was born. I was wrong to do that."

He noticed Avery below, listening. He tucked the drug away in his jacket pocket and stood, and suddenly he was pale, faltering. He put a trembling hand in the small of his back. Wincing. In that instant, the whole performance collapsed, and Miranda saw the man for what he was, every bit his age, more frailty than fright about him. He straightened with a kind of insect-like precision, but when he took a step toward Miranda, his left leg seemed to give. She took a step back, and he went past her, limping slowly up the hill toward the church. She thought of wood eaten away by termites, holding its shape yet somehow reduced. He did not look back.

Though he beckoned her, over his shoulder, with a crooked finger.

Avery wandered deeper into the long grass, away from the cooler, the crypt, the shadow of the church. Merging with the landscape.

Miranda went up the hill. In back of the church, burned oak pews were given over to nature, saplings where once a sanctuary had stood. She found the preacher kneeling near a heap of dirt, the dirt grown over with weeds, clumps of yellow toadflax blooming. He took up a stick, drew a circle in the earth.

"It was struck by lightning," he said over his shoulder. "Long before Lena and I bought the property. Maybe over a hundred years, it's been here, this holy, rotting place. Lena, she found it. One of her walks. She loved to come out here and walk among the trees. It was her idea, to be buried here. In its cold, black crypt."

A warm breeze soughed among the pines.

The old preacher's voice had lost its fervor. Found a tremor.

"Lately, I come out here most ever day," he said. "Some nights I sleep down there. Just to be near."

He drew a line down from the circle, arms, legs. Picked a sprig of toadflax from the mound. He placed it over the circle he had drawn, then laid another beside it, and another.

"Lee wanted things I could not give her. Happiness beyond measure . . ."

Miranda looked at the drawing he had made: a stick figure of a girl, sprigs of yellow toadflax for hair.

"Oh, for the early days," he said. "Cadillac years, Lee called them. Once, that old house overflowed with the children of Lena's flock, and I marshaled for their joy a little brass band, a parade. Can you picture it?"

Miranda remembered the night Littlefish was born, the remnants of Lena's flock smoking fearfully between their shotgun houses. "No," she said.

"She has Lena's gift, you know. This child. She sees."

"Sees what?"

"All ends," Cotton said.

Miranda flashed on the vision of herself, asleep beneath the tree, her quiver empty. Despite the summer heat, she felt a chill work its way all along the length of her spine.

"Do you believe in God, Miranda?"

She did not answer.

"When I was younger," Cotton said, "I never understood it. How a man could simply be washed clean of the past. A man *is* his past. Can he simply shed it, like a suit? Why would he? Why give up the thing you are, that all of nature conspired to make you? To split yourself. Ever after, you look into a mirror, and two men stare back."

"I don't care about belief," Miranda said. "I care about trust."

Cotton looked at her now. Eyes rimmed red. His voice was flat, hard. "Can I trust you, Miranda?"

She looked away.

Abruptly, he scrubbed his drawing and stood. The motion drew a sharp intake of breath, a pause to steady himself.

At that moment, a wind blew through the church, made the pine tops groan and creak. Something caught Cotton's eye, drew it to the great oaken doors of the church, one of which hung askew, an archway of light and trees beyond. Suddenly the preacher went rigid. Miranda's eyes darted from him to the doors.

Voice barely a whisper, Cotton said, "Do you see her?"

Miranda followed his gaze, saw nothing but the distant woods framed by the arch, through it the grass field at the bottom of the hill where John Avery waited.

Cotton lifted a hand, as if to cup the cheek of some invisible congregant drawing nigh. To the empty air, in a voice hushed with reverence, he said, "Oh, I wish you could see her. She's so terrible. So beautiful."

With his other hand, he drew a pearl-handled straight razor from his pocket and thumbed it open. "She's eager for the end I've promised," the old man said. "But I still have business with you, Miranda."

Miranda took a step back.

The preacher's blade flashed across the hollow of his upraised hand. The razor made a sound, sudden and sharp, not unlike an arrow shot from a bow. The preacher bent double, made a fist, and squeezed, and the blood ran down his wrist. He raised his fist above his head. Then stood upright and locked eyes on Miranda that were wide and gleaming through the pain. He splayed his fingers toward heaven, the slit in his palm coursing red.

"One last trip upriver, Miranda," Cotton said. "Tonight. Charlie Riddle will be waiting for you at the dock. After which, by sunup, you will bring me what is rightfully mine."

The preacher flung his arm down, spattering the toadflax with crimson.

Miranda turned and fled. Down the hill, past the crypt with its heavy iron door, into the long grass, past John Avery, who took up the cooler and tried to follow, dragging it behind, calling after her, but she did not stop, not until the trees were tall around her once again, the old mad preacher and all his devils far behind.

NOT THE LEAST AMONG THEM

Avery walked alone through the woods, caught up with her near the river's edge. She stood staring out at the dark river passing, the trees on the far bank moving in the breeze. The day yet hot. He came dragging the foam cooler behind him, small and weary among the pines. When Miranda turned, he said, "Help me bury him."

After a moment, she nodded.

Avery fetched a shovel from the greenhouse.

He chose a spot in the woods near the river, outside the confines of the crumbling boundary wall, where the soil was moist and a ring of wild hydrangeas grew, their petals white. A length of cross vine wound its way up the trunk of a beech tree, red, bell-like flowers in bloom.

He lit what was left of his joint and smoked it while Miranda dug the hole. She was tamping the soil and raking leaves over it with the shovel when the dwarf spoke. "I was hungry," he muttered. "You gave me no meat. I was naked, you gave me no clothes. . . ." He stared at the freshly mounded grave.

"What?" Miranda said. She wiped her brow with her forearm.

"Something Lena said, day I met her. Long time ago. 'You will not be the least among them, John Avery.'"

Silence fell between them. Avery's thoughts turned inward like knives against himself.

Miranda broke it. "Is it true, what he said? The girl is his?"

"Yes. And no."

"What does that mean?"

"Yes, there was a girl. Once. But I swear I knew fuck-all about bringing her here—"

"When was she born?"

"Before . . ." He hesitated. "Before the other one. The one that didn't live."

"So, what, eleven, twelve years back?"

"Twelve. Billy sent the baby to a whorehouse he and Riddle run. Not the Pink, but another one, across the state line."

"Why?"

"It was Lena's child. But it wasn't *his*. He wanted to hurt her."

Avery took out his lighter, re-lit the nub of his joint.

"Did he?" Miranda said. "Hurt her?"

"Broke her in two," Avery said.

In a tree nearby, a mourning dove called, and another answered.

Avery's voice began to drift like curls of smoke as he spoke, his eyes glassing.

"She never would tell who the father was. It drove Billy crazy. That's when it started: doors flung open in the middle of the night, there he'd be, just standing there, like a ghost. People got spooked, started talking about leaving. Most did, save the ones slinging dope for Riddle. After that came the sermons. Devils and whores and corrupted wombs. Everything she built, he tore it all down. Then she died. Everyone left. Everyone but us. We couldn't, we—"

His voice hitched. He wiped his eyes.

"God help us, why'd we do it," he said.

"Do what?"

"Have a daughter. Here, in this terrible place."

Silence.

Nearby, the Prosper ran softly, surely.

Miranda let the shovel fall and set out through the trees.

She left John Avery standing alone by the grave in sun-dappled shadow.

LICORICE

✦

The Landing came into view and Miranda saw the constable's Plymouth kicking up a cloud of dust as it wheeled away from the gravel turnaround. She killed her engine and turned the rudder sharply, and the Alumacraft beached itself in the sand. She opened Hiram's Old Timer knife and went at a quick run up the riverbank, behind the shed, and onto the front porch, where she found the door to the mercantile broken open once again, the boards she had nailed up prized free and tossed in the yard.

She slipped through the screen door, sneakers crunching over broken glass. It struck her like a punch in the gut: cans of beans, boxes of crackers, tins of meat, all ripped from shelves; paper kegs of oatmeal punched open and spilled in heaps and trails like gunpowder; the floor around the bait cooler and the wall behind it alive with crickets where the wooden hopper in the corner had been smashed, the room full of their song. Glass of the old meat counter smashed to pieces, heaps of Saran wrap unribboned across the boards.

She flicked on the overhead bulb and threw up the leaf that blocked the register. She pressed the dull side of the blade against her thigh to close the knife, then knelt and gripped the beadboard panel and pushed in and to the right.

The girl shoved backward in the cabinet, chewing candy. A thin line of colored drool, like ink, ran down her chin. She sat wrapped in Miranda's white childhood bedspread, clutching the jar of black licorice in her lap. Face round and frightened, two whips in her fist.

Miranda sat back on the floor. Aware of how careful she had to be now, how delicate.

The girl licked her lips. Her tongue was black.

Unreal, Miranda thought, that fate, this land, some force within it, had delivered unto her both of Lena Cotton's lost children.

The right sleeve of the girl's pajamas rode up to her elbow, exposing the scars, the needle stitching there.

She is poisoned, Miranda thought, thinking of her own arm now, the snakebite scars. That long, terrible night in old Iskra's bathhouse.

Do you know who saved you, Myshka?

Red eyes in the steam.

The girl stared at her, chewing still, and Miranda stared back.

I USED TO BE HANDSOME

✦

Riddle called Sabbath House from the pay phone in the back of Shifty's Tavern out on the highway, three miles south of Mylan. He sat on a rickety stool, a rip in the seat taped with duct tape. The phone was near the toilets, the air ripe with someone's morning shit.

The preacher picked up on the fourth ring. "Charlie," he said, as if divining the caller.

"I didn't get her, Billy."

Silence on the line, followed by a low wet clicking sound, something weird and insect-like the old preacher did with his mouth. The sound of Billy Cotton thinking. It made Riddle antsy, this sound. All the years he'd known the preacher, he never once recalled the old man's hesitation leading to anything good.

"She'll take her to the witch," Cotton finally said. "May-hap she has already."

The stool creaked beneath Riddle's weight. He kneaded

the center of his forehead. "She gets into them bottoms, we'll never see her again."

"Have a little faith, Charlie. She'll keep her appointment with you tonight."

Riddle grunted.

Out of the bright day, into the bar, walked a girl, young and rail-thin. She wore tight jeans and a blouse tied above her navel, platform wedges. She had dark hair, small breasts. A collarbone that stood out like a root in the ground. Riddle knew her. Goddamn it, she had no business here. He'd told her, like he told the others. Per Cotton's shithouse-rat instructions, just that morning Riddle had sent them gals at the Pink Motel packing, had given each a bus ticket and said get. Yet here was what's-her-name, Tulip, Petal, Rosalee, something like it, taking a bar stool big as Billy-be-frigged. Sidling up to Marvin Gamble, who'd run Gamble's Garage till it collapsed in rot and ruin. Gamble wore coveralls and a cap with a machinery logo printed above the bill, nursed his second beer of the morning. The girl leaned in close and whispered in his ear.

"Settled everything else like I asked?" Cotton said. "Saw the ladies off?"

Riddle's gaze wandered to Robert Alvin, who sat in a booth by a murky window, drinking hot coffee and skimming the funny pages. "Just about," he said.

"What do you hear from your new friends?"

"They say the dope we brung em's good. Say they want the little man, like I figured they would."

"And you said?"

"Said a deal's a deal. If that bitch don't screw us."

At the bar, Tulip or Petal or Rosalee slipped her hand in Gamble's back pocket, while her other hand was in his crotch, her lips in his ear. Out came the wallet.

"Bitches," Riddle said, "got a way of doing that."

"She had a for-sure look in her eyes this morning," Cotton said. "She won't be happy tucking tail. She'll fashion some scheme of her own." A smile in the old preacher's voice. "To outthink you."

At the bar, Gamble cast a glance over his shoulder at Robert Alvin. When he saw Riddle, he straightened from his stool and left. The front door opened. The front door closed. Tulip or Petal or Rosalee saw Riddle and waved. She picked up Gamble's unfinished beer and downed it. Then started thumbing through the contents of his wallet.

Riddle pictured Miranda Crabtree, on her knees before him, tangled in the sun-withered kudzu along the river's edge. In his right hand, Riddle held the arrow that had split his headlight. In his left, a handful of long, dark hair.

"Say it all goes to plan," he said to Cotton. "What you gone do, after? Light out?"

Cotton made a noise in his throat, something Riddle had never heard before. A kind of settling, like wood groaning in the cold of night. The line went dead.

Riddle hung up.

The girl took a five from Gamble's wallet, signaled Shifty for another beer.

Shifty, pudgy old dollop of a hemorrhoid, slapped a towel over his shoulder. Said something too low for Riddle to hear.

The girl's face darkened.

"Shit," Riddle breathed. He saw it all play out before it did.

"Hey, Shifty," Tulip or Petal or Rosalee said, and she flipped Gamble's bottle in her hand and smashed it on the edge of the bar.

Robert Alvin jumped in his booth, spilling hot coffee in his lap.

Shifty growled and spat and now the whore was screaming, "What was that, motherfucker! What you say?"

Robert Alvin sat looking for all the world like he had no blessed clue.

The constable sighed and rolled off the stool, its legs cracking as though they might splinter and burst like tree branches beneath the weight of winter ice.

Later, the girl—Daisy was her name—lay naked on her belly atop the sheet. Snoring.

Riddle sat in pants and a yellowed undershirt on the edge of the bed, prodigious bulk sinking the mattress as if it were a crippled boat going down at the stern. The afternoon light came streaming through the murky glass. Skull-splitting light, an old familiar ache behind his eye.

He reached for the whiskey bottle in a heap of clothes on the floor. His feet were bare and dry and cracked, his ankles swollen and starred with burst veins, his toenails thick and uncut. He had the sudden urge to pull them all out with pliers.

He took a drink.

The houseboat where Riddle lived was a short, ugly craft, moored along the riverbank ten or fifteen miles southeast of Mylan. Here, the river was wider and deeper and faster, and so, whenever he was home—sitting, sleeping, eating, shitting—a gentle, persistent rhythm worked at Charlie Riddle. It made his heart race, and so he rarely came here, taking most of his meals at Shifty's or the truck stop near the interstate. The boat was sparsely furnished, a wide empty living space with only a ratty chair and a television on the floor and a pressboard cupboard in the galley, which was mostly bare. In truth, Riddle imagined he would very soon sink it all. Maybe after their dealings were done tomorrow, he would drop a lit stick of dynamite down the shitter and crack the old mildewed bitch in two. Watch her sink from the shore. Let Robert Alvin drive him far away to some cool, dry place, where Billy Cotton and Miranda Crabtree would soon be forgotten.

The girl's ass was small and bony, a pimple just east of the cleft.

All the times he'd fucked whores out at the Pink, he'd never brought one here. This one, Daisy, came on a bus one night, six months back. Staggering off in a hard rain and asking that lecherous old night clerk for a room. No way to pay. The clerk called Riddle right quick, who set her up with her own permanent room. Riddle asked her age. "Old enough, Sheriff," was all she said, folding herself down on the corner of the bed and grabbing at his buckle. No money ever changed hands, that time or anytime after. Riddle despised her, maybe more than the others, who had at least been capable of fear. Eight or nine whores out of the whole passel had come from Sabbath House itself, back in the early days, unwed mothers seeking God, finding something else in the ministry of Billy Cotton. They came to Lena and went forgiven to the Pink. She never knew. Not until it was too late, anyway. Babies taken care of—snip, snip, snip. The money was good. So good, they'd set up a second camp, a handful of trailers over the state line in Texarkana. A dozen years or more, and now the whole goddamned enterprise a smoking ruin, burned to the ground on Cotton's orders, just to get that girl and, what, erase old sins, clear the soul's slate? Money lost forever, that's what Charlie Riddle thought. Money lost forever.

"Out of his damn mind," Riddle muttered. "A man does what he does don't ask forgiveness. Just does it. Right. Wrong. Just goddamn do it."

He took another drink. He set the bottle aside and dug into his pocket for a prescription pill bottle, and out of this he tapped three white pills and swallowed them with another guzzle of whiskey. Outside, beyond the windows at the head of the bunk, all along the bow railing, the light was harsh. It hurt worse than his head. It made him stupid. It made him mean. He swiveled on the bed and traced the neck and lip of his bottle along the inside of the girl's ribs, nudging the swell of her breast.

Daisy stirred, raised her head, smiled at Riddle. It was a pleasant smile, though her teeth were snaggled and there were blackheads nesting above her nostrils.

Riddle returned it.

"You got any pot, Sheriff?" she asked.

Riddle shook his head. He held up the bottle of rye. "Just this."

"That'll do," Daisy said and took it and drank, and the sheet fell away and one pale breast was bared. Beneath her arm: a thatch of hair like a charcoal smudge. She popped the bottle from her lips and wiped her chin and passed it back, and he drank, too. "I figured Old Shifty was gonna clock me for sure this time."

"Maybe he would of," Riddle said. "You oughta learn to listen. I sent all you gals packing. You oughta gone like the rest."

"I cain't leave you all alone, baby," she said. She lifted a leg from beneath the sheets and slid her foot into his crotch. "I ever tell you I used to know a fella with no nose? He wore a patch over it like your eye. Had this one eyebrow, too, met in the middle like a damn werewolf."

"That a fact."

"That's a fact. He wasn't sweet like you, though. See this?" The sheet had fallen away from her chest, and she sat upright in the bed and pointed at her left breast, where there was a ring of puckered pink scars.

"I seen it before," Riddle said.

"How come you never asked about it?"

"You want me to know, you'll tell me."

"He did that to me. With his teeth."

"Sure he weren't no werewolf?"

"Not after I got through with him."

"What'd you do?"

"I handcuffed him to the bed and shaved that eyebrow while he slept," Daisy said.

"That a fact."

"You bet. While he was sleeping. I got me a razor and some cream and shaved that sumbitch right off. You know why he didn't have no nose?"

"Why?"

"Cause I didn't stop with that eyebrow."

"You don't say."

"I met up with him again. Couple years later in Lubbock, Texas. He was wearing that patch, black leather shaped like a nose. I tell you, I laughed. He didn't like that. He came after me hard." She stepped her fingers across her breast as if the bite marks were stones across a stream. "He didn't catch me, though."

"Hell of a story, little sister."

"What happened to you?" she asked, tapping her eye.

"I lost it for being sweet."

She laughed, a sputtering laugh, her tongue behind her teeth.

"I used to be handsome," he said. "I was even sweeter then."

Daisy sat up a little straighter and her eyes moved over Riddle's bulk.

"You was handsome?"

"It's true. They used to call me Handsome Charlie."

"No shit?"

"The girls," he said, "they'd smile when I'd walk by, they'd laugh when I tipped my hat. Back in high school they even passed me notes."

"I bet they did."

"This one gal," he said, and his smile slipped away and his grip tightened around the bottle of whiskey. He took a drink. A long drink. "This one gal, I had it real bad for her."

"Tell me her name."

"Tell me yours."

She took the whiskey from him and drank and shook her head, passed the bottle back. "My name's Daisy."

"What's your real name?"

"Ain't no name real. Just some word got said over us when we was born. Names mean shit, baby."

"Well. Her name was Cora."

"She pass you notes?"

"I asked her to a dance once. Slicked my hair, brought flowers. Black-eyed Susans. Picked em by the roadside. She turned me down. Looked at me like I was some kind of Frankenstein."

"You mean the monster," the girl said. "Frankenstein is the man—"

"There was this other old boy she liked," Riddle said. His voice dropped low, and he was not looking at the girl. "Married him, eventually, after he came back from the war. She died of cancer." He took another drink. And another. He was not looking at anything now. "Their kid, she grew up to look just like her momma. I tried being sweet to her, too. But she didn't much want it. She was younger then than you are now."

"I'm pretty young," Daisy said, digging her heel into Riddle's crotch.

"She put her thumb here"—Riddle lifted his right arm and extended his thumb and pressed it against his patch, and the girl's eyes widened—"and pushed my eyeball right to the back of my head and half my world just popped out like a busted light."

Daisy drew the sheet over her breasts, tucked her leg back under. "Girl probably had her reasons," she said. "We always do."

Riddle drank, and at the end of it, with the bottle empty, he gave out a great and terrible gasp.

"Baby, you gone kill yourself, drinking like that." Daisy leaned over the edge of the bed to reach a pack of cigarettes from the floor. "You ought to go on one of them diets where you eat cantaloupe and crackers," she said, tapping out a cigarette as she hung over the lip of the mattress, "you know, the ones—"

Riddle smashed the empty bottle across the back of Daisy's head.

She slumped.

The houseboat moved, gently, in the current of the river.

Riddle got up and went out of the bedroom and into the toilet, weaving in the doorway and steadying himself with one hand on the sink. He lifted the toilet lid, unzipped his fly, and pissed. He looked down, couldn't see his own pecker. Glanced up at the moldy ceiling, a panel loosened a while back, where he'd tucked a few grand in cash away, all the earnings he'd stolen or extorted or just plain claimed from John Avery and Sabbath House. No one there strong enough to fight him for it. What would he spend it on, when it was all over, and the last of it collected tomorrow? A glass eye? Women? *A house made to sit still*, he thought.

In the bedroom, barely conscious, the girl had put her hands flat on the floor and was trying, feebly, to crawl from the bed, hemorrhaging, as she did, from a wide laceration just below the crown of her head.

Riddle looked down at the jagged neck of the bottle where he had dropped it on the floor. He picked it up, stood over the girl. "Yeah," he said. "They used to call me handsome."

BATHHOUSE

Littlefish sat on his knees and paddled his bark through the water with wide, webbed hands. He moved along his trot-lines up and down the bank, each marked by a tethered plastic jug bobbing in the current: six perch, four breams, and a slippery mud cat to show for his efforts, each of these tossed in an orange cooler. When he had reset all the lines, he paddled back to shore and lay out in the sun on a bed of pine needles, letting the warm day dry him. He saw shapes and faces in the webwork patterns the trees made against the sky.

Around midday he heard the gentle saw of a motor on the bayou.

Sister, he thought, and pulled his boat fully onto the bank and ran, cooler in his arms, up into the trees and toward the top of the hill. Once, he tripped and spilled the fish. Ashamed at his own clumsiness, he brushed the fish clean and dropped them back into the cooler and ran on.

He left the cooler on the rear doorstep of Iskra's cabin and went around to the front porch, where he found Baba waiting there on the stoop, looking down the long slope of the yard, to where Sister had emerged from the birches, wearing her bow and quiver. She carried a green satchel in her right hand. Her left was closed around the long, hanging shirtsleeve of a—

Girl.

The boy shrank back to the lip of the hill, among the kudzu.

"We have company," Baba said, smoothing her apron. There was something in her voice, a note of caution, even fear.

From where he crouched: What's company?

But Baba did not answer.

Sister and the girl started up the hill, and Littlefish scuttled beneath the stilted porch and lay on his belly in the shadows in the cool dirt among the clucking chickens. Baba did not scold, only watched him, her face unreadable, and once he had hidden himself, she gave only the slightest of shrugs and turned back to the slope to wait, shielding her eyes from the sun with her hand.

Soon the girl's head bobbed at the lip of the slope. Sister pulled her up and the girl stood clutching Sister's hand through the shirtsleeve, which was too long for her arm. The girl opened and closed her eyes slowly, as if the sun were too bright. Beneath the shirt, she wore dirty pajamas. Littlefish inched forward on his belly for a better look. Baba and Sister spoke quietly. Sister unslung her bow and quiver and set them on the porch steps, then went off around the cabin with Baba and the girl. The boy crawled out from the shadows. From the corner of the cabin he saw the three of them headed up the hill, past the vegetable garden and tattered scarecrow, past the outhouse and the pump, and into the bathhouse where they closed the door.

The old cedar bathhouse stood on its bed of rock and timber and mud. Its black stovepipe curving skyward.

Littlefish did not like the bathhouse. At night, sleeping just up the hill in his shed, he sometimes heard whispering in its walls. Menacing words in Baba's tongue.

But the sun was up now and the sun made such things silly, so he crept quietly to the door and peered through a narrow crack. He could not see Baba or Sister in the gloom, but he could see the girl, sitting on the slatted pine bench. She sat with her knees together, her toes just touching the round river stones set into the hard earth beneath the bench. Her hands were folded in her lap, hair short and bristly.

Does she talk? Did someone teach her how, like Sister taught me?

He heard footsteps and barely had time to leap back before the door flew open, Baba's short, heavy shape filling the frame. "Bring wood," she said.

Iskra piled kindling over logs inside the big stone oven that filled the far corner, a metal pipe running up the wall and through the roof to vent the smoke. Littlefish stood by, holding three lengths of hickory in his arms. He stared at the girl, who sat on the bench without expression, eyes fixed on the dirt floor.

Miranda hung her duffel on a hook just inside the door.

Iskra lit a pine knot with a match and with the knot lit the kindling in the oven.

Miranda could see the boy had questions, but his arms were full of stovewood, so he could not ask. One by one, the old woman reached these from him and thrust them into the oven and poked up the fire with a pair of iron tongs, and when the flames were blazing, she gestured for the boy to take the three cedar buckets that hung from steel hooks on the wall and fill them at the pump. He fumbled a bucket and chased it across the floor, scooped it up with the other two, and was gone.

"Undress her," Iskra said.

But when Miranda moved to do so, the girl shrank back from her touch.

"We're going to give you a bath," Miranda said.

The girl only stared at her.

"We aren't going to hurt you," Miranda said. "I promise."

She reached again, and this time the girl lifted her own arms and let Miranda tug the shirt and pajama top over her head. Miranda gasped at what she saw. Naked from the waist up, body stick-thin and pale, the girl's belly and arms were crosshatched with scars. Fine, meticulous cutting.

"Who would do this?" Miranda said.

Iskra snatched the clothes from Miranda, gave the child a glance. "I am sure she did it herself." She tossed Hiram's shirt over a straw-bottomed chair across the room. The pajama top she threw in the fire.

"We'll need more water," the witch said to Miranda. "Let the boy fetch it, but keep him out."

The girl closed her arms over her chest, sat watching the women work.

Littlefish, meanwhile, came weaving up the path from the pump in back of the cabin, a bucket sloshing at each side, the third filled and ready at the base of the pump.

"Stay out here," Miranda said flatly from the doorway, taking the buckets. "We'll need more water soon."

Who is she? he asked, craning past Miranda.

But Miranda toed the door shut.

She hunkered in front of the girl, who sat upright on the slatted bench, covering her small breasts. Her eyes roamed over Miranda, the bathhouse walls. Back to Miranda.

"Close your eyes," Miranda said. She sat on the bench, reached out, drew a deep breath, then smoothed her palm over the girl's short hair. The girl flinched away, but not before Miranda felt it: a fleeting sense of something peaceful, a sadness at once familiar and unknowable. The melancholy warmth of sunshine on skin. "Put your head in my lap," Miranda said, and held her hand away from the girl's head, an invitation.

After a moment, the girl lay down on the bench and put her head in Miranda's lap, and the weight of her was startling and good.

Miranda released breath she had not even known she was holding.

Iskra handed Miranda Hiram's shirt, and Miranda spread it over the girl.

The girl closed her eyes.

Time passed, as Iskra made her preparations, and after a while, the child's breathing deepened, and Miranda realized she was asleep.

As the loose stones atop the oven grew hot to the touch, Iskra lifted each with a pair of ice tongs and dropped them in a low wooden box beneath the bench. At the old woman's urging, Miranda slipped away from the bench, setting the girl's head gently on the slats. She folded her father's shirt over the straw-bottomed chair back and drew the girl's pajama bottoms down and Iskra threw these, too, into the fire. Miranda checked the girl's legs for more scars, more needle marks, but found none.

Iskra directed her to take up the buckets and pour the water over the stones in the box.

Steam rose through the slats and the room grew very hot.

"Now the cauldron," Iskra said, hooking her tongs on the opposite wall.

Lest the steam and heat rush out, Miranda opened the door only wide enough to set the empty buckets outside. She glimpsed Littlefish sitting atop the stump where the wood ax was buried. She took up the third bucket of water, which the boy had left at the threshold, and closed the bathhouse door. She poured the water into a black cauldron suspended over the fire. From a bundle hanging from a rafter, Iskra took down three branches of dried eucalyptus and set them in the cauldron. Soon the bathhouse was filled with the sweet scent of eucalyptus leaves cooking.

Miranda sat in the straw-bottomed chair, which was set against the wall, just below a cracked square of silvered mirror. She waited and watched, her only measure of time's passage the steady filling and refilling of the buckets when the old woman beckoned. The fire roared hotter, stones hissed, and all the while, dread twisted tighter and tighter in Miranda's chest like a wire around her heart. Some terrible thing was on its way. She felt it coalescing in the air like the steam itself.

Iskra took the eucalyptus branches from the cauldron and brushed the child's body, from the soles of her feet to the crown of her head. She bade Miranda come closer. "Give me your hand," Iskra said. The old woman's filleting knife flashed from her apron, faster than Miranda would have believed, and the knife drew a fine red line across her palm. Miranda gasped.

"Drip it," the witch said. "Into the box beneath."

Miranda saw something in her periphery—a shadow dislodging from a corner. But when she looked at the corner straight on, she saw nothing.

"Hurry," the old woman said. "He is coming. Three drops."

Miranda squeezed her hand over the box beneath the bench.

"Now face that wall, and if you must look, use the mirror, but do not interfere and no matter what do not turn around."

Miranda backed away until her legs bumped up against the straw-bottomed chair. She turned and faced the wall, and in the mirror she saw Iskra take up a eucalyptus branch in each hand and spread her arms like a squat bird spreading its wings. The witch fanned the branches over the girl's body, crisscrossing and sweeping, and the steam rose up hot and thick, filling the room, until finally there was nothing but a wall of white heat surrounding them.

Iskra spoke, in a loud, commanding voice: "Where do you come from?"

The girl lay unmoving on the bench, eyes shut.

Iskra whisked the branches and asked the question again, this time in her own harsh tongue. And then, finally, a third time, in English, each word a thunderclap: "WHERE DO YOU COME FROM, POISON?"

Out of the steam, a voice, small and childlike, a whisper: "... *the needle* ..."

Iskra licked her lips. "And what do you seek?"

"... *blood* ..."

"Is there blood elsewhere?"

Something rippled beneath the girl's face, like the fins of bottom-feeders breaking the surface. "... *yes* ..."

"Then go and find it!"

The girl's mouth tightened. She twitched.

Iskra's voice was steady. "What do you devour?"

"... *the spirit* ..."

"And what do you crave?"

The voice was small, petulant: "... *more!*"

"Are you honey?" the old woman said.

"... *no* ..."

"Are you milk?"

"... *no* ..."

"Are you bane?"

The girl seized and thrashed atop the bench. "... *YES* ..."

"THEN LET THE BANNIK TAKE YOU!" Iskra cried, lashing the child with the branches. "FOR BANE IS THE BANNIK'S MILK! AND BANE IS THE BANNIK'S HONEY!"

Miranda watched breathless in the silvered mirror. Remembering her own time in the bathhouse, ten years past. Whatever words the old woman had called down out of the air that night, Miranda had forgotten all of them save one: *bannik*. Blood crusting her bare feet like socks, poison hissing from an arm that had steamed like hot metal dropped into water, it had come—

bannik

—and now, as a tarry ooze welled up from the holes in the girl's arms and ran slowly in black rivulets over her skin, and Miranda shut her eyes against the terror, even as the girl's flew apart like shutters, the monster came again.

BANNIK

The girl opened her mouth to scream, but it was no scream that came out of her.

An ash cloud erupted from her throat and spread among the rafters like an angry swarm.

Miranda forced her eyes open and saw, in the silvered glass, the walls of the bathhouse dissolve into white, the whole room blinding.

Out of the steam, the bannik shambled forth.

It was a demon, hideous and ugly and goblin-small. A wild mane of hair flamed from its skull to its waist. Its cheekbones were sharp above its beard. Its eyes twin red slits in an ancient, leathery face cracked in a toothy smile that floated in the steam, huge and grotesque. The demon's twiglike fingers seemed to hold the smile in place, as if it were a thing detachable. It was not a grin but a curved saw, a crude surgical instrument from olden times, with two wooden handles, and the bannik was lowering it over the girl's body, from torso to legs, where Iskra's own filleting knife hovered just above the joining of leg and hip.

"Here," the old witch said, and the bannik dropped its saw into the joint and began to cut.

Miranda felt her stomach plunge.

Without thinking, she whirled and cried, "STOP!"

The demon sprang across the child, throwing the old witch aside. It rushed Miranda in three sideways lopes and struck her, locking short, powerful legs around her waist. No time to cry out, she fell over the straw-bottomed chair and the bannik pressed her flat to the ground, smothering her with its weight. Long, stick-like claws seized her throat. Hot breath at her ear, jaws snarling, snapping.

"Bannik!" Iskra cried, eyes on the floor, knife and arms spread over the girl.

"You fear the cutting?" the bannik hissed.

"Forgive her, bannik!" the old witch begged.

The demon struck Miranda's left ear with the back of its hand. Its knuckles burned like sandpaper. *"Peeling is truth! See what you were never meant to see!"* Its voice was rough and phlegmy and possessed of age beyond measure, lips black and thin. *"What would you see? Your old witch's secret, would you know it?"*

"Close your eyes!" Iskra cried.

Miranda did, but still, she saw it: a glimpse of Hiram's face upside down in the dark, lit from below by flashlight. Suspended over a great wide maw—

Laughter as the demon let go of her throat, and then its weight and stink were gone.

Miranda, sputtering. Throat and lungs on fire. Scratches

welling red on her cheeks. She hauled herself up by the wall studs and stood bloody before the silvered square of mirror, each breath a ragged draw.

The bannik let out a cackle and took up its saw from the floor, and now the witch moved her knife over the child's hip, and the demon began to saw again. Black smoke plumed from the wound, and the severed limb began to float, to drift free, and up it rose, into the rafters, where it was swallowed by the cloud that had earlier issued from the girl's mouth.

And yet: the child's leg remained fastened to her body. No cut had been made.

"Here," Iskra said, positioning her knife over the other leg.

The demon's saw drifted, and soon the other leg was untethered and floating.

Each arm at the shoulder. The head, beneath the jaw.

The witch's knife played guide to the demon's cuts, until together they had created a bevy of limbs that bobbed like Littlefish's trotlines in the rafters of the bathhouse, each severed stump spewing an inky stream of poison, each stream feeding into the wider pool of black spreading over the bathhouse ceiling.

It's all the bad, Miranda thought. *This happened to you once.*

She glanced down at her arm, the white scar where the snake had struck.

The fire in the oven threw wild shadows in the steam.

Iskra tucked her knife into her apron.

The demon opened its mouth, drew its breath, and now the dark cloud and the bathhouse steam were pulled in a whirling funnel into the creature, and a sound like a great roaring of some deep river-chorus of frogs filled the room, swelling inside their skulls, until Miranda's head was throbbing with a pulsing horror, thick fingers in her ears pushing in slowly to meet in the middle, until finally all vapor inside the room was consumed, and the sound faded as the demon's jaws, now distended, cracked shut, leaving only silence and the child's severed limbs to fade into the ether in the dim light above the slatted bench.

The air was dry and hot.

"It is done," Iskra said, voice quavering.

Miranda turned from the mirror.

Iskra stepped away from the child, then staggered, went down on her knees.

Behind her, the girl sprang upright on the bench and planted her bare feet in the moist earth. She reached out and spread both hands across Iskra's cheeks. The girl's eyes were huge and white.

Miranda started for the old woman, but stopped when the child opened her mouth and began to sing.

The girl sang with the voice of a child, but it was not hers. It was a rough voice, harsh with grief, and the words she sang were in Baba's deep, guttural tongue, and the song she sang was long and terrible in its warp and weft, as if torn out of the peat-smelling earth itself.

Iskra hung between the girl's hands like a woman enthralled, her own eyes brimming with sudden tears as the song pealed out.

The wail fell silent.

The girl's frame sagged and Iskra, released, dropped

onto hands and knees. She crawled away, toward Miranda, who went to her, put her arms around the old woman.

The girl straightened, blinking away tears of her own. She peered into the shadows and corners of the bathhouse. She settled her gaze on the old witch and Miranda, then said, in a voice that was small and frightened and very much a child's: "Who are you?"

SUNLIGHT

Through a crack in the bathhouse doorway, Littlefish watched, though he couldn't see much, just a vague sense of bodies moving.

The door opened and Iskra came hobbling out. "Help me," she said to the boy, offering her arm, and the boy took it and walked the old woman over to the stump where the ax was lodged.

"I am an old rag," she said. She blew air between her lips and lifted the long tail of her housedress and flapped it to cool herself.

The boy looked anxiously toward the bath, but Iskra touched his arm and said, "Stay by me."

He stayed.

Iskra heard, again, the bannik's voice: *Your old witch's secret, would you know it?*

Great leshii, the witch thought, *has the hour finally come?*

The boy touched her shoulder, his lumpen face twisted with concern.

He made motions with his hands, but these were words the old witch had never bothered to learn. She pressed the heel of her hand beneath her heart. Looked away.

The girl flinched when the towel from Miranda's long green duffel went around her shoulders. The thing with the beard and red eyes had been bad, so bad, but something in the old woman's mind had cried out, a memory more terrible than even the demon's fury, and the girl had heard the song as if from the bottom of a deep, dark well, and that well was herself, so she had opened her mouth and the words were drawn up and out of her. She did not understand their meaning, seeing in her mind only a single image that was the story they told: digging a hole, filling a hole, covering the dirt with rocks.

But there was more.

The demon's cutting had opened other doors, doors within the girl's own heart, doors to her awful power. The cutting had not frightened her. It made things better. This she understood, because it always had, ever since she'd first discovered a pack of razor blades left behind on a kitchen sink in one of the trailers. But the demon wasn't good, and like the greedy thing it was, it had stolen through those open doors and seen everything the girl saw, including the old woman's secrets. Something about this place. It made no sense for the girl to know this because this was not her home, home was where the ladies worked in the trailers and that was gone now, burned, all the ladies ash and bone—*should I cry for them, should I cry for them at all*—because they could not see the black coiling cloud that brought the black-clad men with their fire and axes and guns and sharp teeth, and before that, where was she?

But none of that mattered, not now, because the blackness was not here, not in this place, wherever she was—the bannik was not the only spirit here and his was not the only kind, some were good and green, like the glimmer in the darkness she had seen first waking on the river—and now the woman named Miranda was putting her strong arms around the girl, holding her, resting her chin on top of the girl's head. And that was far from dark. It was nice. Very good. Very soft. Outside, all around, was the green, life. Sunlight instead of shadow.

She had not seen real sunlight in a very long time.

Miranda went to the duffel where it hung on the hook by the door and took out a pair of jeans and a faded blue T-shirt, clothes she had lifted from a drawer in her childhood dresser. From the back of the straw-bottomed chair, she took Hiram's long-sleeve shirt the girl had worn earlier and folded it. She set the stack of clothes on the bench beside the child, whose eyes—a pretty, solemn shade of blue—now followed Miranda with a clarity that had not been present before.

"These should fit you," Miranda said. Her words were craggy, her throat swollen and raw where the demon had choked her.

The girl did not answer.

"You're safe now," Miranda said. "Do you understand?"

The girl's eyes cut to the doorway, through it the old woman and the boy at the stump, Iskra's legs splayed, her dress hiked above her knees.

Miranda wondered at the secrets the old woman held yet. All these years, muttering to the house spirit, dead flies in a spoon, a never-ending litany of bedtime stories, tales brought from another world: new brides carrying fire in skulls; princes sealed in barrels and tossed in rivers; a little mouse, Myshka, taken apart by a demon's magic, put back together.

She felt something, a fluttering, as if—

"She has one more," the girl said.

—as if a little bird had flown into her mind, careened among her thoughts.

Dizzy from it, Miranda closed her hands around the bench on either side of the girl, took a deep breath, let it out. "One more what?" she said.

"Story. She wants to tell you now. She's been waiting so long." The girl's eyes were strange and cold. "You won't like the way it ends."

The taste of blood rose in her mouth. Miranda pointed at the clothes on the bench. "Put those on," she said. She put her hand over her mouth and went out and around the corner of the bathhouse into the sunlight, where she bent by the woodpile and vomited into the grass.

HAND IN HAND

When the girl came barefoot to the door of the bathhouse, wearing the boatman's shirt over Miranda's T-shirt and jeans, only Miranda and Littlefish were outside. Iskra had gone into the cabin, grown pale and waxen, a sudden blanket of years thrown over her. Miranda ran her head beneath the pump, washed the taste of vomit from her mouth and nose, the blood from her face. She gathered her wet hair back and spat in the dirt.

The boy stood beside her, hands fluttering.

"Sorry," she said, drying her hands on her jeans. "Again. Slower."

Littlefish pointed to the girl peering shyly around the bathhouse door. He signed slowly: Who is she?

The only other child you've ever seen, Miranda thought.

She answered with her hands: Ask her.

Littlefish stared, his mind forming questions it had never formed before.

Miranda offered her hand and walked him slowly up the gentle slope, past the vegetable garden where red-winged blackbirds lit on the old scarecrow. Past the tall leaning black oak, the outhouse and its earthy stink. To where the girl clung inside the doorframe as if to a tree in a fast-rising flood. Sensing the boy falling a step or two behind, Miranda drew him alongside. "My brother," she said to the girl, "would like to meet you."

Shirtsleeves unbuttoned at the wrists, so the sleeves hung down over her hands, the girl stepped across the threshold into the sun.

Miranda hesitated, then reached out for the girl's hand.

The girl drew back, put her hands behind her.

"Watch me," Miranda said, then made a shape, three times with her hands.

Slowly, the girl made the shape herself.

"To him," Miranda said, nodding at her brother.

Hello, the girl said to Littlefish.

The boy's heart leaped like a fish in his chest, as it had the day Sister had first taught him to swim in the cistern of the little canyon, her hands behind his shoulders, easing him beneath the surface, the sudden pressure in his ears beneath the water, and then lifting him up, and he, coughing, sputtering, thrilled. It was like that now: the fear and joy of plunging. How many times since that day had he plunged and held his breath, his eyes open, his webbed hands sheathing the rough body of a catfish to lift it, thrashing, out of the water, the weight and struggle of it good?

The boy signed, first at the girl, then, when the girl didn't answer, to Sister.

No, Miranda said. Slower. "It's okay," she said. She reached out and took his elbow. "Why don't you show her your garden?"

The girl watched, curious.

Littlefish took a deep breath, then held out his hand. Palm up, fingers splayed, the delicate webs catching light.

Like no hand the girl had ever seen. She hesitated, long enough for the boy's cheeks to burn red, then pushed her shirtsleeve back from her hand and touched him, lightly, with the tips of her fingers. They were soft in his palm, like minnows. He felt her warmth, and the sensation, the pleasure, was everything. The girl touched his rough skin as if she had never touched skin before, traced the webs between his fingers. Pulling away, then touching again, now the contours of his misshapen brow. She ran her palm along his pebbly cheeks.

Sudden dizziness overcame him, like being swept up in the currents of a creek. He swayed on his feet, and for an instant he saw himself as if he were inside her head, behind her eyes, looking out of her face, and what she beheld was not a mottled, gray-skinned thing, more in common with a fish than a boy, but a shimmering creature of light, every crack in his skin aglow with some inner radiance as bright as the noonday light when it sparkles in a million tiny pieces on the river.

More than that: between the tips of her fingers and his cheek, a band of golden light arcing . . .

She dropped her hand away, put it behind her back, her own cheeks rising red.

I dreamed of you, the boy said, released from the heady

power of her touch. I drew your picture. I *know* you. He reached out his hand once more, and slowly, surely, like a flower unfurling from the end of a stalk, her own hand emerged from her sleeve and this time closed fully around his, and he held her tight, for to let go would somehow be like letting go of his own life, he thought, and as she relented, gave herself over to his hand, his touch, Littlefish felt, too, that she understood his thoughts, could feel them, even hear them, though he had never heard his own voice inside his head in all his life.

"What's your name?" the girl asked.

SECRETS

Day streamed through the cabin's windows.

Iskra sat Miranda at the table, as she had when she was little, always some task before her: peeling potatoes, chopping onions, slicing apples. Now, cheeks red and bloody from the bannik's claws, her only task was to sit. Be tended. But the old woman had lost vitality in the ritual, her strength sapped by magic. She moved slowly, a hitch in her step that had not been there before. From the mantel above the stove, she reached down a black leather Bible and thumped it on the table. She opened the Bible to the Psalms, where the pages were hollowed out in the shape of a bottle. The bottle itself was unlabeled and stoppered, three-quarters full of something clear.

"I had to hide it," Iskra said, "when the boy got old enough to snoop. He got into it once. Never told you, did he. Made him sick as a dog." She put one corner of her apron over the bottle, sloshed it, then touched the damp fabric to Miranda's cheek. Her hand trembled.

Miranda hissed.

"Your father used to bring it to me. To rub on the goat's ass for worms."

Miranda smiled. Winced at the burn in her cheek.

Iskra fetched two jelly jars from the kitchen, plunked them down on the table, and poured from the bottle. She sat in the cane-bottomed chair opposite Miranda and pushed one glass across the table.

Miranda sniffed it. Took a sip. It lit her throat on fire, made her eyes water.

Iskra held up her own glass and spoke words in her native tongue, then swallowed half. "My mother used to say: never tell secrets without a drink. A woman of great secrets, my mother."

Iskra drank the rest of her liquor and poured herself another and drank again. She sat straighter in her chair, clenched her jaw, and stared up at the ceiling. Her chin jutted like a bald rock. Her eyes wandered the edges of the room, the pipe of the stove and the stones of the hearth.

Suddenly all good humor seemed to flee the little cabin, and Miranda felt a gulf between them open up, yawn wide, a chasm set to swallow them.

"Now, Myshka," the old woman finally said. "I will tell you the truth. Let my voice bury my words deep inside you. Before the sun sets, I will tell you secrets you have longed to know. For I was a girl once, too, and like you, I have known sorrows so great there are no words to account for them."

"Baba—"

Iskra shushed her. The old woman's gaze settled on the bread bowl. For a very long time.

"This place, it frightened your father," she told Miranda. "Too many things he could not understand here. A spirit in the walls. A demon in the shadows. Things a body cannot take stock of. Things you cannot bait a hook to catch. Things beyond the land he knew."

Outside, a cloud passed over the sun. Inside, the cabin darkened.

"The song the girl sang," Iskra said. "I used to sing songs like that, when I was young. I sang them for money at funerals. This was before I came here. A long way from this place. In miles, in years."

She poured a third time, stoppered the bottle, sipped from her glass. A more measured drink, Miranda thought. The liquor was working now. The words were coming.

"My father, like yours, did not trust magic. But unlike the boatman, he was a cruel, faithless man. He died in the winter of my tenth year. His coffin we brought up to the church on a buckboard. I remember how the ground was frozen so, it had to be broken with pickaxes. Mother and I watched the men of the town lower him into the earth. I did not sing for Yuri Krupin that day."

Iskra spat on the floor.

Miranda started at the sound of it: harsh, final.

"That night, Mother and I sat round the table. The house was cold. We spoke and I could see her breath. I remember, to this day, her exact words. She said: 'Eight months past, I put my hands over your father's stomach while he slept and whispered, "To the death-bringer who dwells in all of us, I, Hana Krupin, do now take this man upon my back and ascend the Great Tree to stand upon the threshold, where I pitch his bones down among the roots of his eternal home, where the white snake coils, where the white bees hive, where sickness dwells forever. Let this man die. This is my command."' She made a motion then, Myshka, with her hands, I have never forgotten."

Iskra spread her hands wide, very gently, and rested her palms on the table. As if this simple, silent motion were all there was to a man's death.

She took her hands from the table and they whispered in her lap. Her coffin-shaped snuff box appeared from the folds of her apron and she pushed a pinch of tobacco from it into her lip.

"You see, Hana Krupin never wore a witch's shift. She never unpinned her hair. She had no mortar and pestle to fly about in. She did not walk with a stoop or a cane or point bony fingers and scowl the Evil Eye at children. Her eyes were not black or crossed. She was not tall. She was not short. She was, in fact, very plain and ordinary looking. She did not laugh or smile. She had two deep creases here, between her eyes, where worry had drawn its plow. Her way of loving was quick and hard, the way you twist a small thing's head off as a mercy. But it was love. When she died . . ."

Hand trembling, she spat into her liquor glass.

"The lament that came out of that child today," Iskra said, "was the song I sang. The day she died."

Tobacco ran down the inside of the jar, thick and slow, like molasses.

Miranda watched it.

"They came for her. The men. Led by the young priest of the church. Their little colony there on the prairie was not to be a backward-looking place, you see. Never mind that Mother was a healer, a deliverer. To them, she was something so much worse. A *born* witch. The most terrible of all. A born witch carries power in her blood. Secrets, old and eternal. Nothing like a man's secrets, which are petty. Fleeting. My father's secrets were not even secrets at all. The men, they knew he was cruel. That his fists fell against Hana Krupin when he drank. They *knew*. But men, Myshka, look after men."

She spat again.

"They hanged her," Iskra said. "In a field there in Prairie County. From the only tree within sight. The crows came and pecked for days before they let me cut her down and bury her. In a cheap pine coffin. Like you, child, I dug the hole myself. And there, at her grave, I closed my eyes and opened my mouth, and without knowing I was going to do it, I began to sing. A long, harsh wail. I sent my voice into the void, shot the grief from my heart. And when the song was finished, I shut my eyes and listened. I listened for a voice in the deep, dark places where the magic runs. Something to comfort me, to assure me that Hana Krupin had made her crossing. That I had brought her into the next world. I heard nothing at first, but then, the sound of wind in pines, speaking the name of a river. This river. A voice in my dreams, Myshka. Huge, ancient. Eternal."

"The leshii?" Miranda said.

"The leshii." Iskra took up her jar to spit. "Rybka's mother was drawn here, too. Not cut from the same mold as a Krupin woman, no, but make no mistake, Lena Cotton was a born witch. I had only to put my hand in hers that night to feel her power. I held her hand and saw—"

Here, the old woman faltered. A shadow seemed to pass over her face and through the room, and Miranda found herself remembering the preacher's words among the ruins of the church that morning: *Lena sees.*

"What?" Miranda said. "What did you see?"

Iskra looked down at her hands in her lap. Rough, dry, empty hands.

"I saw that she was broken," Iskra said. "By a man who had sworn to love her, but loved only himself. It was a true sin, what he did to her. A sin against her power. Against the power of this place. Everything that happened that night, and everything that has happened since, right up until this very moment, all of it was set in motion by Billy Cotton's razor."

Miranda remembered the slit she had glimpsed in the boy's throat that night. No trick of shadow after all. She put a hand over her mouth. "All these years, I've worked for him," she said. "He did that and I've worked for him . . ."

"We have no time for regrets now, Myshka. Only truth."

The old woman took a deep breath. Let it out. "The leshii has her plans," she said, and spat into her jar. "The boy is part of them. Always has been. The boatman, too, played his part. As I played mine."

One more story to tell, Miranda thought. She grew still, as if she herself were an arrow, nocked and drawn. Aware, suddenly, of every speck of dust turning, drifting in the dim cabin light.

Miranda felt it coming now, like a lever had been pulled, locking up the machinery that made her human. She took a single step outside her own body, saw herself sitting in the chair. At the table. Staring at the old witch and waiting. Like a placeholder for some horrible truth. A fist clenching in her throat. Miranda took a drink, did it again. Emptied her glass. The liquid blazing down her throat and into her gut, scalding the tears from her eyes. Had she suspected it, all along? Forced herself to never think it, because to think it was to follow a train of thought that would swallow her, drown her?

Iskra reached into the folds of her apron and took out the wax casing of a red shotgun shell. She set it upright on the table between them, its end charred where it had been fired, all those years ago.

Miranda stared at it.

She stared at it while Iskra told the story of it. How Hiram followed her to that place of magic, deep in the woods, where she placed the baby in the bowl at the leshii's weird altar of mud and bone. How the ground shook and the bowl overturned and when it did, Hiram made to catch the child, though it spilled out dead. Some foolish instinct born of a parent's breast. Dropping his shotgun, even as the leshii reared unseen from the swamp, ready to accept the old witch's sacrifice. Staring into her lap, Iskra muttered: "The gun was there. Your father's back was turned . . ."

Miranda seemed to have hardened into stone. She stared

past the shotgun shell, past Iskra at the bright day beyond the windows, and waited.

"He was right not to trust me," the witch said. "Hiram was right. My greatest secret was loneliness. For years I begged the leshii for my own blessing, for a miracle. 'Fill my womb,' I begged her, but she kept her silence."

A line of juice spilled over Iskra's chin, and she wiped it now with the back of her hand, then wiped her hand on her apron.

"Then came the boy, so many years later, hideous and strange. There was a silence that night, after the gunshots faded. So loud. All the world hushed. I took up my knife and the blood from your father's throat filled my bowl and swallowed the child, and out of that new, warm blood your brother was reborn. I could hear the leshii's laughter, mocking me. This thing, she had given me. My child. When I had asked her for a daughter. Someone beautiful, someone strong. Someone to share secrets with. Not to keep secrets from. The leshii gave me the boy. But I *took* you, Myshka."

Tears shimmered in her eyes, but Miranda Crabtree did not move.

Iskra let the silence work. The old cabin creaking around them.

Eventually, Miranda pushed back from the table, took an arrow from her quiver, nocked it in her bow, and drew slowly on the old woman. Aligned the broadhead with the witch's heart.

Iskra reached across the table, took Miranda's glass, and poured herself one final drink.

SHARP

Like the bathhouse, the boy's hut was set on a foundation
of timber and dirt. It was narrow and long, the roof peaked
and covered with shingles greened with moss, the outer
walls thick with lichen. Inside, beneath a little window, a
makeshift desk of plywood stood across twin sawhorses,
its surface scattered with tools—a hammer, a screwdriver,
a garden spade. A hammock was strung between the far
corners. It was here that the boy brought the girl, to show
her his books and comics. They hunkered on the floor and
she took up a comic and stared at the cover, where a green
monster reared up from a mob of men armed with shovels
and hoes and axes, a giant pitchfork thrust at the monster's
heart. But the monster was a great promontory of moss and
tree and vine, a creature born out of the earth itself, and the
men broke like waves against him. Behind this struggle, a
woman in a white gown was tied to a tree. A fire at her feet.
The monster, somehow, the only sane part of the picture,

one fist upraised as if to smite, godlike, the mob entire. His eyes burned red, set deep in black hollows. The girl stared at the picture for a long time.

The boy reached out, tentatively, and turned the pages in her hand.

See, he signed.

The creature ripped the tree from the rock, tore it from the earth, and the woman was free, and she was tall and powerful and beautiful, her long black hair fanning out like wings. She conjured bolts of lightning from a blue-black sky. The men began to scream. There was a boy, her brother, and the boy and the sister were safe when the clouds had parted because the men were gone, and where the men had stood was a golden field of flowers.

It was the boy, Littlefish signed. His magic, not Sister's. Turned the bad men into flowers. See?

The girl fixed her eyes on the monster in the final panel of the story, left to stand at the cliff's edge and watch as the woman and the boy walked away, the monster's face in shadow. Bond of love between brother and sister, in the end, as great a mystery as his existence.

"He's lonely," the girl said.

Her eyes went from the book to the boy's hands and then to his face, then back to his hands, the webs between his fingers.

The boy did not notice. He grabbed a coonskin cap that hung from a nail on the wall beside his hammock. This he plopped onto the girl's head. She laughed and took it off and rubbed the fur against her cheek.

She put the hat back on and closed the book and got up and went to the boy's worktable.

She picked up a rusty spring. Put it down. Picked up an arrowhead and slid her thumb along the edge.

A thin well of blood.

Littlefish sprang to her side, plucked the blade from her hand.

She put her thumb in her mouth. "Sharper than a razor," she said.

The boy slashed one index finger across the other.

"Sharp." She nodded.

He grinned, happy she understood, and made the motion again.

She turned her thumb in the light that shined through the little window. The cut was not deep.

The boy led her out of the shed to show her his garden.

AIM

Miranda let the arrow rack out of focus, saw the old woman's center beyond. The center was all that mattered. Beneath apron and blouse and breast, a heart beating. Crying out, perhaps, to be stopped. From the heart down to the hands, knotted in the old woman's lap, the arrow drifted. *Hiram is dead, the boy is alive.* Madness, too deep to fathom. A slit in the boy's throat, resolved in Miranda's memory as a trick of light and shadow. But no trick. Billy Cotton had torn his child from his wife's bosom and cut the boy's throat and *you, you worked for him, all these years, the man who would have killed your brother . . .* Miranda remembered him on the stairs, something in his hands dripping red, and now she imagined a similar mouth opening in her father's throat, made by the witch's knife. She flashed on Hiram trussed up from the black oak in the meadow. Had it been like that? Her father strung up like a kill in some cold, alien bog? *I have no father because of this woman and I have a brother*

because I have no father. I never knew Cora and I did not know Hiram long enough to know him as I might now had he lived and here is this woman I thought I knew but I look at her and see only a collection of strange and ancient parts, but I know the boy and the boy is good and true and I love him and he was born from horrors and you can't change that any more than you can change your birth because all of us come from cracked eggs and nests of thorns.

She increased her pull, let the broadhead swim back into focus, let it drift now to the old woman's eye.

Unflinching strength. This, Hiram had taught her.

To flay the skin from the beast and wear the coat it makes.

This same strength, the old witch possessed. It had guided her hand over Hiram's throat.

Miranda's arm began to tremble.

The boy, the girl: two strands entangled with her own, bright colors among others dull and lusterless.

What terrors the girl must know, to peer into a person and see the whole of her.

We are the choices we make.

She glanced down at the shotgun shell set upright on the table.

Miranda made her choice.

NO SHELTER HERE

A peal of childish laughter from the garden out back, even as the cabin seemed to groan all around the boatman's daughter and the witch, the boards flexing furiously.

"Be still, house," Iskra said. "I am not shot yet."

The cabin quieted.

"Well," the old woman said. "Is this it?"

Miranda said nothing.

The old woman pressed her lips together and made a fist in her lap.

Miranda released the arrow.

The shadow of the half-empty liquor bottle had changed places on the table, moving with the sun. The hollowed-out Bible lay open beside it. The arrow Miranda had shot was lodged in the center of the old woman's table, split into two pieces on either side of it: the red wax casing of the shotgun shell.

The witch seemed to Miranda like a campfire burned low, nothing left but coals and ash. She sat quietly while the children played outside, the girl's laughter carrying. Miranda had gone to the window to watch them, and through the glass she saw the girl following Littlefish through his garden, clouds of gnats drifting in their wake. The boy darted behind a tomato stalk belled with empty tin cans. The girl wore his coonskin cap and carried a comic book and ran between the plants.

Iskra pushed back from the table, trembling, and walked their jelly-jar glasses to the sink, a weave in her gait now, one foot dragging. The old woman leaned against the sink, as if for support.

Outside, Littlefish pointed at a ring of cobalt bottles set over sticks, the bottles heliographing in the sun. He spoke with his hands, and the girl listened, though she did not understand.

"They aren't safe here, are they," Miranda said.

"The preacher will find this place. The leshii will see to it. She will all but steer his boat. If he finds the girl, you see, he finds the boy, and that is what the leshii wants. So, no, they are not safe here."

"Damn your leshii," Miranda said.

"She is not mine. She is no one's. To impede such magic—" Iskra made a dismissive gesture with her hand. "You might as well try and change the course of yon river."

Miranda looked out through the window, to the garden,

where the children played. *The bottoms*, she thought. *I'll take them into the bottoms, hide them. They will not be hurt. I can see to that without bargains and magic.*

"Can you," the old woman said, as if reading her thoughts.

Miranda looked at the arrow in the table. Beyond this swamp, beyond these sweltering lands, there were other worlds. Places she could have gone. People she could have been. She felt them now, these other selves, stirring like ghosts in the grave of her soul. She had let too much of the past, of time and the river's currents, shape her.

She yanked her arrow from the table.

Touched the razor-sharp edge of the broadhead.

Blood welled up from her finger.

"Go," the old woman said. "There is no shelter here."

Miranda went.

ALL THERE IS

The sun set on a day that had seemed the longest in John Avery's life. After Cook's burial, he stayed in the greenhouse among his plants. Sometimes pacing, sometimes sitting. Once, sleeping. At the hottest part of the day, he had smoked the last few buds on his worktable, but the fears that plagued him did not dissolve, only morphed into a paranoid certainty that Charlie Riddle's great fat bulk was lurking beyond the blackened windows. Doubts like drills boring around inside his skull. Stomach churning with fear for himself, his family, for Miranda. This third, final run Cotton had demanded. What cargo was left? All the ready dope was gone, ferried the night before. Nothing remained but the plants, and she couldn't transport them by boat. What was Riddle not telling him? Miranda would be a fool to show up tonight. She was not a fool. *But you are. You should have left already. After you buried Cook. Should have walked out of here right then with wife and child and never looked back. Money*

or no, infant or no. The world beyond these borders is hardly so cruel. So why can't you leave this goddamned place?

When he stepped out into the late evening dusk, the trees were black against a red sky, and the whole of the land seemed cauled with a membrane of blood. The dirge of the insects rang out from the trees, low, atavistic. He crossed the lane to the last inhabited shotgun house, went inside, and locked and barred the door. In the kitchen, he took a long butcher's knife from a drawer and stood staring at his sallow face in the blade. He tucked the knife in the small of his back, didn't like the feel of it, tried the front.

"You cut it off, what good are you," a voice said.

There, in the bedroom doorway, was the woman he loved, wearing shorts and a sweat-stained tank top, one hand threaded through her close-cropped hair, the other scratching her chin. A smile at the corner of her mouth.

Night fell, full and starless.

Later, she ran her fingers through his hair. She stood behind him by the small window in the rush of air coming from the box fan, his head touching just below her breasts. Holding Grace in his arms, Teia holding him. He fed the baby from a warmed bottle she had brought from the kitchen. The baby's mouth fastened tight to the nipple. They stood like that for a while, in the cool of the fan, together, and Avery was grateful for it, this small passage of time in which worry was shut out in the presence of their one remaining hope, this small round flame wavering in the dark. He felt the tug of his daughter's feeding subside. He slipped the nipple and passed the bottle to Teia and threw the baby over his shoulder. Carried her around the room until she burped.

Teia set the bottle on the bureau and dropped onto their bed, their sagging, creaky bed where she had given birth four months past, only John attending. *We did this alone*, he thought, looking down into his daughter's face. *Surely, we can do the rest.*

Teia crawled into the middle of the bed and sat in the depression that the weight of their bodies and worries had worn, her sleeveless T-shirt and thin boxers soaked through with summer sweat.

The butcher's knife on the nightstand, within easy reach.

The baby burped and Avery passed her to Teia. Teia held her and began to croon a lullaby. When the child was sleeping, she put her down near the pillows and scooted to where Avery sat bare-chested with his back to her on the far corner of the bed, his shoulders slumped, his heavy head dipping. She put her hands on his shoulders. Began to knead them. "You got that big strong brow," she said. "Holds all them big thoughts." She kissed his ear. "Where you been hiding all day?"

"Usual places," he said.

"You see the fat man today?"

"Not since early. He's been AWOL."

"Don't feel right."

"No."

"You don't really think he's gonna pay us?"

"Not likely."

"So we go in the morning."

"In the morning," he said quietly.

"Hey. What else?"

"Nothing. It's just funny—" He laughed. Not his usual warm laugh, but a harsher sound, the sound of his laughter turned against himself, the edge of a knife scraping stone.

"What, baby?"

He shook his head.

"Tell me."

"I wanted to preach," he said. "A long time ago. Isn't that funny?"

"Yours is a heart stowing secrets, John Avery."

A camp meeting in a field off a highway, a tent blazing light. A voice, booming, drew him from the dark and he slipped out of the womb of night and through the canvas and was reborn into a sea of souls raising hands. Down the sawdust-strewn aisle, he went like a man enthralled, dimly aware of eyes watching him, as they always did, to the platform, where there was room to stand below. The voice he heard from those dry dusty planks crying love and mercy was a woman's. A siren in a dress of homespun cotton and a boy's lace-up shoes, standing on an overturned apple crate and holding aloft a Bible and preaching into a silver microphone. She was small, but her voice was big, so big, and John Avery, sixteen years of age, looked back at all those people and saw that they, too, were wonderstruck. *Up there*, he thought, *I could be big like her*. Then: from the ranks of the first row of metal chairs, a woman with long dark hair streaked gray fell in some paroxysm, began to flop in the sawdust, and as the men around her stared, uncertain whether it was a fit or some religious ecstasy, the young girl on the platform leaped down and fell to her knees and lay hands on the woman and turned her face up to heaven and cried, "I see it! I see the sickness inside this woman, Lord! Black feelers and tendrils! Loose them, Father, loose them!" She began to wail in a gibberish tongue, and as the crowd closed around her and all laid hands on the woman's twitching body, John Avery stood apart in awe, in terror.

Teia had stopped kneading. She slipped off the bed and around him, to her knees on the wood floor. She put her hands over his, locked them in her grip.

"Maybe I wasn't good at God," he said. "But I never meant for this, for any of this—"

"Look at me, John Avery," she said.

He did.

"Now, you keep them eyes on me, and you tell me what you know."

"Cook," he said.

"What about Cook?"

He met her gaze. His eyes were wet. "Someone cut his head off."

Teia took her hands from her husband, slowly, and rocked back against the baseboard. She put her hands over her stomach.

"There's more," he said.

Behind them, the baby gave out a moan, then quieted.

He told her what he knew. How the preacher had brought back Lena Cotton's long-lost daughter. How Miranda had refused to give her up. He told her about the head in the Styrofoam cooler, how they buried it. How Miranda, tonight, was supposed to be here, at the dock, for one last run. "I think Riddle means to kill her," Avery said. He wrung the covers at the end of the bed. "I can't just wait it out. I can't not help her. She's smart, maybe she won't show. I know we should have left already, I know, but I can't just abandon her, I—"

Quickly, Teia put her arms around him and pressed his face to her breasts. "You're a good man, John," she said. "But you remember us. We three, now, that's all there is. You just keep us alive. Let these fools kill each other, but you keep *us* alive."

He began to sob, great hard sobs like fists pummeling Teia Avery's chest, and she pressed him close, held him there in the cradle of her heart.

INTO THE WOODS

They made camp when the last of the day's light was gone and the moon was above the trees, and though Miranda had staked a canvas roll across a rope strung between two maples, the boy and girl slept out by the fire, crown to crown, each curled on their sides like two halves of the same shell. It surprised her, how fast they went down. She sat at the boy's feet, torturing the campfire with a pine limb that left her palm sticky with sap.

How quickly the boy and the girl had come to trust one another. So openly, so unlike Miranda's own bond, hard-won over a lifetime. Teaching the boy his signs, starting with a few basic shapes Hiram had taught her, then moving on to illustrations in a book checked out from the Nash County Library, never returned. The boy, frustrated and unable to cry or scream when he did not understand. He'd struck her once, hands like mallets. She understood such bruises.

But here was a blind trust she did not know, as if they had met each other already in some bygone time. Born of some weird energy passing between them, minds and spirits linked.

Littlefish jerked out of sleep, bits of leaves clinging to his forearm and elbow.

Miranda poked the fire. Dream? she asked.

The firelight made shadows of her moving fingers.

The boy's eyes shone. Smoke, he said. Everywhere. Choking.

"What was burning?" Miranda asked.

Everything.

She kicked up sparks with her stick, every spark a question.

The only one that mattered: *What will you do next?*

Are you leaving us? the boy asked.

Why would you think that?

He only shrugged.

"I will never leave you." She reached out and cupped the crown of the boy's head, where his hair grew thick and long. She kissed him.

He lay back down, burrowing into the leaves beside the girl, who still wore the boy's coonskin cap.

The Root bow and quiver leaned against a tree near the tent. Miranda moved away from the fire and took up the bow and ran her finger along the edge of the fiberglass, the wood beneath a rich cinnamon. Her hand, despite the cut the old witch had made in her palm, felt at ease in the grip, and the arrow rest was lightly scuffed where a thousand broadheads had rested. Over the years she had shot from trees,

from blinds, standing and crouched—always in her sights a
meal, a hide. She was nine the first time she killed a living
thing. An armadillo, come trundling among Hiram's worm
garden, turning over cardboard and licking the worms that
clung beneath as if they were delicacies. Miranda's arrow
had punctured the shell with a crunch like the collapse of
a rotten log underfoot. The animal leaped into the air and
ran. She found it at the river's edge, on its side, half in, half
out of the shallow water. The arrow had punctured a lung
and the creature lay kicking, gasping, bubbling. Miranda
stared down at it and felt ashamed. She knew she should
finish it, put another arrow through its heart. Its chest exposed, thick hair clinging wetly against the mottled skin.
She did nothing, only stared down at the ringed tail and
small ears and long snout, the black, wizened eyes. She did
not cry. When the armadillo was dead, she picked it up by
the tail and carried it into the woods and left it for the scav-
engers. She never told Hiram.

By the fire, the boy was sound asleep.

She touched the string of her bow, strummed it.

It might be easier, killing men.

Men were deserving in ways an armadillo, a deer, a boar
were not.

They mean to kill you, she thought. *These men who killed
Cook. If you go tonight, Riddle will send you to them with Cotton's promise of one last run, and they will kill you.*

She thought of the long, vague time after her mother's
funeral, the sight of Hiram hammering fresh planks onto
the floating dock, cigarette after cigarette hanging from his
lips. Months of silence, no music in the house. A starving

time. The heavy silence of the days at work in the store, punching the register before she even knew how numbers worked. The long somber reassurances of the old men buying bait, their shuffling away like the rustle of leaves.

She remembered the day when that long time had finally dropped from his shoulders like the yoke it was: the day he had taught her to shoot his bow and her first bolt had punched through the center of the paper target and buried itself in the bark of a black walnut tree at the edge of the woods. She was seven. How the slightest of smiles had crossed his face, and there had followed between them a season of unburdening in their lives, whereupon all the reserves of love Hiram possessed, once thought poisoned, were sluiced over into her, and good memories began.

Had she come to such a day herself?

A moment when all her choices could be reversed, set right?

A day of unburdening.

A new life to begin for her, the boy, perhaps the girl, too.

If I do this, she thought, *it will be like dropping a hornets' nest with rocks. The only thing to do after is run.*

She had tucked enough money away in the hidden spaces of the mercantile to live simply.

She looked at her brother, recalled the old witch's words: *The leshii has her plans. The boy is part of them. Always has been.* To be a fly in the web of some dark god's schemes, whatever those schemes might be.

But it's not the boy's burden, she thought.

And what of Charlie Riddle, who hated her so? He would kill her, if he could.

Soon, she thought, somewhere north, across the river, that one-eyed fat man would stand waiting at the end of Sabbath Dock, where some yet-to-be-revealed cargo needed moving along a dark river that ran ever on, its perils known to Miranda Crabtree since girlhood.

Smoke, the boy had dreamed.

Maybe, Miranda thought, *a fire needs setting.*

She left the children sleeping and backtrailed quickly in the dark. It was nearing midnight when she came out of the trees where the boy's bark was banked. She took it across the bayou, tied it to a cedar branch, and skirted the northern edge of Iskra's island, avoiding the old woman's cabin, the old woman herself. She went through low pines over rock and scree and came to Iskra's dock and from there took the johnboat back to the Landing, where she quickly changed into fresh jeans and a beige shirt that buttoned with faux-pearl snaps. In the bathroom mirror, she examined her face, her bruised throat. Her cheek, the slash marks from the bannik's claws crusted over. She traced these with Mercurochrome, the effect not unlike warpaint. She cleaned her palm where the old woman's knife had sliced her. She wrapped it in gauze. She moved on. From the hall closet she fetched a dozen more arrows for the Root recurve, as well as a brown leather arm guard, shooting glove, a pair of binoculars, and an empty canteen, which she filled at the kitchen sink. She grabbed a threadbare apron Hiram had worn behind his butcher's counter for years. This she rolled and stuffed into her quiver. She took his Old Timer out of his tackle box, too, put it in her jeans pocket. She saw Cook's gun, there in the clutter of old lead and tangled fishing line. Remembered how it felt, to draw it on the ramp, a cold, dead weight sapping her resolve. Useless. She locked the gun away in the tackle box and pushed it to the back of the closet floor. Standing up, she felt the hem of a flannel shirt brush the nape of her neck. She hesitated, then, on impulse, snatched it from the hanger and tied it round her waist. On her way out, she took a box of Diamond kitchen matches from a drawer and tucked these in her own shirt pocket. At the dock below, she took two spare gas canisters from the Alumacraft and filled them with gasoline from the pump.

In all, these preparations took less than fifteen minutes.

Once, she glanced up at the practice target across the water where it was nailed to the tree in the field, the bull's-eye long gouged out. She heard Hiram's voice clearly, as if he were standing on the dock some few feet behind. *Be sure*, he said. *When you draw, be sure.* And his old mantra: *Shoot light. Shoot true. Shoot now.*

She stepped into the Alumacraft and cranked the motor and jammed the throttle forward, loosing herself like an arrow into the dark.

INTERRUPTION

A quick, hard rap of knuckles against the edge of the fly screen. Avery sat up, naked atop the sheets. He touched Teia's arm and she gave him a searching look. He pulled on his jeans and went barefoot through the narrow house and opened the door, butcher's knife behind his back.

Riddle stood in the dark, a great bear of a shape.

"What's going on?" Avery said.

"Need you," Riddle said. "Get dressed. I'll wait."

Avery closed the door softly.

"What's happening?" Teia said.

Avery stood behind the door, his head down. "Not sure."

He put the knife in Teia's hand. Said keep it close.

Then he dressed, moving quietly so as not to wake the baby.

IV

✦

Final Run

CARGO

When Miranda saw the dwarf, her heart plummeted. Avery stood naked at the end of Sabbath Dock, hands cupping his genitals. Trembling before Riddle and his deputy and bleeding freely from a cut above his left eye. Stomach and knees pebbled with dirt and blood, as if he had been dragged over rock. Knuckle skin like apple pulp.

Riddle loomed, a cigarette burning between his lips, his thick fingers looped on either side of his buckle. Sky above him flung with stars. Fedora cocked, he smiled wolfishly at Miranda as her boat drew near.

Avery would not look at her.

Miranda sat unmoving at the stern, a tremor of fury working its way out from her center.

The Alumacraft bumped against the dock. The gentle lap of the water against the hull was the loudest sound they heard.

"Hidy, little sister," Riddle said. He noted the bruise-work on her throat, the cuts on her cheek. "You tangle with a bear?"

"What is this?" Miranda said, standing slowly.

Tenderly, Riddle touched Avery's shoulder. "John, what is this?"

Avery, through a split lip: "It's the way it's gonna be."

The constable's smile widened. "Tonight, your boat's a basket, little sister. And this here is the Baby Moses."

Avery kept his eyes on the planks of the dock.

Riddle flicked his cigarette into the water. "We're selling the secret recipe, you might say."

Miranda eyed the Root and its arrows, strapped inside the gunwale, felt Hiram's knife in her pocket. The grip of Riddle's pistol was smeared with John Avery's blood and a sprig of hair.

Are you fast enough?

To do it now, right now, to hell with the plan?

And if she failed, would she even hear the shot that pitched her back into the murky water, or would failure belong to the fat man, failure to register the arrow that had buried itself in his throat?

His hand already on his pistol above her, the boat rocking beneath her, she made the odds and didn't like them. So she swallowed thickly and tossed the rope, and Riddle looped it around a pillar.

"Help him down, girl. Don't worry, he won't bite. He's cool as a cucumber now, ain't you, boy."

Miranda did not move.

Riddle's deputy cast an embarrassed look at his long feet.

Avery turned his back to Miranda before letting go of

his manhood. She looked away as he descended the ladder. On the third rung, he slipped, feet and legs shaking so. Near the bottom, he stopped and clung there, ugly red welts across his shoulders, as if from a strapping.

Miranda reached for him.

"Don't touch me," he said.

Riddle laughed as the dwarf stepped awkwardly into the boat. He collapsed on the center seat, facing the bow. "Like I said, John," the fat man called down. "Don't you worry none about that pretty wife and baby. A promise is a promise. Besides, they family, ain't they, Robert Alvin."

"You say so," Robert Alvin said.

"See y'all later." Riddle slipped the boat's rope from the dock.

Miranda reached for the starter as the men went walking away.

Right now. How easy.

Arrows in their backs.

But she did not.

She wanted it all too badly to work. The way *she* wanted it to work.

Avery sat with his head down.

She glanced at Hiram's shirt, wrapped around her waist, untied it, and tossed it onto the seat.

He gathered it, clutched it in a tight wad in his lap.

Behind them, Miranda heard the Plymouth's engine rumble. She yanked the starter.

They eased away.

AT THE CAMP

✦

The boy woke. The night was thinner now, the sky to the east warming. The fire was all but dead; he could have put his hand into the ashes. He had dreamed again, fleeting. A single white dove, dead in grass. Blood on its breast. The hot wind of a forest fire raging. Trees like fish bones dripping flame in great orange gouts: the woods behind Baba's cabin, burning.

Sister was gone, only a plugged canteen tossed beneath her canvas tent. The leaves inside had not been slept on.

He touched the girl on the shoulder, and she came awake instantly.

He signed at her, saying that Sister had left, that he was in charge. Her expression blank.

He did not know Sister's mind, only knew she was protecting them from something. The girl, he figured, was in trouble. Somehow, her trouble was now their trouble—his, Baba's, Sister's. Sister had brought them into the woods like two children in a fairy tale. He had a book of fairy tales, the spine mended with silver duct tape because it had fallen apart, he had read it so much. Children in fairy tales were always alone in the woods.

In his dream, the woods were burning because Baba's cabin was burning.

We should stay put, he thought.

I will never leave you, she promised. And yet: she was gone, and now they were alone in the woods. Sister had taken them away from Baba's cabin, which meant Baba's cabin was not safe.

But Baba was alone at the cabin.

Fire, he thought. *Everything on fire.*

The girl watched him, some recognition of his tortured thoughts gleaming faintly in her eyes. "I'll follow you," she said.

Littlefish remembered the sight of himself through her eyes, strong and brilliant and beautiful. He grabbed the canteen Sister had left beneath the canvas tent and kicked dirt over the fire. He took the girl by the hand and pulled her to her feet.

We go back, he signed, then drew his new friend away from the ashes of the camp and into the dark.

AVERY AND MIRANDA

✦

A few miles out from Sabbath House, Miranda cut the engine and angled off the river, and there she and John Avery—now wearing Hiram's old shirt like a nightgown thrice his size—drifted in dark, still water among the trees.

Up the inlet, something large broke the surface of the water and rolled.

"I need to tell you," Miranda said. "These men who want you, I aim to kill them tonight."

At this, Avery made a half turn on the seat. "I'm sure Charlie Riddle means for them to kill you first," he said.

Miranda chewed her lip. "Just makes it easier, then."

"I guess so."

"I need to know you won't get in my way."

He turned his back again. His words were slow, measured. Pointed. "If you try, and you fail, Charlie Riddle will kill my family. He will shoot my wife and smash my baby's head beneath his boot like a gourd. Do you understand?"

"Say I give you over, don't kill anyone," Miranda said. "You think Charlie Riddle won't do those things?"

Avery's silence was heavy and clear.

"You and me served evil men long enough, John Avery," Miranda said. "It's about time we served something else."

COTTON ON THE RIVER

✦

In the hours before dawn, kerosene lantern in one hand, gut-hook machete in the other, Billy Cotton walked down the gravel lane from the manse and stood where Sabbath Dock met grass. Acclimating his eyes to the moonless night and listening, for a time, to the frog and insect roar of the wilderness. He took a deep breath of fetid air, then set the lantern and machete on the boards. Nearby, a ten-foot aluminum skiff lay facedown in a stand of cattails. Cotton dragged it out of the weeds and turned it over to empty it of dead leaves. A copperhead spilled out from behind the stern and shot away into the water. He righted the boat, hung his lantern by a tenpenny nail from the bow, then used the paddle to push the boat into the water. The old preacher stepped in at the stern, and by lantern light made for the river.

As the little boat neared the end of the inlet, his back already quivering with the strain of paddling, Cotton felt a stirring in his chest, an unseen hand dragging nails inside his skin. *It is happening,* he thought, *just as Lena promised.* He set his paddle dripping at his feet and unbuttoned his shirt. Touched his chest, drew back fingers wet with blood. He took off his suit coat, then his shirt, folded both, and laid them on the center seat. He stood, snagged the lantern from the bow, and swung it close. Saw, just below his collarbone, a thin line of blood, running south. He watched it, touched one finger to it, even as the blood seemed to congeal and hang. Pain now, the burn of opened skin.

The boat wobbled beneath him. He sat back with the lantern, kept it close.

Ahead, the inlet flowed into the river.

Pain, the ghost had promised, speaking in his head yester morn as she walked boldly into the ruins of the church, unseen to the Crabtree girl or John Avery. Or any of creation, save Billy Cotton. Her voice a thousand bees drumming in a hive.

Pain . . . will show you . . . the way.

More burning now, fierce and sudden. It sent him to his feet in the boat, crying out. He swung the lantern near enough to feel its heat singeing the hairs that grew thick as a forest on his chest, and now the line of blood curved left, and Billy Cotton opened his mouth to scream, but when the blood turned suddenly above his heart and ceased its flow once more, the scream lodged in his throat. A left turn below the clavicle, then three sharp bends.

A map, he thought, with a kind of wonder. *A map of pain.*

A single tear formed in the corner of the preacher's eye. He stretched out his arms and turned his face up to the starless void. He would have danced had the boat not already been pulled into the river's current. He dropped onto his seat and took up his paddle, steadied the johnboat, and soon was passing Crabtree Landing and then the oxbows, and when his chest began to burn again, the blood to flow anew, he followed it, turning onto the narrow bayou, the way ahead all darkness save his lantern's flame.

Shedding blood and tears now, he felt alive in the pre-dawn dark, alive in a way he had not felt in a very long time.

Is this what belief feels like? he thought wildly, then took up a song, and though his voice was lost in the din of night creatures singing their own nocturnal gospel, Billy Cotton believed that his dead wife somewhere in the black heavens above heard his song and knew his heart and, yes, guided his boat on to that horrible isle where devils held captive her child.

He sang the only hymn he'd never forgotten, the one that Lena, in the early days of her ministry, *their* ministry, had loved to hear him sing.

"'The way of the cross leads home, the way of the cross leads home . . .'"

For the way of the cross, the preacher thought, *is pain*.

Verse after verse, and with every plunge of paddle in the water, every new etch upon his flesh, the land opened up to him, enclosed him, swallowed him. A great expulsion in reverse: the devil sent forth into the snare of paradise.

"'It is sweet to know, as I onward go . . .'"

————

"'. . . that the way of the cross leads home.'"

Two months past.

Cotton sang softly as he blasted the shuddering Caddy west along I-30, passing into East Texas, through towns set down among the rolling fields like ramshackle markers. The Caddy made a clanking sound that got louder the faster he drove. Eventually, grass fields in every direction, he took an exit, then followed the state route for ten, fifteen miles. After that, a county road of rough blacktop that gave way to gravel. Through a wooded bottomland along the Red River, then out into a field, where three trailers clustered around a single oak tree.

He passed through a metal gate, thumped over a cattle guard. The trailers were two-toned, beige and brown, the windows silvered over with tinfoil. AC units hummed and dripped. The trailers had always reminded Cotton of roadside cemeteries he'd seen in Mississippi as a young man: a litter of tombstones beneath a few gnarled pecan trees at the edge of a bean field or a cotton patch. Small and insignificant, lost to memory and time. He parked in mud-rutted hardpan among a handful of pickups.

He swept his beaverskin hat from the passenger's seat onto his head and walked up the concrete steps of the first trailer and knocked. The wind blew strong and harsh and carried with it the creak of a tire swing rope, the wide, empty sound of nature.

It was a long time before the door opened. He heard a whispered, furtive conversation, the voices of women. But when the door cracked, hooked by a chain, it was a man's eye staring out, hard and green. Thick fingers, a beard long and scruffy. Cotton didn't know him. He smelled cigarettes and pot and something else, some rank, sinful funk. "I'm here to see the child," the preacher said.

The man's eyes traversed the whole of Billy Cotton. "No kids here," he said.

Cotton caught the door, pushed against it. Said his name.

Silence. Then the chain slid free and the door opened, and the preacher walked into the gloom of the trailer.

He was told to wait, so wait he did. He sat in a gold recliner that rocked, gently. The doorman lumbered down a dimly lit hall to a closed door. He knocked, lightly, then went inside. Cotton looked around. A woman with black hair and red lips sat slumped and braless on a ratty antique divan on the opposite side of the room. She wore cotton underwear and a thin nightie, a pair of marabou heels. A window unit blasted cold air above her. Her eyes were closed, a line of saliva slicking her chin. Cotton stared at her for a while, then let his eyes move on to the bare pine-paneled walls, the lamps shaded in red silk.

A thin, ragged woman whose face might have once been pretty came out of the back, cinching a satin robe over nothing. Her feet were bare. She stood over Cotton, who sat politely with his hat in his lap. She lit a cigarette and eyed him. He eyed her back. He ran a hand through his hair as if to make himself presentable. She blew smoke. "Ain't seen you in a while," she said.

"Been a few years."

"Lot more than a few. You come to take her back?"

"I came to see what all the fuss is about."

"Fuss is you ain't paying me enough for this shit. Like I told Handsome Charlie, that girl's a loss. I got overhead."

Through a placid smile, Cotton said, "I'll see her now."

She *hmphed*, then made a gesture with her bright nails. He followed her out the front door and along the length of the trailer. The woman walked barefoot in the grass, a series of purple bruises running up and down her left calf. She took him out back, to an old Bounder motor home parked beneath the boughs of a Texas live oak, tires flat, roof littered with years of shed leaves. Behind it the Red River, a great muddy snake.

The woman opened the door with a key, then stepped aside and gestured for Cotton to go in. She shut the door behind him.

Inside, all sunlight was extinguished.

Cotton let his eyes adjust.

A girl lay on her stomach on a bed at the rear, legs bent up behind her in a slant of sunlight. She wore a T-shirt and a pair of dark jeans. At the sound of the door, she rolled over and moved to the edge of the bed, one foot turned inward, bare toes grabbing at the carpet. A book in hand, thick, without pictures. Her thumb marking her place.

"Who's that?" she called into the gloom.

The preacher felt a sudden eruption of sweat beneath his armpits. Her voice was small, delicate. Nigh twelve years she had been here, seven since he last saw her. How many times had he longed to come here? To confess the horrible things he had done to her mother?

I sent you here to break her. I tore you from her, and in so doing tore the first great hole in her heart.

Cotton moved through the musty coach, noted the clean sink and stovetop, the dining nook immaculate, a package of crackers and peanut butter on the table, nothing else.

I promised her they would do terrible things to you, then paid them not to do them. In the end, I tore enough holes in that heart to sink it, to drown it forever.

He stood in the narrow doorway to the bedroom, hat in hand.

The girl sat in the dim light, little more than a silhouette. "Ma'am let you in?" she said.

"She did."

Hesitation. "You here for business?"

"Business?" he said, his tone sharp. "They got you working?"

She did not answer.

Gentler: "I'm here to look after you's all."

"I don't know you, mister."

"No, but I knew you when you were little. Used to come here and read you stories." He took a step toward her.

"Don't come any closer," the girl said. She set her book aside and reached from beneath a pillow a pair of men's tube socks. She quickly pulled one sock over each hand and up her arms, brightly colored rings at her elbows. "Ma'am said, ain't no one to touch me no more. Said it ain't worth the grief."

"What's been happening to you, child?"

The girl looked down at her socked hands in her lap. Spread her fingers inside the fabric so the cotton stretched like webs between her hands. "Ma'am says it's just dreams. But they ain't dreams."

"They're visions," Cotton said.

"What do you know about it?"

"My wife, she saw things, too. She always said it was her gift from God."

The girl shifted on the bed, set her book aside. "I sure never thought of it like that."

"What do you see, when you touch people?"

"Bad things, mostly."

Cotton took another two steps toward her.

"Are you here to help me?" the girl said.

"I'd like to," he said.

"Some of the ladies, they came to me, asking me to touch them. Like I was some fortune-teller. But I didn't want to, so they held me down. Grabbed whatever they could grab. It wasn't good. What they saw, it scared em so bad two of em just up and left in the night. Ma'am was plenty mad. All the rest is spooked. She says I'm all-around bad for business now."

Cotton's throat constricted, an odd prickling over his skin. "Show yourself to me, child," he said.

The girl hesitated, then reached out with a socked hand and switched on a lamp, and Cotton's breath caught at the sight of her. Her head was crudely shaved, a few plugs of hair like brush fires here and there. The girl regarded him with large, frank eyes, both enveloped by dark, storm-cloud bruises. Her lip was split.

"Who did this to you?" he said.

The girl did not answer.

"How long has this been going on?"

She shrugged.

Sweat beading beneath his scalp, running down his cheek, Cotton looked past the bruises and the grotesque head and the socked arms. In her face, he saw his wife, the small ears, small nose, eyes that turned down at the corners, forever sad. He saw nothing of himself, though, was helpless to wonder, even in the midst of the child's suffering: whose bed had Lena warmed, even as her own lay cold? Cotton was trembling. He gripped the brim of his hat with both hands.

"Would you touch my hand?" he asked.

The girl recoiled slowly, drawing her legs away from the edge of the bed. She folded her arms across her chest, shook her head.

Like a snake striking, Cotton shot toward her and snatched her arm.

The girl screamed, jerked away. Shoved back against the pine paneling.

He grabbed her left arm, yanked the sock away. Was dumbfounded by what he saw: little white scars up and down the length of her flesh, some fresh and raw. And in the crook of her right elbow, where the sock there had slipped, half a dozen pinprick scabs. She snatched her arms away, corkscrewed past him for the door. Cotton seized her bare foot with both hands.

The vision came like a swift blow to his breast, at first darkness, then pain, deep down, infected cells coursing through red streams, the dank smell of roots, cold stone, blood pattering, a razor—

The girl jammed her other heel into Cotton's chin and scrambled across the linoleum to the narrow bathroom and locked herself in.

Cotton sat back on the bed, gasping. The pain subsiding.

"Go away!" the girl sobbed.

Outside, the preacher staggered into sunlight.

The woman who had shown him to the motor home stood nearby, chain-smoking. She tossed her butt into the grass. "Well?" she said, stalking over.

"You put poison in her?"

"Only way I could turn a goddamned dollar on that creepy little slut—"

Cotton struck her, hard, felt the snap of something in the woman's face beneath his knuckles. She went down in the grass, a slice of bare leg exposed in the sun, all veins and tendons and loose flesh. "I PAY YOU!" he roared. "I pay you and you don't touch her. That was the deal."

"Fuck you," the woman spat. "You ain't ever here, you or Charlie fucking Riddle—"

Cotton seized her throat. "You've signed your own death warrant, whore."

Her eyes bulged, red bursting. Face going purple.

Cotton heard a thunder of footsteps, looked up, and saw the big man who had opened the door rushing him. The man hit him like a freight train. He seized the preacher around his throat and dragged him around the trailer and threw him in the front yard, where the ground knocked everything out of him, made him bite his tongue. He sprawled in the dirt, mouth filling with blood. He pushed up and staggered in a circle. The big man put him down with a single punch.

When Cotton woke he was stuffed behind the wheel of his Caddy. Through the cracked, dusty windshield, he saw the trailers, and in his half-coherent mind, he marked them for his wrath. *She was there, Lee, at the end. She was with us in that cold, black place. She* will *be there.* His mind fixed to this thought.

All the way back to Sabbath House, hot air blasting through the Caddy's window, keeping him conscious when the pain in his head wanted to send him right off the road, into oblivion, Cotton thought: *I was wrong to send her away, Lee.*

She is a lost dove. She is ours.

OURS.

On it drew him, into the bayou, far ahead Iskra's island and the coming dawn. The lure of blood, the selfsame blood that drew his dreams at night to the witch's clearing, to the girl's waiting hand, blood channeled by the will of some force greater than its bearer, a creature old and powerful and unknown to Billy Cotton, whose chest wept red to show the way. The bayou narrowed, the trees wound together, and beneath the harsh nightsong teeming and the sound of his own voice singing out, the old preacher never heard the true world whispering, reshaping itself in the dark, making ready to receive him.

THE MEN WHO KILLED COOK

Beneath the lee of the railroad trestle, the Alumacraft settled with a damp sigh against the bank. Miranda climbed
out and moved quietly beneath the bridge and over the
granite riprap and up the concrete escarpment. As the grade
steepened, she dropped to the balls of her hands and feet,
climbing until she was nested in the abutment. Avery came
up on her right and lay belly-down beside her.

She lifted the binoculars she had taken from Hiram's
toolbox and glassed the barge and boat ramp some sixty
or seventy yards upriver. At the top of the ramp, four men
were clustered in a halo of blue light. Two were the men
she had met the previous night, the giant and his sharp-
toothed partner, their white Bronco parked at the edge
of the trees. Beside the truck were two Shovelhead bikes
gleaming chrome and black in the bloodless light, their
riders tall and bearded and slack-faced, clad in leather from
boots to waist. They stood in a ring, each looking out on

the water. The giant and one of the riders smoked. They did not move, save to ash their cigarettes in the grass. The two men she had never seen before wore sidearms in shoulder holsters, six-shot pistols, tattoos inked in their necks and bare arms like dragon scale. The man with the teeth held a pig-knuckle shotgun at his side. The giant had no firearm Miranda could see, just a long, curved knife in a scabbard that dangled from his hip, lashed there by a length of steel chain around his waist.

She passed Avery the glasses.

"These are the men who killed Cook?" he said.

Miranda slid backward on her belly beneath the I-beams of the bridge. She and Avery perched in the deeper darkness there, listening to the predawn shuffle of bats among the iron. She thought: *So.* The word like the plop of a stone in water, unremarkable. And that was all her life would be, should she lose it in the next few minutes: one more small thing the river had claimed. She thought of her mother's grave beneath the gum tree. Her father. She thought of Littlefish and Iskra, the lives they had made on the bayou. The life they had given her, in turn.

"These are the men," she said.

She slid silently down the concrete and over the rocks, back to the Alumacraft.

Avery followed.

SAFE

Littlefish came out of the trees and saw Iskra's island across the bayou in the warming violet light, the top of his pine tree along the ridge shrouded in mist. It should have given him some comfort, the sight of home, but over the last few hours, as he and the girl had backtrailed through the bottoms, a slow, nameless dread had been rising in his heart like water filling a boat. Now he saw his little bark on the opposite bank, run ashore among the trees, and knew that Sister had used it to cross in the night. He felt alone, abandoned. Where was she? Would he find her just over the hill, back at Baba's cabin? He didn't think so. Across the way, he saw the narrow, root-threaded path that wound up like stairs into the gloom of the pines. Remembered his dream: smoke and fire and everything burning, and suddenly their crossing seemed urgent, as if the sun itself were the fire he had dreamed, rising higher and higher behind the trees.

He made gestures to ask if the girl could swim, and she

understood right away and shook her head. "I'm sorry," she said.

By her overlong sleeves, he drew her hands up and around his shoulders. She understood and linked them behind his neck. He corkscrewed within her grasp and bent forward and she clambered onto him in the reeds and mud, and like a funny, shambling creature, they went into the water.

They went slowly until the boy's feet left the bottom.

He kicked once, and they were swimming.

Webs between hands and feet expanding and contracting with every thrust, his body streamlined itself, and were it not for his ragged jeans and the girl on his back, pushing her neck above water, the boy would have seemed wholly at home in the bayou.

They had covered less than half the distance between shores when the current yanked at the girl and she panicked. Closing her hands around his throat, her forearms locking beneath his chin. A sudden surge of color at her touch, the world refracted through a diamond: dawn sky blazing, treetops gleaming amber, sunlight glittering gold. Water went up his nose. She struggled. He thrashed. She slipped. Littlefish felt her weight leave his back, and when he looked sideways he saw her, crying out, flailing in the sundappled bayou. He surged after her, his form a sleek missile. He caught her by the waist, lifting her, as best he could, above the water. Struggling to hold her, one arm locked around her chest.

Through a stand of reeds and onto the pine-needled bank, they fell in a heap together, choking and sputtering, the boy's lungs burning. The girl's coonskin cap lost to the bayou. A spasm rolled up from her gut and she coughed brown water onto the bank.

Littlefish rolled over, gasping at the morning sky.

The girl sat beside him.

He touched the back of her hand, to ask if she was okay. She started.

Suddenly, the green in the trees around them was aglow, purple wisteria uncoiling in bloom from the pine tops. Littlefish could hear the rush of life in the veins of the plants, and the morning sky blazed with the last of the night's stars that blurred into lines and back into points, and the bayou where the rising sun struck was blinding, and the boy was filled with a shuddering delight.

The girl, too, was luminous, her skin glowing as if from within, her eyes blazing out the purest blue. From a clump of wildflowers near the water's edge a butterfly rose up, the size of a hawk, beating its great wings of orange and black fast enough to blow their damp hair back from their ears, the movement like the rapid shuttering of light through the trees when the boy's bark was moving swiftly in a current. The girl laughed as it probed her face with its legs, then drifted away, leaving a sky overhead that was pink and gold and studded with clouds like stones across a clear blue stream.

Was this the place Baba had told him about, when he was little? The land within the land? *All I need do, Rybka, is draw back the veil of the air, and there it will be, the magic.* And always after this, her laughter, dark and puzzling to the boy.

Littlefish closed his eyes, and when he opened them, the world had taken on familiar shades and contours. In the wildflowers now, the butterfly fluttered small and fragile, and the world was simply the world again.

"I like your world so much," the girl said.

Together, they went up the hill to the base of the boy's tree, to the ladder there, the boy walking in a crooked line, dazed, the girl smiling. All urgency in their flight was gone in light of their glimpse of this green, mysterious world. It flickered across his mind that the vision he had seen might somehow be a trick, or a sort of lullaby, tearing him away from some pressing pursuit. Even now, he could not recall any sense of urgency, and anyway, if there was danger ahead, then surely his tree would be a safe place. He began to climb but did so carefully, lest he fall. Looking back, he saw the girl staring up at the eastern sky, where the sun had risen. Now she wore no smile, no dreamy, faraway look. Instead, she watched the sun rise and seemed afraid, as if it were not light spreading in the east over Baba's cabin but a terrible darkness, welling out from a blackened sun.

He beckoned her to follow.

After a moment, she began to climb.

TRESTLE AND FIRE AND WATER

Miranda drank and offered the canteen to Avery. They sat on
the bank beneath the trestle, beside the boat, letting the sky
lighten. Beyond the bridge, a wall of honeysuckle hid them
from the ramp around the bend, where the men with guns
waited in expectation of a girl, a boat, a dwarf. The morning was damp, heavy with mist that clung to the trees and
water like netting. *Might help with cover*, Miranda thought.
She slipped her arm guard and shooting glove on. The latter
she drew carefully around the cut on her palm.

"Current's strong," she said.

"Don't worry about me," Avery said.

She took another drink from the canteen. "You ain't out
when it lights—"

"I'll be out. You worry about you." He drank the rest
of the water when she passed the canteen back. He spilled
some down Hiram's shirt and brushed at it.

"Ain't we a pair," she said. She offered the dwarf her gloved hand.

Surprised, Avery took it. Held it.

She got into the boat and took up one of the metal canisters from the stern, emptying gasoline over the seats and into the bottom of the boat. She tucked the can quietly near the bow. Avery climbed in by the stern and stood, waiting as Miranda slung her bow and quiver over her shoulder and took up the second fuel can. She stepped out of the boat and onto the bank and took her father's wadded apron from her quiver. Next, she sat on a rock and drew three arrows and stuck them in the ground. She used Hiram's knife to cut the apron in six long strips. She wrapped each of the three broadheads with two strips and cinched these around the shafts. Finally, she unscrewed the fuel canister's lid and dipped each arrow into the canister.

Avery's eyes followed her hands from where he sat by the tiller.

"Everything we do from here out tells how long we live," she said.

He gave a single nod.

Miranda slid the arrows carefully home, one by one, and shouldered the quiver. She grabbed the Root bow from among the rocks and handed Avery the second fuel can. He splashed the rest of the gas into the Alumacraft and set the can softly in the bottom of the boat, between his feet, the fumes wafting up from the hull and swirling in his head and lungs.

"Remember," she said, lifting the boat off the rocks by its nose and easing it back into the water. "Wait in the trees until it's safe. Then follow the bank to me."

"How will I know it's safe?"

"I won't be dead."

He put one bare foot against the transom, bracing himself, one hand on the starter cord. The big shirt hung around him.

"Count ten, then go."

Miranda disappeared into the screen and scrub that littered the slope, rocks dislodging, clattering behind her.

He counted ten. He pulled.

The engine cracked the morning's silence, but it did not catch.

"Shit," he hissed.

He pulled again. And again.

Sweat burst across his brow and he thought: *It's no good.* They would be discovered before their plan was even in motion, and John Avery saw the future that lay ahead: a lifetime in bondage to terrible men of terrible purpose. His wife and daughter fed to the wet moist earth of the bottoms, fat Charlie Riddle whistling as he shoveled them under.

He prayed, as people long bereft of belief will pray, the belief having lain dormant, awaiting some moment of terror such as this to germinate it, to bring forth a shoot so delicate and small and dear.

Dear God, John Avery prayed, *let it work. Dear God.*

He pulled.

Some muscle or tendon screamed in his arm, but the engine caught and spat and all thought and pain and resurrected belief fled in a rush of adrenaline.

He steadied himself as the boat leaped forward, then goosed the throttle, and the Alumacraft left the shadow of the trestle and shot across the bend toward the boat ramp, where the men who killed Cook were pointing in the boat's direction, calling out to one another.

Raising their guns.

Avery jumped from the boat. Was swallowed by mist and water.

Miranda charged up the slope to the top of the bridge, heedless of the briars and nettles that tore at her legs. She came out of the brush breathless, to her right the bridge spanning the river, to her left the rails stretching away between pine ridges in the moonlight. She clambered over the rock-strewn berm and up onto the trestle, where the ties were spaced inches apart and she could feel the wind blowing up from the emptiness between them. Crouching low, moving quickly, smell of gasoline and tar thick in her nostrils. At the center of the trestle, she stood astride two ties with a clear view of the river below and the ramp.

The Alumacraft—empty now, save two spent canisters of gasoline—came chugging out from beneath the bridge, slewing right of the boat ramp, headed for a thick nest of tangled honeysuckle along the riverbank.

Two of the four men had fanned out along the bank toward the water, pistols drawn and trained on the boat. The giant and his partner remained at the top of the ramp, watching.

Miranda propped her three doused arrows on the rail at her feet. There she crouched, and from her shirt pocket took the box of kitchen matches and struck one, cupping the flame with her hand.

The men along the bank were shouting orders at the empty boat.

She touched the match to the first arrow and the flame shot across to the other two. She dropped the match and stood and nocked the first arrow. She brought it back to half draw, then full, heat from the flames blistering the knuckles of her bow hand, Iskra's cut in her palm opening up in her glove, beneath the gauze. She drew a bead on the Aluma-craft, which had now run aground among the shore brush just downriver from the ramp, where it sputtered and churned like a child's forgotten toy in a bath.

The two riders moved through the brush toward the boat, breaking branches and shoving into tangles of honeysuckle and pasture weed and sow thistle.

Miranda glanced at the big man and his partner at the top of the ramp. The small, sharp-toothed man's gaze was on the boat below, the men approaching it.

The giant was looking directly at Miranda, smiling within the dark folds of his hood.

Blood ran freely beneath the bandage that wrapped her palm, into her shooting glove. It trickled down her wrist, along her arm.

She let the arrow go, knowing immediately: a miss.

The shaft cut a flaming arc across the river and guttered with a whisper just short of the boat's stern.

Miranda bent and took up the second arrow.

The giant let out a cry, a high trill. He pointed to the bridge.

The men in the brush looked, saw. Raised their pistols.

Miranda drew to her anchor point, felt the feather

against the corner of her mouth, and this time the pain in her hand did not matter and the blood was not a distraction and she did not waver at the moment of release. The arrow struck the boat and the gasoline went up, threw lashings of fire over the boat, the water, the low scrub trees along the bank. The man nearest the Alumacraft caught a wash of flame and his gun went off and the other man behind him flew backward into the brush, struck. The first man's legs grew tangled in the kudzu. On fire, he fell.

Miranda snatched up the third arrow from the rail and drew and shot.

The bolt struck the fallen man dead center.

On the boat ramp, the small man tossed his shotgun in the grass and took a pistol from the rear waistband of his jeans. Before Miranda could get a fresh arrow from her quiver, he fired. The bullet glanced off the iron rail at her feet, driving a sliver of something hot and metal across her shin. She did not waver. She nocked a fourth arrow. The flames from the burning boat and scrub lit her target. She drew. She released. The arrow struck the small, sharp-toothed man in his heart. He dropped to his knees and rolled down the ramp, the shaft of the arrow snapping in two beneath his weight.

The giant ran for the Bronco at the edge of the trees.

Miranda drew a fifth time, and it was in the midst of drawing that she felt the first vibrations beneath her. Light bloomed around her, her shadow stretching long on the rails and the ties.

The train that came from the south gave out its first long bellow.

Stupid, oh God, the train, how could you forget the train—

Miranda searched out her target across the water.

Took three breaths.

Shoot light—

The giant had made it to the Bronco's door. The truck's dome light flared on a high-powered rifle on a rack in the rear window. The big man's hands closing around it—

Shoot true—

The train's white eye bearing down—

Shoot now.

She let fly, but the arrow only glanced off the pickup's hood.

The giant smashed the dome light with his fist and slid across the seat, pushing open the passenger's door and propping the rifle's barrel on the open windowsill.

The train bathed her in light, a perfect target.

Miranda gauged the distance and knew she couldn't make it to either end of the bridge. She would be shot, or she would trip and fall and the wheels of the train would separate her like the bannik's saw and send her in pieces to the river below. So she tossed the Root over the side of the trestle and followed after it.

The rifle cracked.

The train blew past overhead.

She plummeted.

Down. Down.

Down.

She hit the water.

THE LORD'S BUSINESS

The sun had just cracked the eastern sky when Cotton's skiff drew nigh the old weathered dock. He emerged from a narrow channel, bare-chested and bloody, half the bottoms mapped upon his flesh, and before him lay the old witch's island, crowned in mist where it rose out of the murky bayou. Beside the dock, an old dead cypress festooned with all colors and sizes and shapes of bottles. Hung by strings or set neck down over the ends of branches. Clinking softly. Some held webs and spiders, others darker, mold-furred things. Cotton swayed when he stood, then tied his skiff to the dock and clambered over loose and rotten wood onto land. He pulled his jacket over bare skin, set his hat on his head, and followed a well-worn path carpeted in leaves and needles until it became sumac and saw briars. Hacking and slashing with the gut-hook machete.

When his breath was with him, he sang. Loud and clear to drive away the lingering shadows. With each rise and fall of the blade came a phrase, a verse, hymns of blood that cleansed the soul. Up and down came the machete. Spittle formed at the corners of his mouth. Up, down, up, down, and when the trees had no more to give, he burst through into a clearing, panting through a grin in the knee-high grass, dark trousers and suit sleeves covered in beggar lice. The shack stood like some homely crown on a brow of red dirt and vine. An old withered figure on the porch. Right out of his dream, save the sun. Cotton threw his arms wide and bellowed up the hill, filling his voice with all the fury he could muster: "Grandmother of the Bog!"

On her porch, the old woman sat rocking, implacable in her regard. She picked up a tin spit can from the boards beside her chair and spat a stream of brown tobacco. She set the can back on the boards. Across the knees of her apron, like the ready hammer of a Roman soldier, lay the long black length of Hiram Crabtree's twenty-gauge double barrel.

Cotton moved slowly up the hill, smiling broadly through the old familiar pain returning to his bowels and hips, his kidneys. He sang a few more verses until he reached the top of the rise, where he put his boot to a chicken that had come out with three others from beneath the porch to pluck at the scant grass.

"What brings you, devil?" the old woman said.

Cotton laughed. "Devil? Oh, grandmother, no. I come on the Lord's business." He reached up with his left hand— in the right dangled the machete—and removed his hat and held it over his bloody heart. "The Father Hen has come to call his little chicken home."

"You and your blackhearted God can kiss my ass, Billy Cotton," the old woman said.

"Now, grandmother, I will not stand for blasphemy."

"Walk back down that hill," the old woman said, "or you will not be standing a-tall." She closed one hand over the steel barrel of the gun and hauled it up and took it by the stock and stood.

"You and that Crabtree gal have something that belongs to me."

The old woman leveled her aim at Cotton's chest. "There is nothing here for the likes of you."

A silence passed between them, filled only by a set of wind chimes made from the bones of some small forest critter that clacked in the cool morning breeze.

"Your whore goes to her death this morning."

"I will count to three."

"I am washed in the blood of the lamb. Are you?"

"One."

"He is my deliverer. Who is yours?"

"Two."

"Where is the child I seek?"

The old woman did not speak the final count. She pulled the trigger. Braced against the blast and the sight of the white-haired man coming apart all in red, she gasped when all that issued from the shotgun was the dry click of a misfire.

"Praise God," Cotton said, and he went quickly up the steps and struck the old woman with the machete.

She lurched beneath the blow, the blade passing through the meat of her left shoulder, cutting deep and lodging there like an ax in wood. The shotgun clattered to the porch and the old woman fell backward on the boards, knocking over her spit can, sending a wash of sweet-sick-smelling liquid across the planks.

Cotton bent down and pulled the machete free, slinging the blade like a wet paintbrush that sent a fan of crimson across the wall of the hut. He did not feel the sudden hum in the boards beneath his feet, or, if he did, he mistook it, perhaps, for the slow, building current of the cicadas in the woods. Nor did he notice, as he fixed his mad, gleaming eyes on the old woman gasping, that the nails in the planks beneath his wing tips had begun to inch free of their boards, or that old Iskra's blood dripping down the wall behind him had begun to sizzle. The old cabin trembling, gathering its rage.

"Where is the child, grandmother?" he asked softly.

THE GIRL, IN A TOWER

Her clothes were still damp from the river when she woke.

The boy—Littlefish—was gone.

The dream had been there, waiting for him in the dark. It had hurled him out of sleep, this dream, sent him scrambling for the knothole where he kept his pencils, then over the side, down the tree, gone. The girl knew this because they had climbed to the top of the tree and plunged into sleep, exhausted, cradled in each other's arms like children in a story, and his dream became hers. A new sensation, intimate and strange. What fearful things he wrestled with. She saw herself, standing in the clearing at the bottom of the old witch's cabin, one hand in the hand of a man, a man in a black suit and a dark brimmed hat—*the preacher, I remember him, I do*—and next she woke to see the boy had scratched in the wood with his pencil an act of remembering, like the drawings in his picture book. *I know so much about him. I saw the whole of him, the beautiful perfect whole.*

She sat with her back to the rough bark of the tree, drew her knees against her chest. She touched the rough planks, where a shape had been scratched, the shape of a girl. A little girl in a dress. Stick arms, stick legs, no face, only the grain of years-weathered wood. Yellow hair in big loops, made with a colored pencil. The girl ran a hand over her shorn scalp, wondering what the boy knew that she did not.

From the right hip pocket of her jeans, she took out the arrowhead, swiped from the boy's table in his shed. She held it by the stem, turned it before her, marveled at it. Like a snake's head, fangs bared.

Hair takes time to grow, she thought. *Do I have time?*

A blue-tailed skink ran across her foot.

She jerked her feet apart and saw, then, written in darker pencil on the wood, two words: *SAFE. STAY.* The letters large and crude and meant for her.

And now the bright morning world they had shared grew dark, eclipsed by the thing she had seen earlier, gathering in the sky over the trees, where the old woman's cabin stood, a black mass writhing and dripping long tarry arms toward the earth. Above the mobile homes in Texas, this same shape had coiled for three days, and on the fourth the bad men came and the last thing she thought, before the black smoke became her world, was this: *He has sent for me. That crazy old preacher has sent for me. Just like he promised.*

And now, to this black and coiling shape, the boy, her friend, had run.

SAFE, he had written on the wood. *STAY*.

She thought of the boy's comic book, the woman lashed to the tree, waiting on the green monster to save her.

No.

She put the arrowhead back in her pocket and crawled to the edge of the platform and rolled onto her belly and pushed her legs out into space, then lowered her body until her feet found a branch. Grabbing hold of the rough planks, she edged along until she reached the ladder. She closed one hand around a slat and put her foot on the next. She shut her eyes and pretended she was not a small and terrified creature clinging to a pine tree high above the ground.

She stepped down one rung, found the rung below.

And the next. And the next.

THE BLOOD-SPRINKLED WAY

The old woman lay on her back on the porch. She put her weight on the arm that was not ruined and forced herself to sit up, as best she could. Cotton left her and went into her hut. Inside, the light was dim, the morning sun having not yet penetrated the gloom. "Hello?" he called out, though he knew, from the settled silence of the house, that no one was here. He saw, on the table, a Bible, open to the Book of Psalms, the pages hollowed out in the crude shape of a bottle, and the bottle next to it, unmarked. He set his bloody machete on the table and unstoppered the bottle, gave it a sniff.

In the old woman's bedroom, he saw two unstruck matches near a candle on a straw-bottomed chair, and these he tucked into his hatband. He pulled her mattress and sheets from her bed and dragged them out to the living room, near the table.

Behind him, a floorboard creaked.

He looked around, saw no one.

With a grunt, he ripped the wooden mantel free of the brick hearth.

He took the bottle from the table and poured it over the mattress and mantel, which he then set afire with one of the matches from his hatband.

He took up his machete from the table.

The flames were licking and spreading when the front door of the cabin flew open and a fuselage of tiny missiles shot through the air and struck the old preacher. He staggered beneath the blows, each like the sting of a wasp. As the flames rose up behind him, he looked down and saw half a dozen two-inch nails lodged in a cluster, just below his right rib cage.

Behind him, the rear door bucked in its frame.

Machete in one hand, Cotton pulled nails free with the other. First one, then two, then three at once. He cried out, spittle spraying from his mouth.

The window above the kitchen sink exploded.

The preacher threw up his arms against the flying glass. Was yanked from his feet by a force unseen, then dragged across the planks toward the rear door, one leg thrust up to the empty air. The door flew open as he was hurled through it and slung sideways into the yard, where he rolled to a stop against the chopping stump, one pants leg hitched up to the knee. He lay on his stomach in the dirt, dazed, spine and groin shrieking, machete still clutched in his fist, beaver-skin hat yet snug on his head.

On the porch, the old woman had crawled to the rail

and was drawing herself up, getting her feet beneath her. She left ribbons of blood on the wood.

When she was half standing, leaning against a post, she felt the house spirit behind her.

She felt its anger. Despair.

Felt its love.

"You go on, now," she said. "Do not mind me."

Cotton came shambling-limping around the corner of the house, machete at his side, as smoke began to billow through the open front door. He came up the steps, grimed in dirt and blood, jacket sleeve torn at the shoulder seam. "Where is the child?" he asked a third time, as he laid the machete's blade against the old woman's cheek.

Iskra spat on his shoe, a stream of brown slop that ran down her chin and dripped from her whiskers. "You will know fire, Preacher," she said. "Hotter than any dreamt-up hell. Your chickens will answer"—she laughed—"before that fire is snuffed."

Cotton reared back his blade to strike.

"Meantime," the old witch said, "you go fuck yourself."

She began to laugh. A laugh that quickly rose in pitch and became an old crone's cackle, as blood and spit and tobacco flew from her mouth.

The preacher went at the old woman with the machete, just as he had gone at the brush of her beautiful isle. When he was through, the blade was red and dripping and the blood was running through the cracks in the planks and pattering on the ground beneath the porch, and the fire inside the cabin was roaring.

Cotton limped around the side of the cabin, singing as he went. He sang even louder and brighter than before, as if now he were a man on a military march, and again the old cancer pain in his back and groin subsided, a validation of his efforts. God's hand at work.

He walked up the crooked, root-thick path between the cabin and the outhouse. In its pen at the top of the hill, the old woman's goat stuttered and tramped. Before this, a little shed where Cotton saw a garden in the tall grass, with its multitude of strange contraptions, colored bits of glass on string.

"'The way of the cross leads home,'" he sang.

He went to the shed, kicked open the door, and was shocked to discover the room of a child—no ordinary child, but a child of nature! Pelts on the wall. A knife on a table. A quiver of arrows and a bow leaned upright in the corner. He thought of the Crabtree girl, but knew, somehow, this was not her room. It was a boy's space, had a boy's musty smell, and beneath that something else, a kind of fishy tang. He saw the books, too, on their low pine shelves. He knelt and ran his hand over the spines with a sense of wonder. Something about the room felt familiar, as if it had been a place he had visited before. But it was not, and this made it seem like a trick or a snare or a lie. He tipped the books, one by one, from the shelf. Then, fury blazing in his chest like a pine torch, he kicked the bookshelves flat. He tore comic books in half. He upended the table beneath the window and put one dark shoe in the middle of the bow, snapping it. The arrows he took up and broke over his knee, one and two at a time. When it was done, he righted his hat, which had gone cockeyed on his head, and went out into the sunlight, where the old woman's cabin was still burning, and the girl was yet to be found.

Littlefish watched through the cracks of the bathhouse wall as the old man from his nightmares passed by on his way up the hill. Blood-soaked and threadbare, he limped like Baba's old scarecrow come to life, and Littlefish was sore afraid. Directly, he heard a commotion from his shed and knew the old man had gone inside. He wrung his hands around his three-pronged frog-gigging stick, grabbed from behind his shed as he came out of the woods at a low trot. Now he heard the roar of the cabin blazing, heart pine exploding. *Go,* he told himself. *Go find Baba. Help her!* But he could not. Fear rooted him in the shadows, and it was a very long while before the sound of things smashing and breaking ceased. When it finally did, the boy heard the old man call out in a ragged voice: "I am thy Father Hen, little chick! Harken to my wing!"

Father?

Littlefish knew this word, knew it well from books he had read, and what he knew of fathers—that they were good, strong men who protected children—made this man's use of the word seem like a terrible lie. He thought of the girl, her arms around his neck as they had crossed the bayou. The giant butterfly. Her shimmer. Her touch a strange new warmth, like and not like Sister's.

Surely, she was not *his* child, not this awful man's, no, she was good, she was—

"Little chick? Where are you?"

Footsteps, coming back this way, the tall man's thin silhouette passing outside the bathhouse. Humming. His black shoes covered in dust just visible through the crack beneath the door, where he stopped.

Littlefish moved quickly, before the door handle had turned. He shoved his stick into the rafters and ascended the wall studs in two quick steps, putting one webbed foot on the crossbeam of the frame. He reached up to the rafter and threw his feet up and wrapped his legs around the beam. Now he hung upside down above the door. Hooking his elbow around the beam, with his other hand reaching his stick out of the rafters, the boy was poised to strike.

The bathhouse door opened.

The Father Hen stood black against the fire.

"Little chick?" he said.

MIRANDA AND THE GIANT

Moments passed, though it seemed hours later when she broke the surface of the river near the barge and bobbed in the water, arms flailing for purchase along the old boat's hull. The Root trailed in two pieces behind her, the bowstring tangled around her arm. The world a distant roar in her ears. Her shoulder came up against the port bow and she grabbed the chain anchoring the barge to the shore, most of it underwater and slick with river slime and frog jelly. For a handful of breaths, she clung to the chain like a thing washed up in the tide of a flood, lungs burning.

The sun rising behind the trees now.

The roar in her ears the roar of the dam upriver.

Miranda closed her eyes.

Unconsciousness like arms enfolding her.

No.

Pain in her left side, bright and burning. Her quiver was gone, her arrows with it. Above, she heard the deck wood groan. She bore down on the chain with her weight, shrugging free of the flotsam of her bow. She reached up out of the water for the lip of the barge, steadying herself, and found she was looking up into the black bored eye of a rifle.

The giant, who had descended the boat ramp in great long strides, loomed above her, the steel toe of one boot very near her fingers. He peered down at Miranda from behind the scope of the gun.

Water dripping from her chin, she laughed. She could not help herself. Holding fast to the barge, she let go the chain in the water and pulled the knife from her pocket. When she lifted the blade out of the water, opened and ready, she saw the big man smile.

"Good for you," he said. He took three steps back from the edge of the barge and set his rifle stock-down against what was left of the pilothouse.

Miranda pulled herself onto the barge. She stood, slowly. Allowed no weight on her right leg, lest it buckle. Shifting her weight to the left, gritting her teeth against the pain in her side.

"You're tough as hell, Does-It-Matter," the giant said.

The barge swayed beneath their feet.

Miranda took one halting step. Two. Went down on hands and knees.

Her left side bleeding freely.

Shirt hiked up, she could see the wound, a red slice along her ribs. The work of an arrow, she realized, in her fall to the river. One of several that had tumbled free of her quiver must have cut her in the water when she struck.

"Pitiful girl," the giant said. He came toward her.

When he was within striking distance, she swung the knife, but he stepped back easily and caught her wrist, squeezing. The knife dropped to the deck. With his other hand—his big, wide hand—he hauled her up by the throat and held her before him in the air, brought her to his eye level, her sneakers clearing the barge by a good three, four inches. The muscles in his arm straining, quivering, rippling. Tightening, as he squeezed. She clawed at his wrist, old pain become new in her throat, and he, gently, and with a kind of patience, closed his free hand about hers and pushed it away.

Behind the big man, a small shadow crawled wet and dripping and naked out of the river, onto the concrete boat ramp, moving quickly through the grass and onto the barge. Snatching up a rusted, three-bladed propeller and raising it above his head.

Miranda's vision blackened.

With a fierce cry, John Avery brought the prop down into the big man's hip.

The giant's leg buckled.

Air rushed into Miranda's lungs as she was dropped to the deck.

The giant whirled on Avery, who had already shoved himself back against the pilothouse, beside the rifle.

The big man threw the propeller into the river.

Avery grappled with the rifle, long and unwieldy in his arms.

The giant smacked the gun away and caught Avery by the ears and lifted him fully from the deck. Avery seized the man's arms to support his weight lest his ears be ripped off.

He hung naked, face a grimace of pain, a scream rending, as the big man began to squeeze the dwarf's head between his hands.

Miranda grabbed her father's pocketknife where it had fallen on the deck and lunged. Her lunge was weak, and the short steel blade glanced off the giant's coat and folded, slicing the knuckle of her index finger. The giant threw his weight into her, sent her sprawling. Still, he held the dwarf between his hands, and still, he squeezed.

Miranda snapped the knife blade back into the locked position, got to her feet, and plunged it fast and hard into the big man's right shoulder, buried it to the hilt, then drew the knife down with all her weight, through leather, sweatshirt, tissue.

The giant yelped once, harsh, like a wounded animal.

Avery fell against the pilothouse.

Miranda lost her balance and caught herself on the chain between the deck rail posts, and there she hung. The giant step-staggered toward the gangplank and into the grass, thumping for the blade in his back. Leg bleeding through a ragged tear in his jeans where Avery had struck him with the prop. She watched him angle up the slope, tripping lightly over the edge of the ramp. Blood slicking his hands. The knife stayed in. He moved slowly, uncertain of each step on the rough, corrugated surface. Eventually he shambled out of sight over the top of the hill. Then came the sharp crackle of a motorcycle. The engine idled for a long time. Long enough that Miranda, who had risen to her knees on the barge, wondered if the giant had passed out on his seat.

But then came the long stutter of acceleration, the big man's bike roaring away, then fading.

Avery had pulled himself into a tight ball against the pilothouse.

The distant brush along the bank smoldered, among it the bodies of two men, one burned, a third dead on the ramp.

It felt as if a wheel with many teeth were spinning inside Miranda. She hung her head over the side of the barge. She did not throw up, and when the feeling had passed, she knew that something else was there, in the hollow place the wheel had made, something solid and heavy. She moved away from the edge of the barge for fear of falling into the river, where she would sink like an anvil with this new and heavy thing inside her.

She crawled to Avery. She touched his arm and met his eyes.

She took up a long and rusted push-pole from among the detritus on the deck. Using it as a crutch, she pushed herself to her feet and went to the corpse on the ramp. She saw the small man's filed teeth in the glimmer of the dying fire. The river lapped at his bootheels. She bent over the body and rifled through his vest pockets. Found a single Ford key on a rabbit's-foot chain. This she pocketed. She pulled her arrow from his chest, tossed it into the water, and stripped the corpse of its T-shirt and tied it around her torso, binding her side.

Avery came after her through the grass. He went to the next body, which lay facedown, and began tugging at the dead man's leather jacket. He wrapped it around himself as best he could.

Miranda glanced at the charred corpse tangled in the kudzu along the riverbank. The skin of the man's cheeks was blackened, his lips fused to his teeth.

Together, she and Avery stumbled up the ramp.

A single Shovelhead remained beside the Bronco, a key dangling from the bike's ignition. On the ground near it, where the other bike had been parked, she found her father's knife, slick with the giant's blood. She wiped it on her jeans and pocketed it.

In the Bronco, Avery sat on the passenger's seat, sooty and bloody in the leather jacket. Miranda put the key into the ignition and cranked it. She worked the clutch, put her foot on the brake, and grimaced at the burn in her leg and side. She jammed the gearshift and soon the river and the dead men were far behind them, and the long gravel road turned out onto state blacktop, and from there she wheeled back southeast, toward the Arkansas state line, beyond it Nash County, the Landing. Safety. At least, she thought, for a while.

ISKRA'S PATH

◆

As the old witch lay dying, metal reek of her own blood thick in her nostrils, she remembered the path she had walked since emerging from the trees a lifetime ago, when she had first looked up and seen the long-abandoned cabin atop the hill. Her new home. How she pulled vines loose from the porch pillars and swept mice and spiders clear inside, later venturing on foot into town to trade for nails and boards. Her first goat earned by delivering some bottom dweller's baby. She built fences, plowed a crude garden. Chopped wood. At fourteen, her hands were callused and raw. An old barn now a bathhouse, the stone hearth her own handi-work, each rock lugged up from the bottoms. The spirits were there, from the beginning. The cabin itself groaning pleasantly with each new board she laid. Every night the bannik woke her with its mad cackle.

On her sixteenth birthday, the leshii came boldly into her dreams, a thing hungry and eager for a girl who knew magic, whose mother had known the same: old spells of the rich black earth, flame and water and blood. It drew her to a wide, muddy shore where the tree rose out of the mist and white bees spilled to hang in a cloak-like fire on arm and leg. There, it welcomed her.

Years later, she would come to the tree again, would dig her fingers between the roots to close over something papery and soft, pieces of it breaking off in her hand. Brittle, dusty. "Is this it?" she cried. "How many babies have these hands pulled from fresh, pink wombs, even as mine shrivels like a honeyless comb?"

WHAT USE IS A CHILD TO A LOVELESS BREAST, the leshii pronounced, its voice huge and ancient, *TO A SELFISH HEART? YOU DO NOT LOVE.*

"I love," old Iskra gasped on the porch, the cabin burning behind her. "I love . . ."

Blood pooling beneath her, she stared up at the unpainted boards of the porch ceiling, a sheaf of plywood hanging free, inside a bird's nest, flakes of eggshell. Black smoke billowing around it.

I have seen this before, she thought.

In the final moments of Lena Cotton's life, when the preacher's wife grasped Iskra's hand, the last of the woman's strength ebbing out on the bed. The strength of her grip startling, behind it some last reserve of self, and then, in a rush of blood to Iskra's head, the vision: a torrent of black smoke, the bird's nest, a slice of blue sky, a line of black ants upon a board. The last moments of Iskra Krupin's life. Everything the old witch had ever feared—to lose her family, to die alone—all of it writ true in a headlong plummet that began at Lena Cotton's bedside and ended here, on these dry steps, with the smells of smoke and her own blood choking her. And the rest of that awful night, too. All its horrors laid out in an instant, each moment a step to be taken toward some final end that was not hers to fathom. Leaving the bedroom with the dead child in her bowl, the boatman at her side, scattergun in hand, stepping lightly among the palms, unwitting escort to his own doom, both of them crawling through a narrow break in the wall.

I HAVE NOT FORGOTTEN YOU, WITCH.

Words the leshii would speak as Iskra stood with Hana Krupin's bread bowl in her arms, the spirit's voice alive in every drop of moisture, every fiber of root, every speck of decay. A voice without sex, without end . . .

Iskra began to crawl away from the blistering heat at her back, just as she had crawled through thorn and vine that night, pushing the bowl ahead of her. Blood bubbles popping between her lips, she crawled on her belly for the steps that led down into the yard, beyond them the kudzu yet green, the sky yet blue. She faltered when she saw, six steps below, a line of black ants crawling over the final step, and this was it: the last thing she had seen before Lena Cotton screamed, and the vision shattered like so much glass.

Now here it was, that board, six planks below . . .

No, not yet, not ready—

Silence for a time, save the crackling of the cabin, and out of this the heavy tremble of the earth. Shaking the wind chimes made of bird bones. The air itself humming with current, as if some hideous dormant pendulum were finally on the verge of motion.

WHAT HAVE YOU BROUGHT ME, WITCH?

Lifting the bowl, her mother's bowl, brought to this country across five great bodies of water, the last of Hana Krupin's life across the sea save the secrets in her heart and the blood in her veins, this bowl that held the cold gray fulfillment of the leshii's promise, a child for Iskra. The leshii's cruel laughter shaking the ground. Tumbling the bowl from the altar and as the boatman dove to catch it, she arose, her great black shape unseen against the starless sky. Iskra recalled the cold steel of the shotgun's twin triggers beneath her fingers, then the thunder, and finally the leshii's voice: calling her closer, to the mound of earth and the hole where the demon's vines had caught the boatman's body and drew him up to hang above that unholy well of mud and sticks and bones. A flash of knife, and when the bowl was full, spilling blood like a dishpan, she set it down among the reeds and set the dead child back in it and hunkered to wait, to watch, as the boy began to breathe through the slit in his throat, to stir, and the old witch lifted him out of the bowl and lay the child on the moss and tumped over the bowl to spill the boatman's congealing blood.

Miranda's beam swinging wildly through vines and thorns. Her small voice crying out, startling. Snake. Flight. The old witch searching the mist that wrapped them both. Vomiting, the boatman's daughter, arm red and swollen, baby breathing and kicking weakly on her chest, and the old woman hesitating now. For the space of two breaths: one for the life she had known before that night and one for the life she would live ever after, its expiration already set . . .

Both mine, great leshii?

Silence.

Both mine, the witch answered.

Iskra opened her eyes, felt the hot wind of the cabin burning, lashing her back.

Her heels were blistering, the rubber soles of her brogans melting.

She remembered, no, not a memory, or was it? Could it be happening all over again? Or was the vision still playing out, Lena Cotton yet to scream and let go of the old witch's hand? Was there a choice yet before Iskra, one that would not end in bloodshed and grief?

The old woman put her hands flat on the steps and pushed up, at once wet and heavy with blood yet weak from the lack of it.

This was always your path . . .

Iskra pushed herself over onto her back, her last great effort.

All she saw was blue sky.

There was never another choice . . .

In this moment—no straight line between Lena Cotton's hand and now; rather, time folded back upon itself, two moments touching across the years, the last decade of Iskra's life merely a step across a threshold into the same small room she had left—the old witch summoned up one final memory.

Miranda at seventeen and the boy six, sitting here, on the steps beneath the same blue sky, the girl shaping the boy's fingers into words, teaching him a language Iskra would never know. Conjuring a magic far stronger than any the old woman or the house spirit or the bannik or even the leshii, perhaps, had ever wielded. Iskra had stood within its circle and without it, over the years, had been a part of this magic and, yet, apart from it. Jealous, yes, but also proud, proud that they had found it, forged it together. They had loved one another.

A breeze like a breath blew gently over her, curled away the smoke, the ash, the scent of her own dying, and the woods and the wind and the creatures in the trees sang out their lament for Iskra Krupin.

She closed her eyes.

She died.

A BY-GOD DEVIL

Cotton stood at the bathhouse door, machete in hand. He peered into the gloom, into the corners, and stepped fully inside.

Something struck him in the back with its full weight. The preacher feared for an instant he would flail headlong into the oven, where the last of a fire was dying, but he fell wide, crunching his shoulder against the rock. His machete skittered in the dirt.

Something small and clawed and menacing—

boy, monster, a by-God devil!

—dropped down in the open door.

A reek of fish.

Pain in his left calf.

A two-pronged gigging stick buried deep in the muscle!

Cotton let out a screech and seized the shaft of the spear and yanked it free. He charged, and the monster-child-thing scuttled backward from his advance, tripping in the doorway and falling prostrate in the dirt, where, in the gray light of day, Cotton saw the thing in full, and it brought him up short and breathless.

He saw Lena, pale and bloodied, the old witch lifting an abomination from crimson sheets. His razor flashing, his wife screaming. He had held it by its heel until the blood had all run out. The old witch's arms trembling to take back the hideous blight. Lena, in his periphery, dead, too. And dead the thing had been, yes, as the old woman laid the pillowcase over it in her bowl, dead, dead, *DEAD*!

So it could not be, this *thing* before him on the ground, which even now rolled over as Cotton limped from the bathhouse into light. "Thou art not of me," the preacher said softly, prodding the creature with the gigging stick.

It jerked away and opened its mouth as if to holler, but it made no sound. Its teeth small and jumbled.

Cotton wrung the stick in his hands and struck the thing twice about the arms.

It rolled over, covered its head, and Cotton reversed the stick and raised it high and drove the tines into the creature's right shoulder, forcing it facedown into the dirt like a speared frog.

Spittle flying: "Thou art not of me!"

Sound of the cabin burning like a mighty wind as he ground the stick in the monster's flesh.

"Scream, devil! I want to hear you scream!"

But it made no sound, no matter how hard he twisted. He cast about for his machete and instead saw a wood ax embedded in a nearby stump. He went to the ax and yanked it free and lay the blade against the creature's neck.

He raised the ax.

The girl saw the preacher from the cover of trees at the top of the ridge, ax upturned above his head. She knew him at once, though his chest was bare and bloody and his dark suit was tattered. The man was a living tendril of shadow.

She edged through the branches, breathing hard, then saw the boy, sprawled beneath the ax.

She opened her mouth to scream.

"STOP!"

Cotton whirled.

The girl plunged out of the woods through the tall grass, knocking aside cans on string and bottles and little castles made of old scrap tin.

Cotton lowered the ax. The head touched dirt and the handle slipped from his grasp. He caught the girl by the arm and pulled her close, so relieved to see her, but she beat her fists against him and cuffed his ear, knocking his hat from his head. The preacher staggered back. The girl ran for the boy, who lay trembling and afraid, gigging stick hooked in his shoulder. Cupping his ear, bending for his hat, the preacher saw the tenderness with which the girl knelt over the boy. He backed away to fetch his machete from the bathhouse, and when he returned, she had pulled the gigging stick free and tossed it aside. She saw the machete in Cotton's hand and threw her body over the boy, eyes upturned fiercely, teeth bared. Cotton met her blue gaze and seemed, for a moment, to lose himself in it. In the memory of his vision: the cold stone floor of the crypt, the razor. Blood.

The girl kissed the boy's mottled, ugly cheek. Pressed her hand over the wound in his shoulder, and the boy relaxed, grew still. His eyes closed. "You leave him alone," she said, not looking at the preacher. "I know why you want me, and you can have me. You can have me if you just leave him alone."

Cotton was dumbstruck.

She kissed the boy again, on the crown of his head.

She stood. Held out her hand.

Cotton took it, haltingly, and the preacher's head was suddenly full of light. So bright he had to shut his eyes against it. He dropped his machete, staggering as the light resolved into a book of Bible-thin pages and the pages were his mind and the girl's dirty fingers went fluttering through them, as if searching out a passage. Settling, now, on a page, chapter and verse, numbers and letters all a jumble as the girl sussed them out, saw the truth of what the boy was to Cotton, what Cotton was to the boy, what he had done with his razor, and then the book slammed shut and the preacher stumbled backward, the air between them made blistering hot.

The girl tore her hand away. "How could you do that?" she cried, eyes brimming, spilling clean trails down her face. "How *could* you? She *loved* him!"

Benumbed, Cotton had no answer, and so he turned and walked away and waited near the corner of the burning cabin. After one last ministration to the boy, bending over him, whispering "I'm sorry" in his ear, she followed, though she did not take the preacher's hand again. Cotton let her lead the way down the steep red-clay path through the kudzu. Partway down, he realized his machete lay in the dirt by the boy, where he had dropped it. He did not go back. Instead, like a child himself, he simply followed.

Atop the hill, the witch's cabin collapsed in flames, sending up a plume of smoke like a black hand grasping at heaven.

The preacher and the child passed into the trees.

A COLD CAMP

✦

Littlefish opened his eyes to a warm, dry wind blowing ash across his face. His shoulder hot and throbbing. Baba's cabin smoldering. Only the old woman's iron boxwood stove, one scant section of wood frame, and the porch pillars remained upright, the fire still glowing along the timber, the rest of the house a charred heap like the morning campfires he and Sister had kicked dirt over when he was younger.

A cold camp means time to leave.

Sister's words.

Why had she left them, if not to come back here, to protect Baba?

He stood, wincing at his shoulder wet with blood. His gigging stick lay near the edge of the cabin, tines of the fork flecked with bits of grass and dirt and flesh. Littlefish saw his cooler on the rear stoop, half melted, the fish he'd caught yesterday a heat-blistered soup. One window remained in its frame, the frame and box blackened.

Beyond the window, on the porch steps, he saw the most terrible thing of all.

The boy opened his mouth and gave out a silent cry, the cords in his neck straining with the effort. He charged through the smoldering wreckage of the house, hot boards leaping up beneath his feet, sparks firing only to wink out.

The old woman's dress and apron had burned away and her skin had burst where the heat had swelled her. Her white hair was all gone, her skull blackened, ears and lips melded with bone. Littlefish fell on his knees on the steps. He made frantic signs at her face, urging her to speak, to move, to breathe, but after a while he stopped. The old woman was dead. He wept silent tears. He smoothed his hands along the scraps of her apron, what had not burned away.

Sister, oh, Sister, where were you?

Littlefish went down the steps to the edge of the hill, where the kudzu crept and swayed in the breeze like a green surf rolling in and rolling back. He pulled lengths of vine and carried these back to the old woman's body and laid them over her, covering her from feet to neck, and when he went to lay the last few scraps across her face, his rough cheeks wet with tears, he saw where the Father Hen's blade had cleaved the old woman's head. Littlefish placed the last of the vine over Baba's face and kissed her forehead through the leaves; they still held the faint green taste of spring.

In back of the cabin, he saw the Father Hen's machete in the dirt. Crusted red.

The girl. The Father Hen took her.

The boy ran quickly up the path and into the woods, crossed the canyon to his tree. He climbed fast and hard.

Between the ground and his lookout, he felt the wound in his shoulder tear anew. The platform was empty. He saw the words he had written on the boards: *SAFE. STAY.* He felt his strength go all at once, as if a hand had yanked a string to unravel him.

Gone. Lost her.

Over the trees, to the north, he saw the bird's skeleton on the cross, mocking him.

He thought of his book in his shed: *This Is Where I Live.* He had not shown the girl that book. How could he have explained or made sense of its pages to her, the things he had drawn?

Here is the church, here is the steeple . . .

What had the old man been singing?

Something about a cross.

The way of the cross leads home.

With the red crayon from his pencil box in the pine tree's knothole, he drew an arrow on the wood of the platform, pointing toward the red cross beyond the river. He went over and over it, until the crayon was blunt. She would see this. She would know.

Sister. I am sorry. I cannot wait.

He flew down the ladder to the ground, where a dizzy-making pain in his shoulder sent him to his knees, bent forward over the pine-needle carpet as if in prayer. When the pain had passed, he touched his wound and drew back a hand glistening red. With this hand, he grabbed hold of the lowermost rung on the ladder on the pine's trunk to pull himself up, leaving a webbed, crimson print.

He made his way slowly back to his shed, where he

snatched an old burlap feed bag that hung from a four-inch steel nail. He saw his bow and arrows, broken against the wall. He rummaged through books and boards, the rubble of the Father Hen's fury. He saw his spine-cracked picture book facedown on the floor beneath his desk and shoved it into his bag. He put on his belt of pelts and went out of his shed.

Down the hill, the machete lay in the dirt. He picked it up and bagged it.

Then he went back up the hill and past the goat pen, where the goat huddled in terror behind the milking shed.

At his tree, he stopped. He saw his handprint there.

He took the picture book from his bag. Flipped to the pages he had marked and colored upon waking from his dreams, then draped the book over his bloody handprint. As if working his own incantation, he made the sign of *Sister*, an L-shape thrust down from the jaw. *Find this, Sister*, he thought.

He set out down the ridge, to where his bark was drawn and ready on the bank.

ICE CREAM

Miranda took the curve too fast and the Bronco slewed in the loose gravel, Avery clutching at the dash as they bounced over the wooden bridge that marked the last hundred yards to the Landing. Pine thickets stretched away on either side of the road, which ended ahead in a turnaround, the store just hidden by the trees on the left. Miranda slowed the truck to a crawl, easing onto the shoulder where they remained out of sight. She cut the big engine, and the hot motor ticked in the silence of the morning. Miranda got out and went at a funny lope through the grass and into the woods, keeping her weight off her right leg. The tree line broke at a clearing, within the clearing the store itself, the embankment sloping down to the river. Here, she crouched behind a rotten log and watched for a quarter hour. The front door of the Landing gaping wide where Riddle had twice destroyed it. The drive was empty. She heard nothing, save a woodpecker launching volleys against a nearby pine, until finally the Bronco's door creaked on its dry hinge and Avery came softly through the woods to squat beside her, dead man's leather jacket cinched by the sleeves around his waist. The cut above his eye had closed and purpled, and his lip was puffy and red.

"It's probably safe," Avery said. "They won't regroup so fast."

"Caution can't hurt," Miranda said. She pulled herself to her feet by a low-hanging limb, bit off a whimper.

"How is it?" Avery asked.

"Sprain. Side's worse. Needs sewing. I can't really feel it anymore."

"I can sew," he said. "Steady hands. I wish I had a gun."

Miranda's mouth drew tight with pain. "Weapons are upstairs in the hall closet. Anyone in there, I go in the front, they'll get me before I get them. So I'll go in the back. You see me on the porch, come straight across. Don't dawdle."

Avery gauged the distance through the long grass to the mercantile porch, then hunkered down to wait.

Miranda crept along the tree line to the embankment and scrabbled down among the kudzu, red clay breaking loose beneath her sneakers. She hobbled along the water's edge to the rear deck's overhang, then balanced carefully along the gangplank to the floating dock. Slowly, quietly, she hauled herself up the ladder. Each shift pulling at the crusted wound in her side. Near the top, gasping, shaking, she listened. Heard only the hum of the refrigerator in the kitchen and the freezer on the porch, so she climbed up and fell onto her back on the boards, where she lay long enough to catch her breath. Staring up at three wasps clinging to the surface of the nest beneath the porch eave.

Miranda pulled herself to her feet by the railing and reached into her pocket for her father's knife. She went through the back door into the house and checked the bedrooms and the bathrooms and, once satisfied she was alone, limped into the living room and took down Hiram's Bear from the rack above the couch. To string the bow, she step-staggered through the string and bent the upper limb with both hands and pulled down to slip the string into its notch. Sweat popped on her scalp and along her forehead, and once again her side bled freely through the rag of the dead biker's shirt.

Miranda nocked an arrow from the hall closet and went to the steps that led down to the store. She took each one slowly, easing more and more weight onto her right leg now. By the time she reached the bottom, bringing her arrow to full draw, she was soaked through.

The store was empty.

She let the tension out of the bow. Steadied herself on the same wire rack where Charlie Riddle had gun-pressed her against the wall two nights past, then limped to the broken door and waved.

Avery appeared out of the distant trees and cut a swath through the tall Johnsongrass.

Dizzy, Miranda struggled back to the steps and started upstairs, determined not to pass out until she had reached the hallway between the kitchen and the living room. At the top, she sat down on the step and dropped the bow and arrow and slumped against the beadboard.

She faded.

Avery's voice brought her back: "What do I do?"

"Sewing kit," Miranda said. She pointed to a door. "Bedroom closet. Alcohol in the bath."

She pushed away from the wall and shoved the bow and arrow out of the way, then lay flat on the pine-board floor. She rolled over onto her right side when Avery returned with the kit and a bottle of rubbing alcohol.

"Lift your arm, like this," Avery said, and she crooked it over her head.

With scissors from the kit, he cut her shirt from the wound.

"There's a gun," Miranda said. "In the closet. In the tackle box. If I pass out."

Avery poured alcohol over her side.

Miranda blew air through her lips.

Avery took out a spool of navy thread, licked the thread, and sent it through the eye of a needle. He hesitated, only for an instant, when he saw the swell of her bare left breast.

"What, goddamn you?" she said.

"It's just not the week I pictured," he said.

"Just get it done."

He took a deep breath and bent to the task.

When she woke, she was covered in a homemade afghan from her father's bed. A pillow beneath her head. Avery stood at an open window in the living room, keeping watch on the road. He had fashioned a kilt from one of Hiram's shirts and stood bare-chested in a billow of drapery. The cuts on his knees and face were cleaned. Cook's pistol lay on the windowsill. Miranda sat up, and the afghan fell away. Her shirt hung in tatters. She drew the afghan to her chest and inspected her side, which was stiff, sore, and dry, bandaged with improvised wrappings of two maxi pads and medical tape. She saw Hiram's Bear on the steps where she had dropped it. Clutching the afghan, she got to her feet in a series of slow, careful moves, the pain in her leg dull and tolerable now.

"I'm sorry I couldn't lift you into bed," Avery said from the window.

"How long?"

"Less than an hour."

Miranda wrapped the afghan around her and limped into the kitchen, one hand on the wall at every step. She went to the fridge and took a carton of Coleman's Neapolitan out of the freezer, a spoon still lodged in the strawberry where she had last dug in. She set the ice cream on the table and fell into a chair and went to work on the chocolate.

"Spoon?" Avery asked from the kitchen door.

She pointed at a drawer.

He got one and sat down and set Cook's pistol on the table and plunged into the vanilla. "Oh," he said. "Oh, that's good."

They ate quickly, and Miranda felt the ice cream working, smoothing the hard, rough edges that remained in her throat, the bannik's claws a lifetime ago. She ate until her head hurt. She closed her eyes and pushed at the space between them, and when she looked up she saw Avery holding his head between his hands, too, his spoon dripping vanilla down his arm, and their eyes met and they laughed, and they sat together, laughing, ice cream dripping over their chins, in pain with brain freeze, but alive.

After a moment, Miranda got up and went to the sink and dropped her spoon into it. She wiped her face with a dishrag.

"I should have left by now," Avery said. He stuck his spoon in the ice cream. "I shouldn't have stayed. My wife, my daughter."

"You could have taken Hiram's boat," Miranda said. She leaned against the counter, drawing the afghan close.

"I don't know why I didn't," Avery said.

Miranda stared at him.

"But I need to go now."

"I can take you," she said. "Let me put on a shirt."

She went out of the kitchen and into her bedroom and threw the afghan and her rag of a shirt on the bed. She pulled open a bureau drawer, drew out a faded gray T-shirt, and tugged it on, easing it over the wound in her side. The maxi pads bulged beneath the cotton. She saw her reflection in the bureau's mirror: cheeks scratched, throat bruised, eyes sunken.

Avery was dozing at the table when she returned to the kitchen, his head still in his arms. She took his spoon from the carton—a silly, domestic act, out of place, to clean up after yourself when you had shot men with arrows and leaped from a bridge and bled and been stitched up—and went to toss it in the sink. Thinking of the children she had left in the woods with a sharp pang of guilt. She looked up through the window, across the bottoms, to where the treetops were silver with late-morning mist. *I should go and find them. Keep out of sight until Riddle and Cotton get hit back, and it's over.*

She saw it then, a heavy gray column of smoke rising from the trees to the south.

She remembered the boy's dream.

Everything aflame.

In an instant, she understood that she had been wrong.

The fire was not hers.

Avery lifted his head at the sound of the spoon dropping in the metal sink.

She rushed past him into the hallway and snagged Hiram's Bear where it lay on the floor, along with the single arrow beside it, her body stiff and tired and hungry and sick and crying out, *No, no more,* but she ignored it and ran out onto the porch and down the ladder to the floating dock, where she tossed her weapons into the johnboat that had borne her and the witch and the baby and the boatman deep into the bottoms. Metal smeared red from the deer flank she had brought out Sunday eve. Avery stood at the back-porch railing, calling down to her, but she paid him no heed. She yanked the starter cord until the Evinrude caught, and then she was gone, bent full throttle for the oxbow downriver, beyond it the narrow entrance to Iskra's bayou, another world—*her* world, now burning.

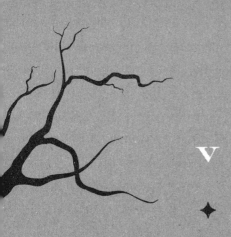

V

✦

Revelations

THE NATURE OF FRIENDSHIP

Riddle sat on the Plymouth's hood, smoking a Marlboro, Robert Alvin behind the wheel with his head cocked back, mouth open wide enough to shove a fist through. The hot summer wind scoured the flat croplands that lay beyond the empty parking lot where once had stood a truck stop café: a tattered awning offering SALISBURY STEAK and SOUP now speckled with mildew, plywood where windows had been. Heavy gray clouds rolled in from the southwest. Far across the bean fields, a swarm of race cars on some dirt track made a sound like a hive of bees. The inside of the Plymouth was warm and dark, and Robert Alvin began to snore.

Riddle took a walk across the parking lot, kicking the crumbling asphalt, bending to pluck the odd dandelion and watch its seeds swirl away. The wind pulled smoke and ash from his cigarette, his tie whipping over his shoulder. Riddle's eye watered behind silver-mirrored shades. He felt a headache creeping. It had started dead center in the back of his neck, an auger turning, twisting up his nerves like the strings of a marionette.

He thought, inevitably, of Miranda Crabtree. Pressed back against the wall of the grocery, wet with sweat and blood, and cringing. He put his fingers to the center of his forehead, where the auger had settled its bit. By now the bitch was dead and the midget was a bedroll on the back of some biker's hog. And soon Mr. Skull Face would show on a thundering machine to inform the constable it was done. Saddlebags of money would be stowed in the Plymouth's trunk, payment for John Avery, and the little man with the sharp teeth would take out a bag and present it like a prize to Charlie Riddle. Inside it, a single gray-green human eye. *Miranda*, Riddle thought, *she always had her mother's eyes.* But this was not the end, no, for waiting back at Sabbath House, still, was Avery's wench: black, lean, and sassy, how she'd crumble when the news came that her husband had been sold into bondage. "Like your ancestors," Riddle might say, and then he would laugh and put a cigarette out in her ear and let Robert Alvin hold her by the arms so she could watch as he hammered her baby's brains into pulp with the butt of his Schofield.

By God, it was all so good.

So why is my fucking head splitting?

The auger bored deeper and the nerves wound tighter. He drew on his cigarette. The tip burned red.

The plywood over the old restaurant's door was loose, so he pried one corner away and wandered for a while inside the blessed gloom of the gutted building, torn pages of a phone book and old paper menus scattered about like dirty feathers in a barren nest.

When they came, they came from the west, a gang of motorcycles rolling up the blacktop that lay like a long hot tongue over the flatlands. He heard them from inside the building, and when he stepped out the door, he saw that Robert Alvin had heard them, too. The deputy stood half out of the driver's door, one boot in the car, one on the pavement. They rolled into the parking lot two by two, six of them. Twice they wound round the Plymouth, slowing on the second run and revving their engines, and Riddle saw what was going to happen the instant before it did, and it made no sense to him. The sensation was like a loss of balance, when the world pitches against your stride.

A woman with thick arms in a white T-shirt torn at the midriff rode double on the third hog. She drew a scattergun from a sheath near the chrome piping on the bike's flank. In the roar of the motorcycles, Riddle didn't hear the blast, but he saw the flame, blue smoke, and the window of the open Plymouth door exploded, blowing Robert Alvin back into the car.

The circle of steel ponies opened up and trained toward Riddle, where he stood his ground beneath the old restaurant's tattered awning, his antique pistol already out of its holster, hammer thumbed back.

The bikes spread wide and charged.

Riddle fired three times, and two in the center fell, bikes

slewing left and right, riders on either side veering off to keep from spilling. Still, four came on, gunning.

Riddle shoved through the plywood sheet that hung askew across the door. Inside, he made for the far corner, where a section of the roof had fallen in behind a metal and glass countertop, the ceiling hanging like an unhinged jaw. He took cover behind the counter and slipped three bullets from his holster into the Schofield.

A crescendo of engines rose outside, and a single bike exploded through the plywood sheet.

Riddle stood up from behind the counter and fired.

The rider was jerked sideways from his mount, which shot away into the pine-paneled wall and lodged there.

Riddle heard the rise and fall of engines. He caught a glimpse of three bikes through the demolished doorway, drifting back to idle out of sight. Directly, the big engines cut out, the only sounds the faint buzz of the racetrack far across the fields and the sputter of the man dying on the floor not ten feet away. The man lay in an ever-widening circle of blood.

He went cautiously around the counter, his boots crunching broken glass, to hunker beside the dying man. His hair was long and bright yellow, and he wore a red paisley bandanna at his throat. His teeth were clenched, and Riddle saw that he had an overbite, a fine dusting of grizzle on his jaw.

"Didn't have to be like this," Riddle said.

The man's eyes slid fearfully at the constable.

Riddle put his hand over the man's mouth and nose, almost gently, felt the sputter of his breath, the dampness of his face. "We should of been friends," Riddle said. He pinched the nose and clamped the mouth shut, and when the man began to struggle, Riddle dropped to his knees and put his whole weight into the task, and he felt the man beneath him wanting not to die, the muscles tensing, the body pushing against him with everything it had, and it was almost a kind of miracle healing, like bringing a man back from the dead instead of sending him there, the way the biker's broken body fought against the end. Finally, the fight went out, and the man lay still beneath the constable's hand.

Riddle wiped his palm on his khakis and stood up, his right knee popping, a sound like the period of a sentence. Through the broken plywood, he could see the Plymouth, the driver's door still open, Robert Alvin's right heel on the dash, his khakis hiked above his boot.

"I wanted us to be," Riddle said quietly. His hand shook as he fumbled another bullet from his belt into his gun. Then, hurling his voice through the open door: "I WANTED US TO BE FRIENDS, YOU MOTHERFUCKERS!"

Something dropped through the roof in the rear corner of the building, a bottle, long flame trailing from a piece of rag stuffed down its neck, and then the bottle struck the tiles and exploded, and the flames rolled out and gathered back and the building was on fire.

Riddle backed away to the smashed entrance where he knew the last three waited in ambush. He cocked the Schofield pistol. "You can all go straight to fucking hell," he said, and he plunged through, shooting.

WALL

The bark emerged from a narrow waterway a mile upriver from Crabtree Landing. Littlefish took his long arms from the water and let the current turn him. He had never ventured as far as the river. Here, the air smelled different—less of peat and murk and more of fish and gasoline and the faint tang of wood smoke. He felt unsettled, exposed, so he put his arms back in the water and paddled upriver with wide, webbed hands, until he came to a narrow, jagged inlet. He could see, through tall dead trees pocked with bird holes, a big white house bestrewn with moss and bright green mold, as if it had somehow risen out of the bog itself. It was the house he had seen in his dreams, and the sight of it here, in this lonely, muted place, was terrifying. Littlefish paddled on, remembering what Sister had taught him when hunting, how to go wide round your prey, out of its line of sight. Being careful. Being quiet. Unable to shake the feeling that the house, with its lidded windows and open white maw, was somehow watching him, he rowed on.

Once, he happened to look down and saw a snake corkscrewing behind his fingers as they lingered in the water. He pulled them out quickly, and the snake vanished.

The boy had chanced on a snake once before, down at Baba's dock, where it warmed itself in a shaft of sunlight. Lazy, crooked, wicked. He thought to scare it by tromping the boards, but the cottonmouth had cracked at him like a black whip. In the end, the boy had pinned it to the dock with his gigging stick and cut its head off with a pocketknife. He remembered, now, how the jaws had worked on in death, dripping poison. Later, he'd brought Baba down to show her. "This," she said, picking up the head, a runnel of blood and tissue and the candy-pink mouth yet open, "is the only way to deal with a snake."

He thought of the Father Hen, who had come a-roaring out of the woods and struck at Baba like a bold black moccasin.

He heard a rustling off to his right, from the bank. Caught motion in his periphery, the sound of branches cracking, shifting, breaking. His bark slowed in the opposing current. Suddenly a sheaf of branches drew apart on their own, like a curtain opening, and through this new, ragged hole in the tree line he saw a high, crumbling wall of stone, angling deep into the woods.

Curious—

Had the trees just moved on their own?

—he banked his bark among a deadfall of branches and

stepped out onto a narrow beach smooth and sandy. He gathered his sack and went up the bank.

He touched the wall, ran his fingers over the rough, tumbled surface.

Feels like me, he thought.

The wall stretched into the trees as far as he could see.

He heard the sound again, that cracking-rustling, and turned and saw that the opening in the brush through which he'd stepped had closed, the trees settling back like Baba sometimes settled with a groan in her big rocking chair.

He thought of Baba's skin, blistered, blackened. Her head a cloven ruin.

His friend, she was out here, somewhere. He pictured the Father Hen, all in black, standing before the low stone building in his dream. Now, as if a waking vision, Littlefish saw the girl beside him, her hand in his, tears streaking her mute, stony face.

The boy looked down the length of the wall, some hunter's instinct at work inside him.

The only way to deal with a snake.

Littlefish followed the wall inland.

MIRANDA AT THE CABIN

Miranda ran out of the trees, breathless, and saw, atop the hill, the old woman's home destroyed. She charged up the slope, slipping twice in the red clay, but she did not fall, pulling herself up by vine and root to the top where, panting, she bent over a prone mass draped with kudzu on the porch steps. She pulled away the vine and saw a round knob of blackened bone and gristle, and there, on a last patch of skin, unburned, were three silver whiskers. She pressed the heel of her bow hand against her forehead. She pushed hard against her skull, as if to hold back a flood tide of grief and rage that threatened to break her, drown her. She covered the old woman's face and looked to the burned-out cabin, to the yard beyond, chickens clucking stupidly in the boy's garden. She stood upright, her side oozing warmly into the pads, and called his name, her voice carrying up the hill.

In back of the house, she found the boy's gigging stick on the ground, the prongs red. She saw where the boy had lain. She ran her hand around his shape in the dirt. There were two other sets of tracks: the girl's small bare prints and a pair of man's dress shoes. She saw the boy's tracks, too, short and wide and webbed and leading away from where he had fallen, and she followed these. She followed them until they tracked back on themselves, and she realized he had crossed his own path, had come back from the woods to his shed; a quick glance through the door told the story of a scattered departure. Here, she lingered, surveying the damage the old preacher had done: torn comics, overturned shelves. The boy's bow and arrows broken. Destruction so vicious, so personal. Heart in her throat, she went into the woods, and there, on the carpet of needles, over roots and knobs of pine white with old sap, she saw the blood. One or two drops every few steps. They led her to the boy's tree, his ladder, where she saw the book, the handprint, the blood on the boards.

A hard, hot lump rose in her throat. She swallowed it.

She reached for the book.

Miranda remembered the story Hiram had told her, a memory she did not possess. Her mother had given her the book, reading aloud each night the simple sentences at the bottoms of its pages, and Miranda had memorized it by the time she was three. Cora Crabtree's joke to show Hiram how his infant daughter had learned to read. "Read the book for Daddy," and Miranda on her blanket on the floor, holding the book open on her lap, would point and recite the words, and Hiram's eyes would well with wonder. Cora laughing, Hiram saying, "What? What's funny?"

She opened the book.

This is my church, the page said, the words printed beneath a white-steepled country church painted in watercolors, beside it a bright green tree. *This is where I go to worship God.*

The boy had drawn flames billowing from the porch and windows, from beneath the eaves, and atop the steeple he had scribbled a bright red cross.

This is our minister. He is very nice.

The picture, once of a smiling man in a black shirt and priest's collar. Over the priest's head of well-combed chestnut hair, in black crayon the boy had drawn a dark hat. Over the chin he had scratched a graphite beard. Over the throat: a red slash that ripped the page.

She dropped the book on the ground and tested her weight on the first rung of the ladder, and when it held, she began to climb. All the way up, to the lookout she had helped him build, and at the top, she saw it right away, drawn in red at the center of the wooden platform: an arrow, pointing north. Across the bayou, over the vast bottomlands, to the red tower thrusting up from the trees, at its pinnacle the horrid cross, upon it the bird skeleton crucified.

She flashed on the torn page, the preacher's gouged throat.

No. He cannot do that.

His blood on the wood below was still tacky.

She scanned the waterways, but his bark was nowhere in sight.

Leg and side slowing her up, she descended the ladder and made for the bank where she had left his bark among the cypress trees the night before. She found footprints, more blood, saw scuff marks in the dirt and bent blades of grass where he had run the raft out.

She ran back up the ridge, through gorge and woods, past the ruin of the cabin where old Iskra lay in her funeral vines, hens pecking around her blistered head. She ran down the hill and through the woods to the dock, where the boat that had carried her father to his doom was moored. She forced all thoughts of grief and despair from her mind save one: the face of the boy, crude and ill-shaped and the one thing she loved most. The only real magic she had ever practiced.

TEIA GOES TO CHURCH

✦

Teia left the shotgun house walking, Grace in her arms, to the iron gates. There she stood, looking down the gravel county road, as if peering into the gullet of the world even as it made ready to swallow her. Across the road, behind chain-link, the windowless Holy Day Church sat like a brooding, mindless thing.

She spoke, none but Grace and the wind to hear. "Where the hell you'd go, John?"

Inside, the church was close and dark and hot. The choir loft behind the pulpit was littered with hymnals and empty music stands, a drum set featuring a bass someone had put a sledge through. Secondhand microphones and amplifiers thick with dust. The great wooden cross torn from the wall and hurled down the aisle, scattering chairs. The shape of it still visible on the paneling, like a picture unhung after years.

Teia propped open the front doors to let in light and air

and sat down in a metal folding chair near the back. She sat for a long time in the musty silence, Grace a counterweight in her arms.

She fixed her gaze on the absence of the cross.

If I were to beg you, she prayed, *what would I beg for? All the old salvations? To know where they took him? Where's my John?*

At the back of the room, at either end of the altar, twin doors stood ajar on darkness. John had told her of a time when Billy and Lena Cotton's lost children had streamed through those doors, service after service, some in tears, others sagging with relief, all with heads cast down at the wasted lives they'd led. Scrawny boys and round-bellied girls, needle marks on their arms. Back there, in a windowless room, they made their confessions to emerge with holy purpose writ on hungry faces.

Back when Avery himself had still believed, dressed in a vest and polished boots, a striped tie and hair like a lion's mane. He'd showed her a picture once, when he was high. They'd laughed at it, made love.

Sweat dripped from her brow. She wiped it.

I was never hungry for you. Only him.

She came to Sabbath House a runaway junkie, lifted by a dwarf out of a pile of cardboard on Beech Street in Texarkana. Two years homeless and hungry, her hair falling out. No family to speak of, no one to love her. Except John Avery. Before he had even known her, he had loved her, little more than a sack of bones, an open wound of need. And maybe she had loved him, too, from the moment their hands touched and she felt his strength. When together they walked to a shelter three blocks down, where she was fed and bathed and clothed and given a concrete room and a mattress and a bedpan and the means by which to heal herself. Long nights of shrieking visions, sweating, fingernails raking flesh, the moon like death's sickle outside a small, narrow window. When it was over and the door opened, it was John Avery who opened it.

And so she came to this barren place, no better prospects. By then it was years after Lena Cotton had died. The old preacher a recluse, a rumor. And Charlie Riddle, well, he was no different than a hundred pimps and pushers Teia had known, something stolen in his pocket, ready to sell. John told her stories of better times, when the church was full without room for standing and a choir played instruments of brass and wood and they all sang hymns and lifted hands together in praise, but Teia never saw it, never heard it. After one year, she begged him to leave, to shed this place with its ghosts and rot.

"Where would we go?" he said. "What's out there for us?"

"Don't you see that preacher for what he is?"

"I've always seen him for what he is."

"These men ain't good to you," she said.

"They need me."

"They use you. They ain't good people."

"Neither am I," he said.

She stared up at the shape of the cross. *John gave me walls, a roof. A bed of my own and love to warm it. What'd you ever give?*

Quietly, yet hopeful, she had saved. Not much, a ten here, a twenty there. Most everything John earned growing dope for the preacher and Riddle he put back into their coffers, just to keep the lights running. She kept what little she could in a plastic bag in the bottom of a rice jar in the cupboard. Then came Grace, and just like that: the money vanished. Every day that passed, they needed more.

Had she thought of leaving him? Once, maybe, when the baby was yet a seed unsprouted in her belly. Sabbath House, for any and every reason she could imagine, was no place to raise a baby. She knew about the girls at the Pink Motel, the mystery of Lena Cotton's affair. But the thought of life without John Avery was somehow worse, like opening your door onto an empty, howling plain.

Five years of her life had already passed at Sabbath House, when Grace was born. She was twenty-seven. After the baby, every knock on their door became a dread. Every payment Riddle had skipped: a promise of numbered days. Lately, between her ears, she heard a fierce roar like rain pouring on a metal roof, drowning all voices save her own: *Get out.*

Now, sitting in the sanctuary, smell of mold in the air, Teia looked up at the dingy ceiling panels and the wall where once a cross had hung and saw cruelty and despair and a great black appetite for human hearts.

To that absence, she said: "I don't beg, you hear? But I want my John back, you heartless bastard. You owe me that. Bring him back to me. You do that and I swear, any man who blocks our way, I will kill that man where he stands. Yes, I will."

She looked down at her daughter, sleeping in her arms, and there, in the soft round contours of her face, Teia Avery found her husband. She began to cry.

LOST

At Iskra's dock, the johnboat's motor refused to start. Miranda sat trembling, staring at the Evinrude in disbelief. She checked the shifter, the fuel tank. The vent was not clogged. She tightened the hose clamp, gave it three hard whacks with the boat paddle. Ripped the starter cord. It came to life, belching smoke. She lit out up the bayou, for Sabbath House, for the red tower. For Littlefish. The dock and the old witch's bottle tree disappearing behind her.

For a while, sunlight broke through the gray clouds and splintered among the trees, where a white mist was woven. The banks rose up, tangled with tree roots, the bottoms stretching away for miles in all directions. She passed the familiar bones of a pine struck by lightning, covered over with limbs and bracken that had risen with the river long ago and snagged there. Soon after, the bayou would narrow, the woods would thicken, and the water would open suddenly onto the river via an almost invisible slip in the trees.

But none of this happened.

The trees thickened, yes, and the way ahead grew narrow, but here was a bend Miranda did not know, a tree she had never seen.

Suddenly the engine's roar seemed to fade away, though the boat sped on.

She heard the low hoot of an owl deep in the woods. The susurrus of the trees, the trickle of water. Gray clouds like autumn leaves driven by the wind . . .

A memory, sudden and strange. Looking back at her father from the bow, where she perched like their very own maiden of the mast. Pretending they had struck out not for a fishing hole in the bottoms, but for the very mouth of the Prosper itself, which would, in turn, give way to a larger, wider river, and then another even wider, until finally they would make the ocean, where the currents ran in all directions, and the sky and the water reached for each other but never touched. The two of them drifting into the great wide world to find everything they had ever lost. Out there, perhaps, waiting for them on the shore of some island where horses ran wild, was Cora. Barefoot in the gray sand. Miranda knowing that one day she would look over her shoulder from the bow and he would not be there, the boatman, like her mother, like all parents, claimed by the coming of a slow, inevitable end, the ultimate consequence of growing up, getting old.

But it had not happened that way . . .

The low, steady drone of the Evinrude gave way to the high, electric buzz of the cicadas, singing out from the canopy-dark. The two sounds merging into a weird, alien pitch that seemed to bore into the very center of her.

Beneath it, something else: the crack of tree branches.

Something moving in the woods . . .

So many times she had set out into the bottoms to find his body, boating deeper into the bayou from Iskra's island, and every time she had come back filthy and bug-bitten and scraped empty as a slit fish, the land slowly and surely hollowing her out like an old stump at the mercy of time. One day, she had thought, long ago, she would be old and brittle, and she would break apart like the logs in the woods that crumbled by the handful, spilling little black beetles. Funny thing, to feel that way when you're just a girl, not even thirteen, fifteen, then twenty-one—

The trees on either side of the bayou began to sway, to bend, the land itself conspiring, cracking.

Tired, she thought, eyes and limbs and heart as heavy as they'd ever been. *So tired* . . .

Her chin touched her chest—

She jerked awake and saw, too late, the cul-de-sac ahead, a cove speckled with a thousand late-blooming lily pads, each the size of a pie plate, some as big as hubcaps. She cut the motor, but she was already in them, and the propeller chewed the pads like twine. They tangled, choked the blades. The motor cut out and the boat was yanked to a halt.

Miranda spun gently between banks of sickly brown cypress trees, their branches forlorn with great beards of moss. Dragonflies swirled among the lily pads and little brown birds perched on the blooms to snap them up.

The air was oppressive, hot and still.

Miranda put her head in her hands, elbows on her knees. She sat like this for a while, and when the urge to scream and the urge to weep had passed, she looked up and around and turned on the seat to lift the Evinrude as far out of the water as she could. It hung halfway. She held it upright with one hand and with the other tried to reach down into the water and strip the pads from the prop.

The motor slipped from her grasp, splashed back into the water.

She yanked the cord and when the engine sputtered back to life, acrid exhaust pouring out, she reversed and the boat spun free, but she had overcompensated the throttle, and now more pads were tangling in the blades.

She cut the engine again. Pulled the motor out of the water and locked it off. She tore at the thick, rubbery stems until the blades were clear, then dropped the engine back into the water.

It would not start.

A dozen times she tried, standing in the boat, bracing her foot against the stern, ripping the cord until her arm burned and her side bled freely, and now she did cry out, let her voice echo back her frustration. Her panic startled some heavy-winged bird from a branch.

In the bottom of the boat lay a paddle.

Miranda locked off the motor, took up the paddle, and plunged it from starboard to port and back to starboard, heading back out of the cove, looking for a bend in the bayou where she had drifted off course, but there was no bend. There never had been. The water just . . . went on, straight and narrow, and now she was paddling against the current.

She stopped, looked over her shoulder.

The cove, the lily pads, had vanished.

The bayou behind her was the mirror image of what lay before.

She cussed under her breath. She had come northwest from the island, reversing the route she always took, nothing had changed . . . except it had. The whole damn landscape had just . . . *changed*.

She remembered all those long days walking the woods south of Iskra's island, searching for Hiram, her sense of mounting desperation that each new turn had only worsened her odds, until finally she broke from the trees to find her boat where she'd moored it, though the path she'd returned by had never been the same, not once. Even when she'd tied a string to the boat, only to follow it back through different woods.

Behind her, she heard the creaking of wood, the whisper of leaves, the sudden snap of branches. These sounds like a kind of laughter now, mocking.

The way she had come was not the same as it had been. The bayou curved in the wrong direction. She was sure of it.

"What are you scared of?" she cried out to the trees. Her voice slapped back from the banks. "Are you scared of *me*?"

Sweat dripped in her eyes. She wiped them.

She scanned for the sun, but the sun had fled, disappeared behind thick gray clouds.

Wound in her side ablaze, soaked through in the wet

summer heat, she paddled, and with each new stroke the space between her shoulders burned and her lungs grew hot and full. Maxi pads sodden, her hands raw and red, each stroke falling in time with the furious beating of her heart, and soon there was only the great red drum between her ears.

THE FATHER HEN'S HOUSE

Burlap sack over a shoulder, Littlefish had been trailing his webbed fingers along the brick—the wall had bent twice more through the piney woods—when he saw the road, and was drawn to it through the thinning pines. He had never seen a road before. He knew the word from his books. His hands were helpless not to make the sign for it when he saw it. He followed the wall along the road, the sun hot and beating down, the ditch full of bent aluminum cans and old faded plastic wrappers that spoke foreign symbols to the boy. After a while, atop a hill behind a chain-link fence, he came to a low building with no windows. Beside it the tall metal tower, and up, up, up at the top of the tower, the red cross and bird-skeleton he had long seen from his tree.

Church, his hands spoke.

The building from his dream.

This is where he *lives.*

He crept from the cover of the trees, across the dry gully

of pine needles and trash, and into the road. The gravel underfoot was warm. He closed his fingers around the fence. Imagined a section of it in his vegetable garden, bean vines growing around it. He thought of Baba, how she had laughed at his garden contraptions meant to scare crows and red-winged blackbirds, even as she reaped his harvest of blackberries and squash. Tears wet his eyes. He brushed them away.

The day was quiet.

Behind him, across the road, were twin iron gates, and through these he could see the big white rotting house. He wavered, briefly, thinking he could just turn around and go back to the river, back into the woods across the water, to the world he knew. It was not the same world now, but there were islands other than Iskra's. He could camp, fish, hunt. Survive. Sister had showed him the right places, how to live in them. Little islands all throughout the bottoms, humped up out of the water like turtle shells. The boy knew all he needed to know to be another crawling, stalking thing among them.

After, he thought. *After the girl is safe and it's done.*

He moved along the fence, walking his hands over the chain-link, until he came to the open gate. Beyond it, a path led up a small hill lined with cracked flagstones shot through by dandelions. It reminded him of Iskra's hill, her cabin perched among the vines.

He went up the path and to the doors, which stood wide open as if to welcome him.

Here is the church, here is the steeple, open your hands . . .

The place was empty, dark, musty-smelling.

He went up the center aisle, leaving mudprints on the thin blue carpet and dragging his burlap sack behind him.

At the front of the church, on the wall, was the shape of a cross, the cross itself hurled among the metal chairs, many of which had been knocked askew. He saw things he had no reference for: metal boxes on legs, round white kettles that looked like toadstools. The piano in the corner was coated in a skein of dust, and at the foot of the raised platform was a long, scratched table, the words *DO THIS IN REMEM-BRANCE OF ME* cut crudely into the wood and lacquered over. Atop the table, a pair of ceramic hands were clasped in prayer beside an arrangement of faded silk flowers, a big, heavy book open beneath them. Its pages thin as locust shells, their edges trimmed in gold, and the words were the tiniest print the boy had ever seen. Some of the words were red. He did not know them all, but he recognized a few.

. . . the way, the truth, the life . . .

He ran his mottled finger over the words.

. . . the Father . . .

Turning the page: *branch, fire, burned.*

Love. Life. Friends.

The girl was his friend.

Slowly, he closed his hand over the page and the sound the paper made as it crumpled was crisp, satisfying, like biting into a fresh apple. He tore the page from the book and let it fall, and it lay on the carpet at his feet like a broken-winged bird. Littlefish took the corner of another page and tore it. The sound was very loud in the near-cosmic silence of the church.

A voice from the dark spoke: "Don't."

Littlefish whirled.

A woman stood in the back, a baby in her arms.

"Please," she said. Her voice was soft.

Littlefish bumped into the table, and the ceramic hands tipped over and rolled, but they did not break. The boy's own hands fluttered before him, and he saw that the woman was following them with her eyes, but she did not understand. She opened her mouth as if to speak a question, but the question faltered on her lips. She had seen the webs between the boy's fingers, and on the woman's face Littlefish saw astonishment, even as she drew her baby tightly against her.

The boy fled along the outside aisle, knocking over dusty sprays of flowers. The woman called to him, stepping out of shadow, but Littlefish ignored her and rushed out into the muted gray light. He ran down the hill and into the trees. He ran without stopping for what seemed the longest time, until his legs and chest were burning, the bottoms of his feet scratched and bleeding. He ran until finally the trees parted and he found himself on the road once again, and there he stopped in the center of the gravel lane, in the sharp bend of a curve, gasping.

Doubled over, thinking he might vomit, he remembered his burlap sack.

He had left it on the floor of the church.

Blood pounding between his temples, the sound of his own breath so great, he did not hear the car careening around the curve—rocks popping and skewing beneath its tires—until it was too late.

In the stillness after the dust had settled, the white Plymouth having disappeared around the curve and into the compound gates, John Avery stepped from the trees over the ditch and stood, shoeless, on the roadscape, wearing only the fashioned skirt of Hiram Crabtree's shirt. He had kept to the trees but followed the road, three, four miles, long and tiresome, and thrice he had sat and rested, back aching, legs trembling. Once, he fell asleep with his head against his chest and woke ashamed. At the sound of the car, he had hidden himself among the pines and watched as the white Plymouth passed, the fat constable slumped like bloody death behind the wheel.

In the ditch, a figure lay unmoving. A boy whose skin was mottled and cracked like the bed of a long dry river, strange pigmentation ranging from the color of stones to apricots to an almost iridescent sheen along his shoulders. The digits of his hands and feet were widely spaced, webbing between them. His face was lumpy, the line of his jaw crooked.

Gun in one hand, Avery took up a stick with the other and touched it to the bottom of the boy's foot. When the boy did not move, he edged closer to see if he was breathing.

"John?"

Avery looked up.

His wife stood a dozen feet away, Grace in one arm, a burlap sack in the other. She came out of the woods, stepping over the low, rusted wire fence that bordered the trees. Her eyes moved over him: bare chest, bloodied feet. The gun in his hand.

"John?" she said again, a tremor in her voice.

The day was hot and quiet and still, and it seemed, for an instant, as if the world itself had ceased to spin.

THROUGH THE WHITE

Fog ahead, a breathing wall between the riverbanks, curling on itself, catlike.

The space between Miranda's shoulders throbbed with heat. Her hands were raw and blistered. She stared at the fog through a curtain of wet hair and thought that whatever lay beyond must be the way. She had no other choice now; the land had given her none. She wiped her brow with the back of her arm and thrust the paddle into the water until the handle was slick with her own blood.

The johnboat slunk into the white.

The world behind and before and all around was erased, not even the sky above distinguishable.

Miranda ceased paddling when she felt the hull scraping stumps in shallow water, though she saw no trees, no bank, not even the bow of her ten-foot boat. She slumped, her stitched side a red, fevered mouth. The boat eased a few feet more, then hitched up against the stobs.

How long she sat there, like a woman out of time, swept into some eternal place, she did not know. The mist broke against her skin. She breathed it in, cool and damp.

She put her paddle out and took the depth of the water, which was barely ankle-deep. She stepped out, the boat wobbling beneath her. The water was warm. She stepped around cedar knobs and sprigs of green that grew out of white-oak stumps, their little branches bejeweled with dragonflies and wasps that flew away at her passing.

All around her, the world grew hushed.

She stopped to listen. Heard something moving in the water, but far away.

Soon, the silt bed beneath her feet became a muddy bank and she was sinking, step by step, until finally she pulled her left foot out of the muck and her sneaker was tugged free. She wobbled, kept her balance. Bent for her shoe.

Ahead, the fog peeled away, and she saw the trees, the wide muddy shore before them.

The skin of her snakebit arm began to itch, the old white scars to burn.

Standing atop a rise of red clay that sloped down from the edge of the tree line, looking implacably at her, was the white crane she had seen at the Landing and later the inlet to Sabbath House. Its undercarriage still grimed with black swamp mud. It lifted its leg and took a single, slow step, as if remembering how to walk, then disappeared into the trees.

Miranda took off her other shoe, tied both around her neck by the laces, and went after the bird.

THE GREENHOUSE

✦

The boy lay deeply unconscious among the thick growth of Avery's plants. Teia wet a rag beneath a spigot that jutted from the brick foundation of the greenhouse and washed the lacerations along the boy's left arm and leg, the flesh shredded finely where the car had grazed him. His arm was swollen at the elbow. She wrung the washcloth over the crusted puncture wounds in the boy's shoulder, her gaze drawn back to his child's face, his eyes closed beneath a heavy, crooked brow, flickering behind their lids. A strange, hypnotic beauty in the boy's slow, steady breathing, his lips parted slightly. Avery, at her side, held Grace, Cook's revolver on the gravel beside him. Teia reached for the first-aid kit she had brought from their bedroom closet, set atop a pile of fresh clothes for her husband.

The generator out back coughed and chugged, and the lights overhead flickered.

"Is it bad?" Avery said.

"Maybe only a sprain at the elbow," Teia said. "He's lucky. Some swelling here, on his side. Maybe a busted rib. These other wounds—wherever they came from—are deep. Could be on the way to infected." She emptied a bottle of antiseptic over the wounds. Pressed them with a gauze pad. Blood seeped through. She taped a fresh pad in place.

Avery set the baby on a blanket and changed into a T-shirt and jeans while Teia worked. Pulling on his boots, he said, "We have to get the hell out of here, as soon as we get some things together—"

"Tell me where you've been," Teia said harshly, still bent over the boy.

"Baby," Avery said.

"You disappeared last night," she said, tearing tape with her teeth. "I was scared. I was so scared, I thought you were dead, so you tell me—"

He went to her and dropped to his knees beside her. He touched her shoulder. "There'll be time," he said, "for explanations—"

But she pulled away, taped a final bandage over the boy's leg.

Avery got up and picked up the baby and went to the greenhouse door and pulled a strip of electrical tape away from a blacked-out pane and looked out at the constable's Plymouth, parked crookedly beneath the oaks. He held Grace and hummed softly, a lullaby or a hymn, the words long forgotten.

THE EDGE OF THE ABYSS

✦

Torn from a deep, dreamless slumber, Billy Cotton sat up in bed.

"BUHHH . . ."

A man's voice, hoarse and full of pain. Downstairs.

Cotton winced. It felt like someone was splitting stove-wood over his skull. He lay in his trousers and shoes, the sheets beneath him dirty with leaves and blood. The gouge in his calf angry and throbbing. Wounds on his chest crusted red. The cancer sending up its own wretched howl from his hip.

"BUHHLEEE . . ."

The preacher rolled out of bed and limped shirtless out of the bedroom. At the top of the stairs, he put one hand on the newel post to steady himself and stopped, staring down at the grisly sight in the foyer.

At the bottom of the stairs, Charlie Riddle slumped against the wall, half upright. Beaten, it appeared, within an inch of his miserable life. A string of red drool ran from his chin onto the star above his flabby breast. He shouted again, unaware Cotton stood above him, staring down at the wreck he was.

The preacher came stiffly down the stairs, red suspenders flopping at his sides.

Riddle fell silent and turned his massive head, his one good eye rolling open in a lump of purple. "Licked em," he spluttered through a bloody grin. "Licked em, Billy."

"Did you," Cotton said.

"Tonight . . . said they'll come . . . kill us all, Billy, they'll—"

"They'll be too late, Charlie," Cotton said. He stepped around the constable and onto the porch. Behind him, Riddle made more noises, then fell silent, head slumped on his chest, which rose and fell yet. Cotton saw the Plymouth parked thirty, forty yards away, the driver's door wide open.

He stepped over rotten boards and vines and sat down on the wide, sagging steps, pain lancing through him as if he'd set himself down onto a spike. He took off one shoe. The gold toe of his sock was torn. He smiled sadly at what a pauper he had become. He picked up a rock from the grass and considered it, then tossed it away. He had seen, days before, among the weeds, a green-glass soda bottle, webbed white inside, and this he found and smashed against the crumbling brick foundation of the house, a little brown spider spilling out of the neck, which he held in his hand. The spider fell among blades of grass high as Cotton's ankles. It crossed a single shard of bottle to disappear forever into the forest of the yard. Cotton tossed the neck and took up the shard and tucked it deep in the toe of his shoe. Then he slid his foot back into the shoe. He pulled the shoe tight and laced it, and the sudden new pain was clear and bright and focus-bringing.

From the west came an eruption of thunder, but when the ground began to shake, Billy Cotton realized it was not thunder at all.

It was the earth itself, starting to heave.

TREMORS AND ECLIPSE

In the greenhouse, a pair of garden shears slipped from their hook on the wall when the first of the tremors hit. A glass pane dropped from the ceiling and shattered among the plants. The fluorescent grow lights overhead flickered in the saucer pans, went dark. Came back. Teia clutched Grace against her, one hand cupping the baby's head. After a while, the world was still. The low drone of the generator out back unwavering.

Avery sat with his back to the potting table they had tucked the boy under. The boy's chest rose and fell slowly, and his breath came out in a high, soft whistle. His burlap sack was open at Avery's feet. Avery held the bloody machete he had found in the sack, turning it in his hands.

Teia was looking at it, too. "Who is he, John? *What* is he?"

Avery slid the machete back into the sack and looked at the boy, remembering the night Lena Cotton died. The old witch's bowl, his glimpse of what lay beneath that red-stained pillowcase as it passed. A small gray foot pushing out. Webs between its toes. Limp and lifeless.

A stronger tremor hit, and mortar dust shook loose from the brick foundation and a clay pot fell from the table and cracked in pieces on the ground.

Avery went to the front of the greenhouse and opened the door.

"Don't . . ."

"It's okay," he said. He walked out beneath the oaks.

The light was strange. The shadows of the trees and the manse and the Plymouth all slanted at the right angles, but it was too dim for this time of day. The world had taken on a muted, filtered look, like the sun was beaming through a glass of dirty water. All along the gravel drive and the grass where he stood, the boughs of the oaks threw blurry, half-moon shadows. Gray clouds had walled up the sun, obscuring whatever mystery was happening.

Dread crept over Avery's heart as the cicadas from the surrounding woods took up their evening chorus early.

Billy Cotton stood gazing up from the front yard of Sabbath House, as if some secret only he could read were written in the sky. He worked his hands up and down his red suspenders. Took no notice of Avery. After a moment, he limped back inside the house.

A third tremor hit. Dead limbs fell from the oaks, the whole world shuddering like a great iron ship firing its engines.

In the greenhouse, he found Grace safe in Teia's lap.

"Maybe the world is ending," he said. And tried to smile.

Teia looked up with dread at the glass overhead.

They sat quietly, fearing it was too late to do anything now, that some terrible machinery in the earth had been set in motion, wheels and gears and cogs grinding, and they were but silent players upon a shifting stage.

ROCK AND TREE AND MONSTER

✦

The sky dimmed, edging toward darkness, though Miranda, near-delirious with exhaustion, had yet to notice. She had staggered free of the mud as the first of the tremors rumbled. She fell against a tree, waited on the creaking of the earth to subside. She wiped the mud from her feet with a handful of dead leaves, put her shoes on, and forged ahead, the crane still in sight, though always on the cusp of disappearing, flapping its black-tipped wings and shooting off, to land some distance farther.

It made a steady graceful line among the trees, all the way to the grove of saw palms, where it alighted beside a rotten log and put its bill in the earth to root for grubs.

The earth shook again.

Miranda remembered this place: undergrowth and briars dense, great long thorns growing among them. She froze, listening, for what she did not know. Her own voice, eleven years old, crying out her father's name only to have it come echoing back, no answer?

The crane picked its way with ease among the palms. She followed, first through the maze, which bit and sliced, then on hands and knees through the undergrowth itself, her palms sore and blistered from paddling.

Her old tunnel waited ahead, still intact, if overgrown. New vines and thorns to claw and snare. At the end of it, a faint orange light.

The crane ducked and went through, as if it knew every chink in the forest's armor.

Soaked in sweat and blood, Miranda crawled after it.

When she emerged from the tunnel, Hiram's flashlight lay where she had dropped it ten years past. Burning still, the beam strong. As if no time had passed. She took it up and brushed bugs from the plastic housing.

Playing the beam ahead, she walked on, into the weird forest of toothpick trees, where the streams of black viscous liquid congealed, past the dead owl still mired in the muck, perfectly preserved, over the log bridge, and into the vast, barren wetland, its borders staked by cypress trees that had long since shed their needles, their trunks and limbs a miserable gray.

I remember, she thought.

Strange reeds at the edges of black pools, their stalks a pale uncolor. The pools themselves stagnant. Weird brown fungi and yellow, star-shaped blossoms.

At the center of it all, ringed by a skirt of fog, the rock. Twice the size of old Iskra's cabin and shaped, Miranda saw

now, like a blacksmith's anvil, half submerged, the horn canting upward. Atop the horn: the tree, a nightmarish chimney
in mid-topple. Limbs outstretched like flailing arms. Roots
spilling over the horn and hanging down like the wet, tangled hair of a drowned woman.

The crane stood at the base of the rock. It swung its
long, periscope head in her direction and seemed to regard
her with a kind of satisfaction, having finally brought her to
this moment. The bird spread its wings, took to the air, and
vanished into the trees. She aimed the light into the gloom
where it had stood, saw the glint of brass she expected, the
shotgun shell lodged there in the mud. Swinging the beam
around, she saw, too, the clump of reeds where she had
found Littlefish that night, bloody and heaving at the base of
a mound of earth big as a tractor tire, now grown over with
moss and vines and brambles and daubed with dead leaves
and rotting wood and the bones of small animals—skull of
a raccoon, leg of a fawn. The hole at the center remained,
dark, wide, deep. The darkness there was an inky liquid of
the same viscosity as that of the moat and the streams that
tracked like veins from the center of this place. Its surface
glistened, as if with starlight.

Something dripped into it.

She ran her beam up, and what hung there from the
canted tree made her cry out.

Trussed up from a long, reaching limb, vine knotted
around his ankles, jeans and shirt heavy with mud, was the
body of her father, Hiram Crabtree. He wore the same shirt
he had worn when she last saw him, his left shirt pocket
unbuttoned, as always, to better slip his reading glasses in

and out. A ragged hole in his stomach, a frown in his neck. Dripping red into the pool.

Miranda started for the mound, stopped when her sneaker crunched in the spongy earth. She lifted her shoe. Half buried in her footprint was a thing white and round and it reminded her, at first, of the grinning jawbone of a boar. She toed it out of the ground, shined the flashlight on it.

A claw. Easily the size of Hiram's pocket knife.

A high trill sounded, somewhere in the dark. Followed by a low, wet clicking.

Miranda swung the light at the distant trees, saw nothing.

She turned the beam back to the vine that held her father's corpse. She felt with her hand in her pocket, after her father's Old Timer, but the knife was no longer there. Instead, her fingers closed around the same shotgun shell she had only just seen in the mud. Another phantom object. Tucked in her right hip pocket that long night past and lost, later, to the chaos. It lay bright red upon her palm now and still smelled of cordite as if just fired.

Two shells that night, she thought. But the old witch had only ejected one. The other, the one Iskra had set before her on the table yesterday, the shell must have remained in the barrel long after she'd fired its contents into Hiram's back. She recalled now the sensation of eyes upon her, felt a preternatural sense of déjà vu, wondered if the old witch was yet alive and watching her from the shadows of the rock.

For a moment she teetered, the whole of it too big. Head spinning. She closed her eyes, bit the inside of her lip. Tasted blood. Swallowed. Breathed in, breathed out. Opened her eyes.

The rock loomed.

She tucked the shotgun shell into her pocket and moved closer, eyes locked on her father's corpse.

The rock's surface was damp, a fetid smell to it. Roots stood out from it, large and smooth and slick. Unlike any bark Miranda had ever seen in the bottoms. She closed her hand around one. It was warm and pulsed at her touch. She jerked away, then gathered her courage and touched it again, this time closing her fingers around it. It swelled in her palm. A low hum filled her head, a gentle tremor ran the length of her arm, and suddenly all the aches in her muscles were fading. Even the burn in her side, cooling. She took her hand away. Her blisters were gone.

Heart thudding against her breastbone, she tossed her flashlight on the ground and jammed her foot into a narrow hold, seized two handfuls of root, and began to climb. Finding toeholds, hauling herself up, hand over hand.

Overhead, dark gray clouds spiraled toward the sun.

Frantic near the top, when all the holds seemed to vanish—

Daddy, oh, Daddy, I'm here now, I've found you

—she made one final leap for the summit.

Moments later, she sat on a shelf of black rock, no burn in her chest despite the heave and wheeze of her lungs. The tree reared above her, Hiram's corpse less than a dozen yards away. She crawled as close to the edge as she dared, then stretched her arm, could almost reach him, lacked mere inches. She steadied herself on a low-hanging branch and looked down into the wide black well of liquid below. She took the shotgun shell from her pocket, hesitated, then dropped it into the hole. It struck the surface, hung there a moment, then sank. The vine knotting Hiram's ankles to the branch coiled back to the trunk and down into the rock, strange little hairs bristling along its surface like a million tiny feet.

Miranda judged the weight of the limb, the angle. Her own strength relative to the great desire of her—

Heart.

She flashed on Littlefish in the clearing beneath the oak. The doe's heart in the boy's red-slicked hands.

Yes, a deer, it wasn't Hiram in the tree then and it's not him now, it's a trick, it's the boy you want, not Hiram, the boy—

She shook her head as if to clear it. Backed away from the edge of the rock. "It's a lie," Miranda said quietly.

Silence, save the creak of the branch beneath the weight of the corpse.

Miranda's hands curled into fists. "Where's my brother?" she said, glaring up at the tree.

A wind swept out from the distant tree line, sudden and strong. Blew over the clearing and up the rock and sucked Miranda's shirt against her and threw her hair wildly about.

Thunder cracked. The sky darkened.

The vine that held Hiram Crabtree's corpse uncoiled like a knot slipping, and his body dropped into the dark black well below. Miranda watched him sink, then let out a cry and fell to her knees and began to pound and tear at the tree's thick, fibrous roots.

The rock beneath her began to shake.

Lightning shot down from the clouds.

"I'll rip you out of the goddamned ground!" she cried.

A root tore free from the rock in a red spray, struck her like a great flailing tentacle.

She pitched forward, fell long enough to suck in a single breath before black water sluiced over her. Gritty, oily, a thousand venomous barbs lancing her. She clawed at the mud, felt the sticky remains of recently dead things. Cold liquid seeping into her ears. With a great cry, she dragged herself over the lip of the mound, then rolled into the brittle reeds at its base. There she lay among the toadstools, gasping hoarsely, going numb all over.

The ground was trembling. Something big, pounding up through the earth below.

She could not move.

Miranda closed her eyes when a thing monstrous and impossible broke the surface of the black liquid and reared above her.

The noise it made an eager clicking-clucking-trilling.

Let your last thoughts be of the boy.

From behind and above came a sudden din like dry bones snapping. Something huge whipped past and she heard a crunch, as if a giant bug had been squashed beneath a giant shoe. Whatever had come up through the mound was ripped free and taken high into the air.

She heard it shrieking.

Miranda opened her eyes. What she saw was the tree itself, bending backward, rising up as if a thing alive.

Her mind comprehended it dimly, this thing, impossibly tall—taller than the trees that surrounded the bog, a dark writhing column—yet somehow human in its shape, possessed of a torso glistening green and blue like the iridescent carapace of a horned beetle. It was the tree and not the tree. Its ribs were thick, ropy vine, its arms clawed and barren branches. Its head a long, seed-shaped oval, its eyes knotholes wherein shone a furious white light. Atop its thorny pate a crown of knotted roots and stobs, the headdress of a queen.

Leshii, Miranda thought.

It held, in one of its massive hands, the monster that would have killed her.

Its body was long and white, a wicked tail curving in a dangerous question mark, a stinger at the end weeping venom. A hundred legs working madly beneath a milky abdomen, each one ending in a hooked cat's claw, very like the claw she had found in the muck. Black eye-stalks jutted up from a round, flat head. Its narrow slash of a mouth wide open as it screamed, row upon row of shark's teeth inside. Two giant pincers stuttering open and closed as the tree squeezed and the creature broke in half in a gory spray that lashed Miranda's face. Each half tossed aside into the bog.

Roots twined into two great legs, each one tearing free from the rock, cracking it like a shell as the thing—*tree, monster, demon*—reached down its terrible arm beneath a sky where clouds hung like the clots of a hornets' nest and the earth came apart in a horrible ripping, and the monster's hand closed around Miranda Crabtree and lifted her and rolled her in a palm of moss to face two bright, shining eyes—

bees, its eyes are bees, millions

—and then something flashed, a silent thunderhead, and her mind became so much static.

She was transported.

FAULT

It ran the length of Nash County like a cable buried in the earth.

The first quakes that morning knocked cans from cabinets and dropped panes from windows like loose teeth in rotten mouths.

In the town of Mylan, a stoplight snapped its wires and fell, and Shifty's Tavern lost six good bottles of whiskey to the floor.

At the Pink Motel, a picture window cracked in an empty room, the women who had long inhabited it now gone.

A second round of quakes struck when Miranda Crabtree departed this land for another.

Throughout the bottoms, trees pitched up as the earth heaved.

Thunder and lightning split the sky.

Fat plops of rain began to fall.

Embankments slid away beneath bridges all over the county.

People took to their windows to look out. Some stood on porches and spat tobacco at the ground and listened to the roar of the water on their tin roofs, reminded, perhaps, of a storm ten years past, their thoughts turning to time and how it gets away, day by day.

Twenty miles upriver, just over the state line in Texas, not too far beyond a boat ramp where three bad men lay with arrows in them, a portion of ground sloughed away from an earthen dam sixty feet high, on the other side of which was Lake Whitman, over twenty thousand acres of water surface.

After the last tremor passed, the rain fell harder, and the fissure that had opened in the dam grew wider.

MIRANDA IN THE TREE

First: the void.

Suffocating.

Infinite.

Her senses return, one by one: the clotted stench of mud long unturned from its bed. Tiny pinpricks of light resolving into stars. The rustle of wind in the treetops. A breeze against her skin. The taste of blood. Out of the water she climbs, whole, onto the floating dock, the river sliding past, black and viscous and reflecting no light. Behind her, the mercantile. Upstairs, a light, fanning out warmly. The night strangely silent beyond the borders of the dock. Her body slicked, her clothes soaked.

From above, a sound. Small and hard, a single *chock*.

The white crane stands at the edge of the dock, belly and legs black with mud.

Chock. Chock. CHOCK.

Downriver, the johnboat's Evinrude. The boat emerging out of the dark into the mercantile's lonely glow. Hiram, alone, ties off and climbs out with a croaker sack. The sack is heavy, bulging with weight. Miranda says his name, but he does not hear. He lifts the sack from the bottom and tips it, and the dead crane spills out onto the dock, its neck bent oddly, wings a heap. An arrow in its chest. The meat from its breast will feed them for two, three days.

"You taught me that," she says, remembering.

Hiram looks at her, his eyes sad. He turns away to pull the arrow from the bird, and the sound it makes coming free is the sound of all the violence in Miranda's life, her initiation into a world without grace.

Another sound, falling down from the kitchen.

Chock. Chock.

CHOCK.

Hiram is gone.

Miranda climbs the iron ladder.

Cora cuts carrots in the kitchen by the sink. A small, slight-framed woman, a head of dark curls falling between her shoulders. Her arms in her sleeveless dress pale and freckled. She chops and the knife strikes the board and makes a sound like the ticking of a hollow clock.

June beetles pop in front of Miranda at the fly-screen.

She does not go inside, not yet, only watches the woman in the kitchen.

The blade goes through the carrot into the wood. The carrots roll to the floor, only they are not carrots, Miranda sees, but red wax pieces of shotgun shell.

Cora smiles over her shoulder, and her face is pretty and soft.

Chock. Chock—

Down the hall, yet another sound: soft band music on the Victrola, a woman singing. Drifting through the kitchen.

Miranda yanks open the fly-screen and rushes inside.

In the living room, in the soft glow of a late evening twilight, curtains rustling in the breeze, Hiram dances with a woman in a blue flower-print dress, the dress somehow familiar.

The photograph, she remembers. Her father's service annual. The double exposure of Cora.

The knife in the kitchen cuts: *chock, chock, chock*.

The couple turns and the woman, her cheek pressed close to Hiram's heart, is not Cora Crabtree. Miranda recognizes her from Hiram's funeral, standing alongside the preacher in the downstairs store, holding a covered dish of some casserole Miranda will end up throwing out.

Lena Cotton dances with her father.

They kiss, break apart, and Hiram leaves the room, goes to the closet, passing where Miranda stands unseen, enthralled, and Lena turns away, bare feet on the carpet, to peer out the window into the night. Hiram calls to her over Miranda's shoulder, and when they both turn, the camera flashes, recording the image over the first in the roll that has remained intact inside the camera since Cora Crabtree died. The faces merge, the corona effect in the picture no trick of light but the luminous glow of Lena Cotton's blond hair.

Miranda takes a step backward.

Chock goes the knife in the kitchen. *Chock*.

Lena cuts her eyes to Miranda. For an instant they flash wide and gold like those of the crane. Then dim. "Billy's a liar," she says. "There's nothing of him in that girl. Can't you see it?"

Miranda looks at her father. He's laughing as he winds the camera. A smile she remembers from her youth, like the parting of the clouds to reveal the sun . . . and yes, she sees it, the resemblance suddenly so clear. Outside the bath-house, the girl had smiled at Littlefish just this way, warm and quick. Unconsciously, like a child fidgeting, Miranda's hands make a shape, the word for *sister*.

Lena turns away, to the window, where Cora's hurricane lamps burn like sentinels against the wet, thunderous dark. "Hiram will weep," the preacher's wife says, her voice oddly flat, devoid of emotion. "When he sees how he ruined your mother's picture. And then he'll tell me it's over. That it just can't be." She half turns from the window, and Miranda sees that one hand is across her belly, which is now distended, grown full. "I won't even tell him about the baby. Sometimes it keeps us safe, not knowing the truth. Don't you think so, Miranda?"

The music has fallen silent, the Victrola's needle scratching, bumping.

"Myshka." A voice, behind her.

Miranda turns.

The woman chopping in the kitchen is no longer Cora. Now her smile is ugly and hard, teeth gray and stained.

"Myshka," Iskra says, and the old witch is bleeding from the top of her skull, each fall of knife on board somehow opening a new wound beneath her hair, gash after gash. The blood streaming down her neck and arms, soaking the dress to her skin, which is old and veined and wattled.

Blood courses over Iskra's face and drips onto the linoleum between her brogans. She crosses the kitchen to a cabinet, leaving a trail of crimson shoeprints. Only the cabinet is not a cabinet but a curtain of oyster shells, and from behind it Iskra reaches a jar—green glass from the witch's bottle tree—and holds it out to Miranda. Her legs have taken root to the linoleum of the kitchen now, the freckles along her spider-veined calves darkening the color of tree bark, and each of her ten toes has punched through her shoes and into the floor. Flowers open from her knees, little white blooms, and there are white bees swirling inside them.

Miranda recoils from the jar when the woman-tree-thing sets it on the counter.

River water and silt, out of which the eye comes swimming like a fish to peck at the glass. An iris cornflower-blue.

Handsome Charlie.

"You have other *BUSINESS*," the old woman says. As she speaks, her voice deepens. *"THINGS YET TO SEE."* Cheeks sprout vines that sprout leaves that unfurl like the fingers of a newborn babe.

"You're the leshii," Miranda says.

The creature bows its head. *I AM THE EARTH, THE AIR, THE BORDERS OF THIS GREEN LAND. I AM THE LAND. I AM LIFE. I AM DEATH. I AM.*

The leshii's face weaves anew, hair blooming with yellow flowers. It drops the kitchen knife and the ground begins to shake. The creature throws its arms wide and its limbs are branches punching through the beadboard walls. The floor cracks, splits as the monster grows, filling the room, the very house itself. Growing up through the floor in the center of the living room, pushing through the collapsed ceiling, the trunk of the tree taking shape, wide and strong and old. Within its twin knotholes, roiling still, the light of the sun, the room itself made a white-hot furnace. Light pulsing, weaving along the branches, blood in veins.

"I ain't afraid of you," Miranda said. "The boy's mine, not yours."

Laughter, great and booming, shaking the walls. Dropping pictures from their nails.

YOU CANNOT CHANGE HIS PATH. HE IS DESTINED TO DO MY WORK.

"You can't have him."

LITTLE MOUSE, LITTLE FOOL, WHAT WOULD YOU TRADE FOR HIM?

"Anything, if I have to. Everything."

WILL YOU TAKE HIS PLACE?

Miranda hesitates, then gives a single nod.

The leshii laughs, and now the walls are collapsing, sloughing boards like meat from bones. Miranda flees downstairs into the mercantile, where the leshii has burst through the floor in a great tangle of moss and root and earth. She crashes through the screen door into the night, where the only sound is that of the cicadas, hammering out their frantic song from the trees.

"Dear child," the old preacher says.

Like the pendulum of some hideous clock, he hangs by his feet beneath the boughs of the gum tree, over her father's empty grave.

The grave is open, yawning dark, a heap of wet red clay earth beside it.

Cotton opens his mouth, as if to speak or sing, and out of it comes a swarm of white bees a million bright like the mist that showed her the way once before, when she was stumbling through the night with the child, her brother—

Littlefish.

His webbed hands cupping the deer's heart, holding it out as a gift to her.

All her love poured into the boy, a torrent, cutting new shapes roughly and surely and filling them like a river flooding its banks.

DO YOU SEE YOUR PATH?

"I do."

WILL YOU WALK IT?

"I will."

Beneath a night sky that is not the night, in a place that is nowhere and everywhere, she reaches for the quiver she does not know she has on her back, and the arrow all but springs into her hand. In her other hand: her father's bow, the Bear. She nocks her arrow and aligns the broadhead with the old preacher's heart. She lets fly and the arrow streaks through the air and buries itself in its mark.

The singing of the bees falls silent with a sudden hitch.

When Miranda lowers the bow, the old man is not the preacher.

Her father hangs before her, something of peace on his face.

"In the land of Spain," he says.

Through tears, Miranda draws again.

Aims for the vine that holds him above the black slash of his grave.

The arrow leaves her bow without so much as a whisper.

Hiram Crabtree drops silently into the earth.

Miranda drops her bow and quiver and steps forward to the edge, unfathomable darkness before her, and with a single breath she steps out over the pit and drops, plunging down until she strikes wet earth. Alone in the grave, no Hiram, she thrusts her fists into the muck like a grub burrowing, feels the wet rush of mud and water into her ears, nose, mouth, and is swallowed by the dark. Here, in the void, there are creatures. The same monstrous guardians who would have torn and gnashed and devoured her at the base of the rock, save for the leshii's grace. She cannot see them, only senses them, like great behemoths swimming beyond the reach of light. They took Hiram after the old witch drained him. Took him with their claws and black round eyes and milky bodies. Clawing up from the darkness over which he hung to snatch him away into the deep. Suffocating now, lungs full of mud and black tar, she thrusts deeper into the void as if chasing a catfish in the currents of the Prosper. Finally, the tips of her fingers close around something familiar, and she seizes on the shaft of her arrow and pulls, and out of the sludge with a great wet *CHOCK—*

The sky was flat, gray, pouring rain. The rain fell on what was left of Iskra's cabin. It fell on the bayou. On the woods. On the bog, where the canted rock had split and the earth was ripped open. One half of the rock had sunk in the mud, but the tree stood still, tall and gnarled. After a time, the whole of the clearing flooded and the mound at the base of the rock began to run in little gray rivers among the toadstools. Then, with a great thunderclap, a hand thrust through the ichor, followed by an arm, a shoulder. A head of mud-plastered hair. Shambling up and over the edge of the mound, Miranda dropped into the wet spongy earth like a thing reborn. Clutching to her breast a grisly rib cage, a spinal column, a cracked skull plugged with mud. She rolled to her side and vomited a gout of black water, in her arms the oldest of her heart's desires—the remains of her father. Shivering and wet, the rain pouring down and mixing with her tears, she held him close.

ARROW AND CROSS

The girl sat in the narrow window seat, knees drawn to her chest, turning the boy's arrowhead between her fingers. Outside, all across the bottoms, trees were lost in a silver curtain of rain. She lifted her shirttail, traced a finger over the old scars, every one the expulsion of some awful memory—the cruel snare of Ma'am's tongue, a man's cloying scent smothering, her own hair in bundles at her feet. Cigarettes hissing against flesh. Laughter, cruel and cold. And all the other terrors, not her own. Betrayals, despair. Loss so deep and bottomless. Ends so violent. Now she found a patch of skin, just above her belly button. She thought of the boy, bleeding in the dirt. Was he dead now? She pressed the tip of his arrow into flesh, watched the blood bloom beneath it like a flower. She waited. But there was no release, no separation from herself, only sudden hot tears and a burn in her belly.

In the hall, a key slid into the lock and turned it. The

bedroom door opened and the girl pulled down her shirt and thrust the arrowhead beneath her thigh. The preacher, who had slipped a fresh shirt over his scarred chest, closed the door softly behind him. He put the key back in his pocket. The girl only stared at him, her expression blank.

"What do you see?" Cotton said.

The girl made no reply. She saw many things. She saw a snake in a man's suit. A devil whose reach was short but cruel. A man surrounded by walls that had snuffed souls. She saw a razor and a dove and the true reason she was here: the preacher, his wife, and she, all together in a terrible dark place.

"Death," she finally said. Her voice was not angry. Her voice was not afraid.

Absently, he touched his pocket, the outline of something there, some implement.

The razor, she thought. *But he will not do it now. No, it will happen somewhere else.*

The girl had tried to see her own death. But it was like peering into a deep black lake at night: perfect silence, nothing more. Again, she thought of the boy. With him, there had been no end, only the present. Only the peace of his company, the pleasure of his eyes, and that great open channel to the life of his world. She could never cut these things out of her, she realized.

The preacher sat down on the window seat beside her, grimacing with old aches made new by the morning's exertions, a bit of blood seeping through the fresh white linen of his shirt, and he saw in the pane what she had breathed on the glass and drawn there, earlier, an arrow, pointing toward the horizon, where the smoke from the old woman's cabin had ceased to curl. He breathed on the glass himself and made a cross.

The girl wondered what power this symbol held over him. Just a fading shape in glass, soon to be unseen, forgotten? Or was it somehow his wife, a fading god behind glass? Or an awful beacon, shining out like a lighthouse in a storm, one he had fixed his rudder for, lashing himself to the wheel, her to the bow? Maybe it was all of these things.

"'And the sun shall hide its face,'" he said, looking out at the sky. "The Book of Revelations."

She drew her knees to her chest.

"Every page a promise of fire."

She thought of the old woman on the steps of the cabin, burned. The boy, sprawled in the dirt. His sister, still out there somewhere. The girl could feel her, another kind of beacon, maybe, not like the boy, but Miranda had lived here so long, surely some of the magic of this place had touched her, too.

She held on to this hope, clutched it to her breast.

But she remembered the old preacher's vision, too, the one she had glimpsed so briefly at the cabin, like a bad seed sprouting poison shoots.

A dove, a straight razor.

Two glass coffins.

They both gazed out the window, arrow and cross and the world beyond all washing away.

THE LAND WILL TELL YOU A STORY

✦

The rain kept on, and the water began to rise throughout the bottoms. Whirlpools formed amid the cypress trees, all manner of creatures taking to the air, to the trees, to higher ground.

The currents surged and carried a weary Miranda in her johnboat back to Iskra's dock, which was slowly disappearing in the rising water. In the wind, several of the bottles in the old cypress had torn loose and dropped into the bayou. Miranda tied off. Hiram's skull and spinal column and rib cage lay in the bottom of the boat in half an inch of muddy water, the rain having rinsed away nature's gore from the bones. These Miranda took up as she climbed onto the dock, skull and vertebrae clacking like wooden blocks.

At the cabin, she had to shoo vultures away from the old woman's body. They amassed like a black choir in the dead, kudzu-choked trees, spreading their wings in the rain, a fine silver spray bouncing up from them. Several had fallen to eating Iskra's softer parts—her eyes, her breasts, the insides of her thighs. They shuffled patiently to the edge of the yard. One was slow to abandon the unburned instep of Iskra's left foot. Miranda cussed and kicked it, and it flapped away. Gently, she pulled the blanket of kudzu from the old woman's body. This she laid on the ground and wrapped her father's skull and spine and ribs in it. Then she took Iskra by the hands and dragged her away from the front porch steps and around the side of the house.

She was out of breath when she got the body into the bathhouse. The door would not close. Its peg-lock was broken, the doorframe splintered. Outside, she saw the tracks that were Cotton's and the boy's and the girl's, filling with rainwater. She remembered what Hiram had taught her about tracking: *The land will tell you a story.*

Here was a story untelling itself.

She fetched Hiram's remains and brought these with her into the boy's shed.

She stood in the doorway for a time, staring at the ruins of the boy's things.

She had to go to him, save him—

SLEEP, CHILD.

The leshii's voice, curling, writhing inside her skull.

The rain beat down against the roof and sheeted against the window.

Maybe just a while, she thought, bone-weary.

She climbed into the boy's hammock with Hiram's bones clutched to her breast.

YES, SLEEP. THERE WILL BE TIME. SLEEP NOW.

Helpless not to, she closed her eyes.

It was a mercy that she did not dream.

RIDDLE AT THE WINDOW

One hand grasping at the banister, Charlie Riddle hauled up from his slump against the foyer wall, bones in his leg and back grinding together like rocks. He had expected, by now, to be dead. To have closed his eye and slipped away, but for some reason he had not. He staggered across the hall and through the open parlor door, where some furniture was draped in old sheets. He made it to the dusty sideboard, where he filched from the cabinet a half-empty fifth of Wild Turkey. Through a window he watched the yard, the lane beyond brimming with puddles, all the oaks and magnolias and hydrangeas dripping. The late afternoon light indistinguishable from twilight, as whatever weird thing was happening happened outside in the sky. Between the dwarf's greenhouse and the row of dilapidated shotgun houses, the constable saw his Plymouth in the grass. Poor Robert Alvin, dead in the trunk where Riddle had stuffed him after the fight was over, by now steamed like an oyster in the wet heat.

Riddle laughed.

Pain, instantly, in his ribs. His left leg a sack of glass. His right knee popping every step. Bruised ribs, right cheek-bone cracked and swollen, nose split at the bridge. The way that one bastard had gone at him with a pipe, the old trouser snake would spit blood, if it worked at all.

He grunted, drank some whiskey.

Fucking savages, he thought. *Fucking motherfucking savages.* He'd sent one more to hell before the last two had him. With steel-toed boots and lengths of chain and knuckles of brass, they had him. He took a drink. *Fuck em all. Let em come and kill whichever ones here I don't fucking kill first.*

The Crabtree bitch.

That fucking midget.

Outside, Avery's whore came out of the greenhouse, moving fast.

Riddle watched her, his eye watering. He wiped at it and drank some more.

She went to the Plymouth—the front left fender dented, the hood crimped, the car's ass low on its axle—leaned in through the shattered window, and snatched the Plymouth's keys. She put them in her pocket, then returned to the greenhouse.

"What y'all up to?" Riddle muttered through swollen lips.

He watched the greenhouse and took another long, thirsty pull from the bottle. He remembered the curve, a thud against the fender. Blood in his eye, the tree slewing toward him. Then away, as he corrected.

Upstairs, he heard the sound of bathwater running, the pipes in the walls of the old house gurgling.

He took another swig.

COTTON TAKES A BATH

The preacher grimaced with pain on the edge of the cast-iron tub. He ran the water, tested the heat with his fingers. The girl sat quietly in the wicker chair beneath the window at the foot of the tub, her bare feet just brushing the checked tiles.

Cotton turned off the bathwater and began working the buttons of his shirt, slowly. He folded the fabric back from his chest as if it were the slit skin of a fish. His chest was broad and hairy, old white scars crisscrossing the soft flesh of his belly. Above these, the fresh, scabbed wounds that made the crooked shapes of the river, the bayou.

The girl sat forward on the edge of her chair and stared at his belly in wonder. "You did that to yourself?" she said.

"Pain," he said, "has long been my god."

The faucet dripped loudly in the silence.

THE PLAN

✦

Inside the greenhouse, the hot, humid air sweet with the scent of Avery's plants, Teia took a knee in the gravel beside the boy. He had come awake a while ago but had not moved save to draw himself up beneath the table and shiver, every now and then casting a fearful glance like a cornered stray cat. Avery cracked open the revolver and spun the ball. Five bullets, the hammer chamber empty. He pushed it shut. Outside, the rain had let up, though drops of water still played a beat on the panes overhead.

"John," Teia said.

Avery tucked Cook's gun into the front of his jeans, lifting his shirt out and over it.

"John," she said again. All anger in her voice had fled. She was plaintive, tired. "Why don't we go? Right now. The baby's here, I got these keys, let's just go." She saw that he saw her eyes, wet and pleading, and she saw how hard it was for him to refuse her, but he did. Stubbornly, he did.

"Miranda and I, we started something this morning," he said. "I have to finish it."

Teia stared at the moist floor where tiny clover had sprouted between the rocks. She slumped beneath the nigh-unbearable weight of the next few minutes. Nearby, the baby kicked atop her blanket in the gravel between two big tractor tires of dope. *And now*, she thought, *he will ask me to say it all again, so that he can be sure I am sure.* He was standing and she was sitting and his somber eyes were leveled at hers. He touched her chin, tilted it up.

"Tell me," he said. "The plan."

"You go to the house," she said.

"Yes."

"I take Grace, get the suitcase from the bedroom."

"Then to the car."

"I put the baby and the suitcase in the car."

"And?"

"Then the boy."

"And?"

"Start the car and wait."

"That's right. And how long will I be?"

Quietly, Teia said, "Not long."

"That's right," he said, and he cupped her cheek.

She took his hand away from her face, enclosed it in hers. "Let's just leave. Something terrible will happen if you go into that house, I—"

"The plan," he said, voice calm. "You have to go."

So goddamn calm. "John—"

"Now, Teia."

She saw it in his eyes, the look he sometimes got: steely,

faraway. The look of a man who had spent his entire life looking up at others while they looked over him, beyond him. The look of a man who finally meant to be seen. She kissed him, one last plea. "You have to go," he said.

She wiped her eyes and gathered up the baby. She held Grace in one arm and edged the door open. The rain had all but stopped and the day was steamy. She glanced back once, crossing the grass, and saw Avery slip through the crack in the door and circle left, around the greenhouse to approach Sabbath House unseen from the rear.

THE CONSTABLE INVESTIGATES

✦

Riddle went walking when Avery's whore left the green-house with the baby in her arms. Out the front door of Sabbath House and down the sagging steps he went. The rain kicked up again, fat drops that dampened the blood on his khaki shirt. Teia Avery had gone into the last shotgun house. Riddle made a fractured line for the greenhouse, bottle of whiskey stoppered in hand. He wandered wide, into the lane, bumped against the Plymouth's trunk, rapping twice on the metal with his left hand and chuckling. Then he staggered back across the road to the greenhouse, where the door was cracked just a smidge.

He yanked it open, went inside.

Instantly he smelled something powerfully rank, the stink of long-unwashed skin. Scant gray light cracked through blacked-out panes and sketched the shapes of the midget's tall plants. Far back in the gloom the constable saw, on the packed gravel floor, drawing backward beneath the overhang of a wide potter's table from which it had just been creeping out, another shape, small and odd. Two brown eyes.

Riddle set his whiskey on a low table beside a spade, a rake, a hammer.

Fishing a cigarette from the pack in his left breast pocket, he said, through swollen lips, "Who's that?"

No answer came back save the sound of breathing.

Riddle put the cigarette between his lips. He took from his hip pocket a matchbook from Shifty's Tavern, opened it, tore the match with his teeth, then slid the book between the thumb and index finger of his right hand—had to wedge it there, since the whole damn hand had stopped working— and struck the match. He followed the glow to the back of the greenhouse, where he found a creature cowering beneath a table, a freak-show thing if ever there was one. "I'll be good goddamned," he said.

The match burned his fingers and he hissed and dropped it.

He struck another, and by the match's flame he let his eyes roam over the pebbled landscape of the boy's skin. He stared, silent, in awe of the ugliness before him. And there was something else, wasn't there? Something familiar about this boy.

He took the whiskey from the table, bottle sloshing, and sat down abruptly in the gravel. The jolt popped something in his back. He set the bottle aside, and when it tipped and spilled out, all he said was, "Shit." His head lolled, then righted itself, and he remembered the cigarette between his lips, which he had not yet lit. He went about the tedium of tearing a third match, the last in the book. He lit the cigarette. Tossed the book at the boy. His left hand fumbled in the dirt for the empty bottle, and when he found it, he got up on his hands and knees, wheezing, coughing wetly.

Finally, he stood again. He held the bottle by the base at first, and then, staring at the boy, flipped it in his hand so that he held it by the neck. He pointed a finger and said, "I know you. You're dead. I saw you carried off from here when you was a baby."

Riddle heard the sound of something wet pattering the dirt. Over the boy's already ripe body-stink and the pungency of the plants themselves, he smelled it: piss.

The constable blinked sluggishly. "Maybe you weren't dead," he said. "What'd that witch do, keep you?" He remembered what some of the old-timers who used to frequent the Landing had said about Miranda Crabtree, in the months and years after Hiram disappeared. The old witch raising her, teaching her the black arts. "Miranda Crabtree," the constable said, and he watched the boy, whose eyes swiveled at the name to meet Riddle's one.

"Oh," Riddle said. "I see."

He reached behind his back to his belt and, after a long while of trying, managed to unsnap his handcuffs. He let the cuffs dangle from one hand, the bottle in the other. He staggered forward and reached beneath the table and the boy scrabbled like a cat, but the constable's big hands found an ankle, a leg, and he held on. "Come on, now," he said. "Come here. Come on. Come on, son."

Riddle got one bracelet around the boy's wrist, then

slapped the other around a segment of metal conduit bolted into the brick wall, which ended somewhere as a spigot.

"I don't know how you got here, but take my word for it, boy, you ain't a-leavin."

Riddle swung the whiskey bottle and the boy threw up his free arm to ward off the blow. The bottle made a great *WHUMP* but did not break. Eyes and teeth clenched in pain and terror, the boy slumped, held his arm to his side.

Atop the potter's table, Riddle saw a pair of drop-forged pruning shears, their ends sharp. He dropped the bottle, took up the shears.

"Let's see them pretty brown eyes," he said.

ALIVE

The girl was wringing water from a sponge to soap the old preacher's back, careful not to touch his bare flesh with her own—*I won't touch him ever again, if I can help it*, she thought—when something hard and unseen struck her left arm. She flew backward, slipped on wet tiles, and fell flat on her back. Dazed, arm blazing, she lay staring up at the high slatted ceiling, where black mold came creeping out between the boards.

Alarmed at her fall, the old man shot up out of the tub.

The boy. He's alive. Someone is hurting him, but he's alive.

Scared, so scared, something awful happening—

She closed her eyes, focused on the pain radiating out from her arm, her arm become the boy's, into the dark of a shed . . . the boy's shed? No, not a shed, but somewhere moist and dark, somewhere near . . . a smell: pungent, dank.

The preacher loomed, naked, dripping.

She reached deeper into the darkness, even as she shrank from the old man's proffered hand.

Miranda, she thought.

A PROBLEM IN THE TRUNK

✦

Grace bundled in a light blanket at her breast, Teia crossed the lawn between the shotgun house and the Plymouth, carrying a heavy suitcase and two thick quilts pressed under her arm. When she opened the rear passenger's door, she did not look at the front seat. It was a horror of flesh and blood drying, once-white vinyl shellacked red. Teia arranged the first quilt across the backseat and lay the wrapped and fretful baby on it. She spread the second quilt, doubled up, across the front.

The rain had started up again, a needling.

She fished in her pocket and plugged the key into the trunk and opened it.

She gasped.

The constable's deputy lay inside, a twisted crimson mess.

Teia felt the shakes beginning in her arms, threatening to spread down her legs, up her spine, to her teeth. She set her jaw and reached into the trunk and took one of the deputy's boots and tried to drag him out, but the boot pulled free and she fell backward onto the grass, landing hard on her rump. She tossed the boot aside. Was about to try again when she heard something smash inside the greenhouse.

The door stood open wide, Teia saw.

She listened, heard only the steady chug of the generator out back.

Fear coiled in her gut.

She folded the deputy's long leg back into the trunk and slammed it. She got behind the wheel, started the motor, and eased the car over the lane, parked it in the grass. Left it running, big engine rumbling and popping, and went inside the greenhouse.

READY

Miranda woke in the hammock to the sight of Hiram's skull, jawless, against her breast. His eye sockets rimmed in mud. His ribs reached around her, as if to comfort. Her clothes were dry and crusted, stiff against her. Her hair thick and matted. Through the window she could tell it was still light outside, the skies roiling with fast-moving clouds, the eclipse having passed dreamlike while she slept. Thunder shook the little shed.

"We're getting near the end," a voice said.

Miranda started and saw the girl sitting cross-legged on the floor in Miranda's old T-shirt and jeans. She was reading, an open book in her lap, taken from the heap on the floor.

Miranda pushed out of the hammock, left her father's remains cradled there.

The girl flipped a page. She did not look up. "I'm with the old preacher who calls himself Father. I'm helping him get ready. But I like it better here. It's nice here."

Miranda went stiff-legged and sore toward the boy's table, leaned against it. A coffee can of Crayolas toppled, crayons spilling and rolling to the edge of the table, some dropping into the dirt.

"Get ready for what?" Miranda managed.

"His ritual," the girl said. "You have a ritual, too. Boiling water. The witch's finger." She closed her book and stared over Miranda's shoulder, out the window, where small droplets of rain had begun to patter against the glass. "I like rain," she said.

"I do, too," Miranda said, but the girl kept talking as if she had not heard.

"Boiling water, the witch's finger. A jar, broken. The chickens got that."

"Got what?" Miranda's throat dry as dust.

"The chickens are fighting over it. It was in the jar because the woods and the worms took it and the green lady kept it all this time, safe in the dirt like your daddy's bones, and when the time was right she gave it back to the old witch. The woods took it and the green lady gave it back, just like she gave the old preacher back his razor. She knew he'd need it and she knew you'd need what's in the jar and the old witch kept it safe in the cupboard, but now the chickens have it. It was in the jar and the jar is broken, the chickens have it. The jar is broken. Broken jar. Boiling water. The witch's finger. And blood. Blood and the words. You have to say the words—"

"What words?" Miranda said.

"—say the words, just say the words. Look and see. Look and see. Look and see."

"Look and see," Miranda whispered.

"Look and see, look and see, look and see!" Her voice rose in pitch as she began to cry: "I'm in the bath with the old man, not with the boy, and he's in trouble! He's hurting him, a big man, he's hurting him and he's scared, why are you doing that, why, why are you hurting him, oh, please, don't do that!"

"Where is he?"

"I don't know, I can't see, but you can! Look and see! Jar, water, finger, blood! Hurry!"

Miranda threw open the door and ran into the rain to the smoldering wreck of Iskra's cabin. Repeating in her head everything the girl had said: boiling water, the witch's finger, a broken jar, blood.

Look and see.

REACH

In the upstairs bath of Sabbath House, the girl opened her eyes where she lay on the floor. She had gone away, had split herself between here and . . . elsewhere. The old witch's island. The boy's shed. The ruins of the cabin. Only for an instant, though it had seemed an eternity.

She felt dizzy, had to flatten both hands on the cool tile floor to still the swimming in her head.

The preacher reached down to help her up, but she pushed his hand away with the back of her arm still safe in its sleeve. Tried to slow her breathing.

The old man eased down into the tub and sat back and closed his eyes as if to wait, confident that the girl would recover from whatever fit had gripped her, would take up her sponge and resume the slow, mechanical circling of sponge over skin.

The girl's throat felt hoarse, scratchy, as if she'd been yelling. What had she done? She didn't know, really. The boy's pain had triggered it, a sudden leap across space, time. Picturing the world as that great, transparent jewel, her own face reflected in all facets of the diamond's cut, and then, out of a hall of infinite mirrors, two more faces emerged, Sister and the boy toiling in their own mad nightmares, and the girl had simply reached out for one, fingers parting the diamond's wall like water, and she had *seen*—

She sat on the edge of the tub. Reached into the water and drew out the sponge and wrung it. Then resumed washing the old man's chest, and soon the preacher began to hum his dreadful hymn.

I reached, she thought. *That's what I did.*

And Miranda heard.

In a moment, her heart had slowed, her breathing eased.

AVERY

Avery went up the back porch steps and through the un-locked door and kitchen and into the main foyer. There he stood listening for any sound. A smear of blood on the wall outside the parlor, where Avery half expected to find Char-lie Riddle dead or dying. But the room was empty. He bit off a curse, having already imagined the satisfaction of press-ing the gun barrel to the constable's good eye, John Avery the dwarf standing tall over Constable Charlie Riddle for once. He listened again. Heard the soft baritone of the old preacher's humming. Upstairs.

Avery moved cautiously up the foyer staircase, one hand reaching above his head to steady himself along the ban-ister. Ball of the heavy gun pressing cold against the bare flesh of his belly beneath his shirt. When he reached the top of the stairs, breathing fast and shallow, he saw the master bedroom door aslant, lamp glow spilling out. He could hear the old man humming softly of the sweet by and by.

Avery stepped onto the landing and moved through a knife's edge of light, sure that the sound of the creaking floor or his own heart pounding would betray him. Neither did. He reached out, put his hand on the knob of the bedroom door, and hesitated.

He thought of Cook.

The way Cotton had reached without qualm into the Styrofoam box to take out Cook's head and gaze up the stump of the neck like a boy peering up a doll's dress.

Avery took Cook's pistol from his waist.

He turned the doorknob and went into the bedroom.

RITUAL

The cabin's roof and floor had collapsed and two hens and a rooster clucked and pecked in the exposed earth beneath the hut. Everything had a greasy, black smell. Soot ran the consistency of ink in the rain. She ducked a fallen beam, stepped over the remnants of a kitchen chair. The old woman's bread bowl, scorched black. Only the iron stove and stone hearth and the pump in the kitchen sink—

boiling water

—remained intact.

Miranda dumped rainwater from a blackened enamel pot. She sloshed it full with fresh water from the pump and set it on the stove. She cast about for anything dry, but all the wood was damp. She remembered the bathhouse, where wood was stacked beneath the tin roof of the lean-to. She ran, her side thick and heavy but old in its hurt. She loaded up with as many dry lengths as she could carry, along with a handful of kindling from a pail, and all of this she stuffed into the belly of the boxwood stove back in the ruins of the cabin. She went to Iskra's cupboard and rummaged through the drawers until she found a small box of matches. Inside, there were three.

She struck one, and it snapped.

She struck another, and it would not catch.

She was about to try the third when she heard a commotion kick up among the hens.

She followed the sound into what was left of the pantry, only one wall intact, all the shelves collapsed. The floor here in the narrow space had fallen in, and the joists jutted like the bones of a fish half eaten. Jars had burst and scorched with the heat. The wood made tumorous with fleshy, pulpy things burned black. Down below, in the space beneath the cabin, the chickens were flying at each other, beating their wings. She could see the scraps of a shattered jar, some long tendril of something in the dirt that they were fighting over. She dropped down between them and kicked them away— they fled into the shadows to cluck and fuss—and bent over their prize.

At first it looked like an earthworm, a night crawler. But when she picked it up carefully by the tail and blew on it and brushed away the debris, holding it up to the dull late afternoon light, she saw that it was a squashed human eye, burst like a grape, hanging from a few last shreds of nerve, whatever the chickens had not managed to eat.

A jar, broken.

In the jelly of the eye, she saw a sliver of iris, cornflower-blue.

The house shuddered around her. Wood rumbled against wood.

She knew the eye at once. Remembered the sensation of her thumb pushing it deep into the socket, how it had given way, warm and wet, a squish, a pop. She remembered running with it, not even feeling it sticky and soft in two pieces in her hand until she was on the water, safe. She had dropped it in the johnboat's wake. She remembered that. But here it was now, made whole again among the ruins of the witch's cupboard. Bits of green-colored glass all around it.

The bottle from her vision in the tree.

She imagined Iskra's old hands holding it beneath the bayou's surface, a layer of rich dark silt sluicing in. Stoppering its murky contents on a high shelf in the pantry. A vessel still in want of its final filling, the constable's plucked eye, which one day, week, or year was not there, and the next it was—returned by the river that had claimed it when Miranda threw it in. She imagined these things and knew that this was how it had all happened. She saw the eye growing, suspended in the jar's silty womb like an otherworldly stalk.

She tucked the eye and its tendril of nerve into her shirt pocket and pulled herself out of the hole in the floor—her hands squishing in black pantry goo—as all around her the charred bones of Iskra's cabin began to shake and groan as if they were coming alive, as if the house itself were attempting to stand on the stilts that raised it above the sloped ground.

In the pit of the living room, beneath the joists, the rooster beat its wings as if to warn something away.

An iron poker fell with a clang, and the door of the heavy boxwood stove swung open.

Miranda opened her pocket, peered in closer at the eye, like a hunk of frog jelly. Like the grub she had buried in the earth. Yesterday? The day before?

Working quickly—

boiling water

—she crouched on her knees by the stove and struck the final match.

It flared. She set it among the kindling. The kindling glowed, dimmed.

"No, no, no," she said. She blew on it.

A stiff breeze blew up, as if something had drawn one last breath and sent it through the bones of the house, and a flame caught inside the stove.

The rain seemed to cooperate, too, slackening to a random patter. She left the fire to blaze and went back to the bathhouse, where she knelt by Iskra's corpse. She took the old woman's filleting knife from her apron—the handle charred—and with hands that shook, put the blade against the witch's right index finger. She grimaced and pressed the blade into blackened flesh. She cut at the joint. It was not unlike topping an ear of corn.

Husk, blade, bone.

Now the fire was roaring and the water was beginning to boil. She dropped Iskra's finger into the water and took the gauze from her own hand, where Iskra had sliced her in the bathhouse the day before. But the wound had clotted. And the stitching in her side had held. So she made a new cut, drawing the blade over the palm of her left hand. She had bled so much, did she have any left?

She dripped into the pot and wiped Iskra's knife on her jeans and set it aside on the hearth.

She stoked the fire.

Boiling water.

The witch's finger.

Blood.

A jar, broken, and the words.

Putting a hand over the constable's eye in her pocket, she opened her mouth and started to speak, but she hitched, no idea what the words should be.

She closed her eyes, and in her mind's eye she saw the boy as she knew him, sunning himself along the bank or hopping out of a tree, bow and arrow in hand, smiling, warm.

She moved her hand from the pocket of her shirt to her heart, and from there began to shape a word with her fingers, and then another word, and soon both hands were speaking, and the words were tumbling out silently, and she hoped they were as right and true as the arrows she and the boy had shot together, on hunting trips in the great green bottoms and all along the banks of the River Prosper.

TEIA IN TROUBLE

✦

Teia took the butcher's knife Avery had left on the nightstand out of the waist of her jeans. She stood in the greenhouse doorway, listening, but heard nothing over the sound of the generator. She moved quietly among the plants in their tractor tires, knife thrust out before her. In the back, the boy had drawn up into a sitting position beneath the potting shelf, his knees tight against his chest. At first she thought he was afraid of her, but then he jerked and shook his arms and she heard and saw the handcuffs, one of the boy's hands secured to the water pipe anchored in the brick. She caught a whiff of ammonia.

She heard a sound, hollow, like the plunk of an empty bottle against soft earth, and then she was on her hands and knees in the gravel and clover, a roaring in her ears that was not the generator.

Someone loomed over her, weaved drunkenly. Held a pair of pruning shears and an empty whiskey bottle. The knife was kicked away, into the shadows beneath the plants. She felt a boot in her side, and all the air left her body.

Her vision darkened. She rolled over.

A shape above her, a giant, big and wide and reeking of tobacco and whiskey and something else, something red.

IN THE MASTER BATH

Avery went slowly through the preacher's bedroom, which was sparse in its furnishings save the four-poster bed and a marble-topped bedside table, on it the old man's Bible, unfurled to the Gospels like a lazy, thoughtless maw. He held the pistol before him, never more aware of his stubby fingers, his awkward grip on a weapon made for bigger hands, the inevitable buck that might tear it away should he have to fire it.

He pushed through the bathroom door and saw the preacher hunched forward in the claw-foot tub. Humming still. A girl sat on the edge behind him, soaping the old man's back with a fat yellow sponge. She wore an oversized T-shirt and jeans, had rolled the sleeves of the T-shirt up to her shoulders, which were small white knobs.

Avery stood there, gun in hand, and did not move.

The girl looked up, saw him first. The sponge went still

against the old man's back. Her mouth tightened and her eyes shifted, slightly, to the gun.

Cotton stopping humming. He cocked an ear over his shoulder, as if attuned to the very beating of the girl's heart. He showed no surprise when he looked up, as if this were a betrayal he had long expected. He met Avery's eyes, ignoring the gun. "John," he said.

Water sloshing in the bath.

"Get up," Avery said. "Now."

With marshaled dignity, the old preacher put his arms on the sides of the tub and raised himself, naked and dripping, from the bath. His left calf was swollen red from three raw punctures. His chest stitched with angry red cuts. As if someone had carved a map into the preacher's chest. His arms shook and his legs quivered. A whorl of blood in the water.

"Out." Avery cocked the revolver.

Cotton stepped out onto the tiles, holding fast to the edge of the tub.

The girl, sponge clutched at her chest, backed away from the tub.

"Where's Riddle?"

"Downstairs, last I saw him," the old man said.

"Ain't there now."

"Then I don't know, John."

The girl stepped around Cotton. Clutching the sponge so tightly that water ran from it and pattered on the tiles.

"It's okay," Avery told her, never taking his eyes from Billy Cotton. "I'm taking you out of here. My name's John. What's yours?"

Tears shimmered in her eyes, spilled down her cheeks, as if the girl herself were being wrung now. She shook her head. "I don't know," she said in a voice so very small.

"John," Cotton said.

"It doesn't matter, honey, you don't need a name to come with me. My wife, her name is Teia. Isn't that a pretty name?"

The girl nodded.

"Just give me your hand."

She wiped her eyes. Shook her head. "I can't," she said.

Avery was sweating now, the sweat dripping. "Sure," he said. "Sure you can, why not?"

"I'm supposed to be here. I *have* to be here. I said I would be."

"It's okay, child," Cotton said suddenly. "You can go."

She turned her face up to his. "I can?"

"Sure you can," the old preacher said, never taking his eyes from John Avery. "Sure."

"See?" Avery said, gun slippery with sweat. He let go and held it one-handed, wiped the other on his jeans. Then reached out. "Now. Give me your hand."

The girl looked up at Cotton in the manner of a caged animal turned out, and at that moment John Avery stepped forward and seized her hand. The girl screeched, yanking her hand away, but not before John Avery felt something like a static shock. He saw, at his feet, the long grass of the front lawn, sprouting suddenly between the bathroom tiles, whispering as it grew, grew, and grew, rushing up around him. He cried out as he was swallowed by it.

The girl pulled her arms into her shirt and backed away. "I'm sorry," she said, almost a whimper. "I'm so sorry—"

The barrel of the gun dipped toward the tiles.
Avery gagged, senses clogged with earth and blood.
Cotton went for the gun.
The girl screamed.

LOOK AND SEE

The flames licked behind the grate of the stove. The water in the pot roiled. Miranda finished the words and reached into her shirt pocket and took out the constable's eye. She held it over the pot. She spoke to the ruined cabin, to the ghosts of ghosts. She spoke as she understood. "I've sent devils to hell. I've dug graves for the bodies never buried and called things that crawled right out of the ground. I took the poison of a moccasin. I took the worst of the river and the worst of men. I took it all and I'm alive. You show me that boy. You show me what I want to see."

She dropped the constable's eye in the water.

Look and see.

THE CONSTABLE, SCREAMING

✦

Riddle was squeezing Teia's throat and was about to put the tip of the shears into the flesh beneath her jaw when someone slid a white-hot ice pick into his empty orbit. He screamed and staggered away from the prostrate Teia, tearing at his eye patch, and when he ripped it free he tore with it the veil of darkness that had shrouded his sight these last nine years.

He screamed and screamed, oh, how he did.

Teia slumped against the frame of the shed, drawing heavy, wheezing breaths.

The constable flailed like a man lit afire.

"It burns! Jesus, it burns—"

Teia had no understanding of what she saw.

The boy saw, too. He saw the wetness spreading at the constable's crotch.

The man's mouth open, spittle flying.

Teia crawled, past the fat constable hunched over and wailing. She crawled for the burlap sack set in a heap on her husband's worktable.

WHAT MIRANDA SAW

✦

The air cracked as if lashed by a whip, and Miranda smelled sulfur, and she saw. She hung like a spider in the hollow of Charlie Riddle's eye and saw. She saw the present, the past, moments ago and memories long gone. She was choking a woman—John Avery's wife—but the woman's face was Miranda's. She was hitting the boy, her brother, with an empty bottle. Striking him: the knee, the calf, the arm. Taunting him with sharp shears. His eyes wide with terror. All of this beneath the blackened panes of John Avery's greenhouse that pitched and wheeled as the constable screamed. She watched with horror as the whole of Charlie Riddle's sins unfolded. She saw men and women on motorcycles, guns. Blood and death in the dim light of an empty building. A skinny girl on a houseboat, the woman possessed, like Avery's wife, of Miranda's face. Staring back at herself from the pillow, no expression, and suddenly the face was not Miranda's but her mother's, Cora Crabtree's, contorted in a kind of horrible, imagined ecstasy, then Cora's face—*Daisy, her name is Daisy*—stove in and gone and Miranda, like Riddle, screaming. She saw the railing of his boat, Charlie Riddle looking down into the dim, darkening water as the dead girl sank, weighted with cinder blocks tied on by rubber straps. And there, in the water's depths, she saw her mother, younger than Miranda had ever seen her in pictures, wearing a dress that billowed around her as she sank, her eyes wide, and all around her were flowers, black-eyed Susans handpicked and bobbing to the surface.

GO

Teia drew the gut-hook machete from the sack and gripped it with both hands. She reared up and brought it down hard where the constable's neck met his right shoulder, and the blade cut into him with the softest of sounds. It struck bone, the shock of it traveling through Teia's hands and up her arms. He cried out, more in surprise than pain, then fell to his knees, clutching and slapping at his shoulder as if stung. She pulled the machete free—this time a shucking sound— and stepped back and raised it above her head, a thin ribbon of blood trailing after it, and struck again, and now she was screaming, and the boy beneath Avery's table was scrabbling and yanking at the silver cuff, and this was surely the maddest moment of her life, as she brought the talonlike blade down one last time, into Charlie Riddle's head, and the constable's skull cracked beneath it—a hard sound, like smashing a walnut. He pitched facedown in the gravel, in the little sprigs of clover that grew between the rocks. And

Teia, still gripping the machete stuck in the fat man's head, was dragged with it, until she let go.

From Sabbath House came a single gun-crack.

She heard it, but it took several breaths—she made little gasping sounds—to realize what she had heard.

John.

His name a bell rung inside her head.

She stumbled out of the greenhouse, shook away the darkness that threatened to spread over her eyes and mind like a stain. She wove her way through knee-high grass toward the manse. Halfway to the porch, she saw her man walk out between the briar-wrapped columns. He came down the front steps and stood at the edge of the high lawn, looking around as if disoriented. When he saw her, he lifted a hand, and for an instant the cold fingers that had closed over her heart in the greenhouse loosened their grip. But then Avery shook his head and spoke, his lips making the shape of a word. A blood bubble popped between his lips, but the word upon them was clear: "Go."

After he had said this, he dropped like an armload of wood into the tall grass.

Teia ran to him, fell beside him, but she did not pitch forward as Avery had. *Because I am not dead.* She rolled him over, cradled his head, and saw the hole in the denim shirt he wore, just below his sternum. How had she not seen that right away? Was she blind? She said his name over and over, softly at first, then rising in pitch, but his eyes were already glassy and still. He was gone.

Billy Cotton limped naked onto the porch, Cook's pistol in hand. The old man stood gazing down at Avery's wife wailing over the dwarf's corpse. Cotton watched all of this play out like a drama he had no part in. His expression piteous and sad. He started down the steps, thinking that he might somehow minister to her. She was, after all, the last of his flock. Had endured such hardship in his name. But when she saw him, gun in hand, she scuttled backward, pushing away over the ground, as if forcing herself to abandon her man. She turned onto hands and knees and crawled, then got to her feet and ran, and in a blink of an eye she was in the Plymouth. Cotton imagined what he must look like to her: a naked old man, arms outstretched, gun in one hand. Staggering like a monster.

The car spun its wheels in the grass, tearing up the earth, and shot forward through the compound gates. It turned right on the county road and fled.

Cotton walked as far as the greenhouse, where he stood listening to the Plymouth's fading roar, the cicadas singing out from the trees. The cough of the gas-powered generator behind the greenhouse, a series of stutters, and it died. In the near-silence that followed, he heard another noise from inside the greenhouse, a whimpering, the clank of metal against metal.

Curious, Avery's gun almost forgotten in his hand, he walked through the door.

LAST BREATH

Fading now, the constable's sight. Her own heart slowing in tandem with his. Her brother's face yet before her, wide-eyed, spattered with blood. Beneath a table in a place with blackened glass and harsh light. And a forest of Avery's green plants. Darkness.

Miranda opened her eyes to the smoldering ruin of Iskra's house.

The fire in the stove had died.

A wind swelled through the bones of the cabin, blew ash and smoke and cinders, and Miranda felt the house shudder, and she remembered the fairy tales Iskra had told her when she was little, stories of a witch whose house grew chicken legs and roamed the forest, never to settle in the same place twice. The house hid the witch, she said. It protected her.

The wind died.

The girl appeared as a vapor up the slope, near the stump and ax.

"You have to hurry," she called.

"I'm coming," Miranda said.

A breeze rattled the cans in Littlefish's garden, scattering the vision.

Brother, Miranda thought, *I am coming.*

THE BOY, NOT ALONE

After the woman ran away, Littlefish summoned the courage to look at the dead man, who lay not three feet away on the packed hard rocks. Shirttail half untucked, bulk spilling out the sides, the man appeared to the boy like a great felled pig. And that was how the woman, with the Father Hen's blade, had treated him: like a creature with better uses on the other side of living. Littlefish smelled something bad—and not his own stink of fish and piss and fear.

Dying, the fat man had shit his pants.

Littlefish tugged at the handcuff that held him to the wall. The flesh around his wrist was raw where the metal had already bitten. There were no tools within reach of his free hand. His arm and leg hurt where the fat man had struck him with the bottle. His shoulder burned. Each breath drew pain.

Outside, he heard voices, a woman screaming.

The roar of an engine, too, bigger than the steady drone

that had been sputtering for a while now, just beyond the wall where he was chained.

He closed his eyes and sat back and tried not to think about how stupid he had been. To leave without Sister. He wondered where his friend was, was she safe or dead? If dead, would he die, too?

The low drone cut out.

The pie-pan lights overhead flickered.

The entire greenhouse plunged into darkness.

Briefly, the boy yanked at his restraints, one last try, but the steel only bit deeper into his wrist.

A single shaft of light cut through the darkness.

"Who's there?" a voice said.

A voice that nearly stopped the boy's heart with terror.

He saw a naked man silhouetted among the plants. The boy could only see him from the waist down; the tabletop blocked his view.

"Charlie?" the man said. He squatted beside the corpse, put his hand on the handle of the machete buried in the fat man's skull. In his other hand: a gun. Littlefish knew about guns. Sister had taught him never to touch the shotgun Baba kept in the closet. The boy tried to make himself as small as he could against the wall, but the chain of his handcuff clinked against the pipe.

The naked man dropped his head and crouched to look beneath the table.

The Father Hen's eyes were black pits. He sat down on the rocks, a grunt of pain. He peered at the boy for a while. He leaned over and gripped the machete in the dead man's skull. Yanked it free. The sound was wet, like a ripe summer melon splitting.

The boy heard gravel rustle, and now the girl stood in the long shaft of light, her shape like a cut-out paper doll. He felt a knot of fear inside his chest turn loose at the sight of her, then tighten again when the Father Hen spoke to her.

"Look and see, child, what is delivered unto us."

The girl hunkered low and stared at Littlefish, and her eyes were wide and terrified for the boy. "We gotta hurry," she said. She hesitated, then took the old man's hand and tried to pull him, gently, to his feet. "Bad people are coming. There's a black cloud over this place."

Still, the Father Hen resisted, pulling her closer.

"It's providence," he said, voice soft and full of wonder.

"No," the girl said, pulling away. "He ain't got no part in this. He ain't a part of what I saw."

"But he is, child. He is a part of me."

"I never saw nothing looked like him. Just you, just me. That's the way."

Littlefish heard the words and understood only one thing—

he is a part of me

—a thing he had long suspicioned, waking from his awful dreams. Dreams he and this monster had shared. A truth. The only truth he had ever dreaded knowing, and now that he knew it, he felt it had punched a hole through the hull of his heart.

The girl pleaded, "It's time to go!"

She is trying to protect me, the boy thought.

"All together now," the Father said. "Better like this. Better—"

Fast as a cottonmouth moccasin, the girl leaped on the Father Hen's back. She raised her hand high above her head and brought it down along his cheek and the Father Hen threw her off, staggering into the tall green trees, where he fell. His machete flew from his hand. The girl lay on the ground, breath knocked out of her.

Out of the trees came a high-pitched and garbled scream. "WHAT DID YOU DO?"

The trees parted and the old man shambled out, holding his cheek, blood gushing from beneath his hand. He caught the girl's arm and jerked her up like an unruly mutt. "Who are you?" he demanded. His voice thick and wet. He squeezed her wrist and her hand opened and out fell a bloody broadhead. He clamped his other hand around the girl's throat, and a flap of his cheek fell away like the slit belly of a fish. "I THOUGHT I KNEW YOU!" he roared.

Littlefish yanked at the pipe in the wall.

The girl sputtered and clawed at the hand.

The boy rocked on his back, ignoring the pain in his side and shoulder, and put his feet flat on the bottom of the table above and kicked hard, and the whole thing pitched forward and struck the Father Hen in a clatter of tools.

He let the girl go.

Littlefish reached out with his free hand and splayed his fingers at her as if to beg something for which there were no words, but she did not see him where she had fallen retching on the greenhouse floor.

The Father Hen shoved the table aside with a crash and

fell on his knees and fought clumsily through the boy's thrashing legs. He seized Littlefish's head by the ears and slammed his skull into the brick foundation of the greenhouse.

The first blow made the boy see stars.

The Father Hen made grunting noises, something between hurt and laughter.

The second blow made Littlefish see nothing at all.

TO THE RIVER, TO THE END

✦

The Evinrude cranked on the first try and Miranda went full-throttle down the bayou from Iskra's cabin to the river. The wind blew her hair stiffly behind her, so caked with mud and grime it might have been a crown of twigs. The rain-rushing currents had opened a whirling vortex where the bayou met the Prosper. She eased off the throttle, went slowly around it, beneath the overhang of the trees. A fallen branch was swept into the torrent, and Miranda watched it spin round and round until she could not see it and this was her life, she thought, her entire world become this inescapable end of nature.

She docked at the Landing and went in to fetch Hiram's bow, a fresh quiver of arrows, and a spare shooting glove. She rummaged a box of matches from old stock in the store downstairs, then filled the last gas canister she owned at the dock and set it in the boat.

Then, one last time, she made for Sabbath House.

LENA

Cotton carried the drugged girl in his arms through the dimming woods, the ampule brought to him in Cook's head now emptied into her veins. He cradled her as Mary had cradled Christ taken down from the cross. He strode naked through the pine thicket and came out into the clearing at the base of the burned-out church, the insects singing madly. He carried the girl to the iron door of the crypt, which he had left propped open. Deep into the cave they went, where the walls were made of hand-shaped bricks and bats teemed in the shadows above. The air was cool, dank. His bare feet slapped stone, each step an echo.

He followed the tunnel down into the large round vault, where overhead the foundations of the church were visible among the roots. Between the two caskets on the cold stone floor, the boy lay on his side, fully awake and trembling with terror, arms handcuffed behind his back, a length of rope running from the cuffs to his ankles, which were tied.

Bits of pine needles and leaves were still lodged in his hair where Cotton had dragged him through the woods by his feet.

The preacher laid the girl beside him.

Billy Cotton gazed at the bones of his wife. He did not see skull or crumbling jaw or crooked teeth, the dark orbits empty, but rather the young woman she had been when he had first known her, he already long past the age of Christ, she not yet twenty-five. He had hitched his way out of the Texas oil fields and into a truck stop along the neon-lit borders of Texarkana. *You*, he thought, *that pretty waitress who brought me eggs*. Remembering now how he sat ashamed in a dirty button-down shirt and road-filthy jeans, stewed in his own body's stink, Tony Lama boots pulling apart at the soles, the whole of his insides wrung out from clawing his way across the land. A man without a home, a ragamuffin. A vagabond. A criminal. Washed up in a booth with no coin to buy coffee, no cash to buy food. There in that oasis he had met a messenger of God named Lena Bowen.

How unworthy I proved, he thought.

At the head of the casket, he turned a key in a lock. The key was stubborn, and when it finally clicked, the casket gave a hiss, and the lid's tongue popped free from the body's groove, breaking the seal and releasing the moldered stench of old bones and death. Cotton raised the lid with a grunt. It was heavy glass. The two caskets had been made by a company out of state and shipped here in the winter of 1963. Cotton reached into the coffin to caress the near hairless skull of his wife. "I've brought you someone," he said. He scooped up the heavy boy, whose struggles only tightened his bonds. "Look here," he said, holding the child up like a great fish he had caught in the bayou. "He's come back to us, after all these years."

He spilled the boy out of his arms into the coffin.

The boy's weight crunched Lena Cotton's dry bones.

The preacher closed the lid and locked it.

HER BROTHER'S TRAIL

She bypassed the dock and drove the boat straight through the water grass and lodged it like an arrow in the bank. Armed with bow and shaft, she stepped onto the land and walked the edge of the property, which was deathly still in the twilight. She nocked an arrow behind the first shotgun house and went low around the empty building. At the corner of the porch, she took a view of the lane and the house across the way. She heard only the distant, alien cry of the cicadas.

Blackened panes from her vision: the greenhouse. She moved quickly across the road and through the open door into the dim shaft of light. Right away she saw the constable's body sprawled in the gravel, half hidden by the thick growth of the plants. A machete near his hand. She felt nothing at the sight of him save the cataloguing of his absence, the great amount of blood he had spilled in leaving.

With the end of her bow, she broke out four, five panes of glass, to let in more light.

Now she saw the overturned table, the indentations on the floor where its legs had stood. Beneath it, rocks and earth displaced in the shape of a boy who had been terrified. She touched the metal pipe that had pulled slightly away from the brick, saw the scrapes the handcuffs—missing from Charlie Riddle's belt—had made as Littlefish had struggled violently against them. A little silver key lay in the gravel beside Riddle. She stuffed it in her jeans pocket.

She saw her brother's blood on the brick foundation, a few stray hairs from his head stuck there. The furrows where he had been dragged toward the open door. Blood on the door, and more hair, where his head had banged on the way out.

The blood not yet tacky.

Outside the greenhouse, she saw the trail, stalks of weed broken, the long grass bending away, toward the woods.

The old burned church.

Miranda heard the heavy shuffle of wings. Above, vultures circled in the gray sky. There were more perched in the oaks overhead like ghoulish celebrants. Miranda moved through the grass toward a spot where three of the birds were shuffling.

It is not him. It is not him. It is not my brother.

It was not.

It was John Avery.

She raised her bow and let fly the arrow. It struck the largest bird in the breast. Two more took flight, though they didn't go far. One landed in the lower reaches of a tree. The other perched on the dilapidated porch railing of Sabbath House. The bird she had killed lay at Avery's feet. She knelt beside him, saw where the birds had eaten his eyes. His lips. Part of his tongue. Miranda saw the hole in his denim shirt, too, the wound that had killed him.

She rolled him over, hoping it might keep the vultures from the rest of his face.

She made for the furrow in the grass, her brother's trail.

Into the trees. Where the sign became a furrow of pine needles, broken branches, an old man's bare footprints.

She did not look back.

SHADOW AND ROOT AND STONE

✦

The crypt door was open and issued a cool, dank air. Miranda went down, down. She slogged through a wide puddle of water from the day's rainfall, then stepped quietly onto dry stones. Things skittered along the walls and ceiling above. Ahead, the chamber widened into a vault where lantern light danced. She listened. Heard the preacher's strong baritone as he sang.

"'O, a better day is dawning, a day that knows no night . . .'"

His voice sputtered strangely, full of air and something else, something wet.

Miranda drew an arrow, nocked it.

"'When all sorrow shall be banished and every wrong made right . . .'"

She put tension on her arrow.

"'God will take away all fear, wipe away our every tear . . .'"

She stepped into the vault.

Naked, his back to Miranda, the preacher stood over the raised lid of a glass casket, setting something gently into it. Nearby, a second casket flickered with the lantern's greasy flame.

"'You'll be there . . .'" he sang.

When he stepped away, Miranda saw that the girl lay in the casket, nestled among purple silk brocade.

"'I'll be there . . .'"

The preacher turned to the lantern on the floor, beside which he had set his straight razor. His skin hung loosely from his frame. His cheek, Miranda saw, was a gory red flap, blood sputtering through as he sang.

"'In that better day that's dawning *we'll* be there . . .'"

A muffled thump came from the other casket, which was shut and locked.

Inside, Littlefish was trussed up and struggling atop the bones of his mother's corpse.

A rage swept through Miranda Crabtree like a wind.

Hunkered, opening his razor, Cotton froze at the creak of her string. He looked up slowly, squinting into the dark. His mutilated face registered no malice, no surprise, no emotion of any kind when she stepped out of shadow and into the dancing light. He glanced at the open coffin, the girl inside. His hand moved slowly away from the razor, out of sight behind the lantern.

"Art thou a ghost, too, Miranda," the old preacher said in a hushed voice, teeth shining through his torn cheek, "or are you flesh and blood?"

"Don't speak," she said, aligning her broadhead.

"Thank you for raising my son," Billy Cotton said.

Miranda's aim faltered, briefly.

She heard a metallic click, saw Cotton's hand moving from behind the lantern, saw Cook's black revolver gleaming orange in the light.

The bolt struck the preacher in the chest, buried itself to the fletching just below the red raw curve of Iskra's bayou. The whisper of the arrow's passing made the lantern flame dip. The preacher dropped the pistol and sat back against the wall, pale legs splayed. A thin line of blood trickled from his mouth.

Miranda dropped her bow and went to Lena's casket. She pried at the lid until she saw the key. She turned it. The boy stared up at her from atop his mother's corpse, eyes wet. She touched his head, kissed him. Dug in her jeans for the handcuff key she had found near the fat lawman's corpse. She unlocked each of the boy's wrists and the tension on the rope eased, leaving only his ankles bound. "Put your arms around me," she said, and when he did, she lifted him out of the coffin and set his feet on the stone floor. He clung to her fiercely, shaking all over. She held him and whispered in his ear, "I love you. I love you. I love you."

When the boy's breathing had steadied, his tremors passed, she left him and went to where Cotton had fallen and brought back his razor and used it to cut the rope binding his ankles.

Littlefish gripped the edge of the second coffin and stared at the girl inside.

He leaned into the casket and kissed her gently on the cheek.

Her eyes opened, briefly.

From the wall came a gurgle, a sputter.

Cotton sat with his back to the bricks, blood frothing around the arrow in his chest.

Littlefish held out his hand, made a sign with the other.

Miranda shook her head. "It's done," she said.

He made the sign again, his other hand still open. Expectant.

Remembering the torn page in his picture book, the minister's throat slashed red, she put Billy Cotton's straight razor in the boy's webbed fingers. *I have done the worst of it,* she thought. *He is saved from that. Whatever happens next is his to do.*

Littlefish limped toward the dying man, one leg dragging in a manner oddly reminiscent of the preacher's. He stood over him and made a sign Miranda could not see. The lantern flame flickered in his eyes. He made the sign again.

Cotton's eyes rolled weakly in the boy's direction.

The boy held five fingers splayed above his head, his thumb touching the center of his forehead, a coxcomb shape. Veins ran like lightning through the tissue between the boy's fingers.

Father, Littlefish signed.

He knelt and closed the preacher's razor and put it in his hand, then closed the preacher's fingers around the hilt. Cotton blinked and made a brief wet sound, like water leaving a drain. He shut his eyes.

"Miranda?" The girl's voice, slurred, as she eased up in the coffin. "Do you see?" Her drugged gaze on the crypt's deep shadows. "Do you see her?"

Miranda saw nothing but darkness.

Littlefish looked, too, seemed to squint at something.

Miranda put a hand on the girl's arm. Brushed hair back from her forehead.

"Look now," the girl said.

Miranda did, and there, in the shadows, white as chalk, was the woman who had danced with the boatman by lamplight. Lena Cotton stared from behind the veil of her wedding dress, and Miranda stared back, and for an instant it seemed that hers was a series of faces both strange and familiar, those of all the women rent by the violence of this house, last among them, perhaps, Miranda's. And then there was no face at all, only shadow and root and stone.

Miranda opened her arms and took the boy and the girl into them.

And thus the long season of grief was ended.

All fathers buried, all graves filled.

FIRE AND FLOOD

Night had fallen by the time they reached the boat at the water's edge. Miranda laid the girl in the bottom, signed for Littlefish to stay with her.

Where are you going? he asked her.

"One last thing," she said. "Won't be long."

She took the fuel can and went to where John Avery's corpse lay in the grass and gathered him into her arms and carried him down the lane and across the road. She walked up the steps to the Holy Day Church and went through the open metal doors. She took Avery into the church and swept aside the Bible and the praying hands on the table. Here she placed the corpse and doused it, along with the altar. She picked up the Bible and lay it across the dwarf's chest. She took the box of matches she had brought from the mercantile out of her pocket.

She lit the Bible first, and everything else caught quickly.

By the time she reached the dock, black smoke and

flames were pouring from the low, flat roof. Miranda pushed the boat into the water and leaped in with her brother and the girl. She brought them around and started the motor.

Soon they came to Crabtree Landing.

Miranda cut the motor and watched the Landing grow closer.

She seemed to consider it, as if seeing it for the first time.

She pulled Cook's pistol out of the small of her back, where she had tucked it upon leaving the crypt. She threw it into the river.

The river carried them on past the mercantile, the floating dock.

She let it.

Is that where you lived? the boy asked from the bow.

No, she said.

They drifted on.

She started the motor again.

The rain came again in the night, hard, relentless. Thunder spooked livestock and the lightning forked to the ground and burst along the sky like scattered glass, made Nash County a kind of crucible. Upriver, the reservoir at Lake Whitman began to rise. The fissure in the earth wall everwidening, until the banks that held the structure in place slid away, and the dam collapsed.

A wall of water, thirty feet high, spilled through the bottoms.

Sabbath Dock washed away as the water came welling up the inlet and the gravel lane, flooding the manse and shotgun houses. The windowless church smoldering in the rain, the crane high upon the cross dislodged by the hot winds that had roared up from below when the fire was raging. Only the cross remained, hanging askew.

Out of the wet dark night, the bottom dwellers came. They came in boats, sodden, their eyes hollow, the men among them working tillers and paddles as the women clutched children and dogs, shivering and wet. A silent family of four in a long boat who had, on occasion, taken fish and game from Hiram Crabtree and his daughter, the youngest of them a boy in corduroy pants clutching a small rabbit-eared television.

A Shovelhead crested a hill on the county road.

The hooded giant sat astride his machine at the water's rising edge, watching the people drag themselves in exodus onto dry ground. He touched the crow's foot at his throat, then dismounted and helped a wiry boy and his mother land their boat, even held the nose of the vessel steady as the father came tromping out in soaked boots. The giant wore black jeans and a black T-shirt beneath his sweatshirt, a red rag around his head. He wore a leather scabbard on his thigh, in it the long curved bill of a hand scythe. The family froze when their light strayed to his face, grim and square and painted blood-red, black lines of the skull tattooed in his flesh giving him the appearance of a skinless ghoul. The bottom dwellers formed up together in the rain, trying not to look at him. They walked up the gravel road toward the highway. They did not look back. Later, they would tell themselves they had seen no one at all, or, if the man persisted in their dreams, let him be a kindly ghost in the story of this night, they said, some ferryman of the storm come to bear them onto dry land.

The giant took the family's boat, passing others as he followed the road, which was now a wide, fast-moving river between the trees. He navigated by the beam of a spot he had brought from his bike's saddlebag. Soon he came to the burned-out Holy Day Church, across from it the iron gates to the compound. He went through these and slowly up the lane, the boughs of the oaks above close enough now to brush with the tips of his fingers.

Shining his light, he saw the fat constable's body caught in the broken panes of the greenhouse where the water had washed him half through and snagged him in the glass. A wide crack in his skull.

He circled Sabbath House, the front doors of which stood open, water ever-climbing the wide foyer staircase. He brought the boat back to the porch and tied off to the railing and waded into the house, among the floating detritus of a meager life abandoned. In the foyer, a vulture lay upon the stairs, washed up by the storm. An arrow in its breast, the fletching a blue-gray. A smile traced his bone-white lips. "Does-it-Matter," he said quietly. He went upstairs. Searched every room. The house was empty. From the porch, he gazed out at the row of six shotgun houses in the lightning, their vacant windows, their disappearing porches. All manner of trash and debris swirling past. A chicken coop. A coffee table. A length of board that might have been the painted side of someone's barn.

The giant nosed his boat gently up to the greenhouse, where he broke the windows with his hatchet and paddled in. He drifted among the stalk-tops of the last few plants, hacking and heaping them in the boat. He drew his craft alongside the outer wall and hacked, too, the fat cop's head free of its body. He threw it in the bottom of the boat with the plants. No great satisfaction, but it would do.

He steered into the lane beneath the oaks, where he cut his motor and drifted, listening.

He heard only thunder at first, the patter of rain, the rush of water.

He thought of the woman, wondered if she had set loose all this destruction, brought down nature's wrath on this haunted place. She was strong. She was capable. It made him happy to think she had.

From overhead, he heard a single shriek, like a baby's cry.

He shot his spot into the trees and saw a great gray barred owl, its eyes dark hollows, its face a skull.

Still as death beneath his light.

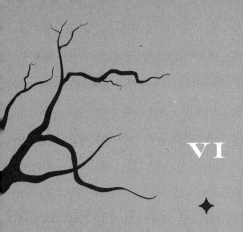

VI

◆

After the Flood

Days later, neighbors were still rescuing neighbors—men and women caught unawares who had struggled onto rooftops, families separated in the dead of night when the water came rolling in, busting windows, collapsing walls. Boats trolled among the trees, voices calling out the names of those who had been lost and were not yet found. Waterlogged bodies drifted out, some snagged in trees. Others were found in hay fields miles from the river, when the water went down. Among them, caught up on a shelf of riprap near the highway, where a bridge passed over a creek, was a man in black leather, sharp teeth like a devil's. An arrow broken in his chest.

For years, people told stories about the things they saw.

A white Bronco lodged in a house trailer like a missile.

A tractor hanging by its front axle in an oak tree.

An antique couch snagged in a deadfall.

Six buzzards perched on the spinning corpse of a mule, riding it like a raft.

Eating as they rode.

One week later, Miranda returned to Crabtree Landing. She rounded the last oxbow and saw the damage and felt a strange lightness at what she beheld. Two supports beneath the rear of the store had crumbled and the whole back half of the place, including the upper porch, had broken off into the river and washed away, along with the floating dock. The wooden stairs rose up from the struts like the spine of a skinned thing. The Landing itself a skull without a jaw. The iron ladder still stood in the river but reached nowhere. Hiram's work shed was gone, too. She banked the johnboat and climbed the embankment and went around to the front door, which the water had torn completely away. The store had flooded, and most of the shelves and what little stock was left were scattered across the floor, mired in a reeking sludge, the odd dead fish rotting in the summer heat. Miranda waded through this to the panel behind the counter, where she bent and reached up inside and took out from among the two-by-four frame a dozen plastic-wrapped packets of cash, one for every ferry to Cook since she was fourteen. No fortune, but enough. She climbed the stairs, aware of the sun on her cheeks as she did, balancing with one hand on the beadboard to her right. In the living room, she gathered her two remaining bows, her quivers, some clothes. She leafed through the pages of the slim picture album until she found the photograph at the pier off Lake Whitman, she and her mother. She took it out, then took the double-exposed photograph from Hiram's war album.

Wondering if Hiram had ever known Lena Cotton was pregnant. She pocketed both pictures and stood in her living room for the last time and looked around. No sounds came from downstairs—no crickets, no compressors. The mercantile was quiet. All the ghosts had fled.

Early fall, Iskra's island. The kudzu turning brown, dying on the vine. Miranda drove the last of the framing nails and dropped the hammer on the plywood subfloor. Down the hill, Littlefish came out of the woods, carrying a stack of two-by-fours on each shoulder. Miranda waved, but the boy had no free arms to wave back. Instead, he smiled.

The girl sat on the platform and tapped nails with swift, sure strokes into the plywood. She had put on weight and wore clothes that fit, and her skin—so pale before—had browned and freckled. Her hair grew long in thick yellow curls.

"Hey," Miranda said, when Littlefish had dropped the lumber at the lip of the hill. She signed: Lunch.

The boy nodded, and the girl signed her agreement: Hungry.

Whatever strange magic brought her, Miranda thought, *whatever nightmares she suffered elsewhere, she will grow up here a girl. She will live in the light.*

They took cheese sandwiches wrapped in foil from a cooler and sat near the graves in the shade of the black oak's branches, the sky above a warming blue. Highest on the slope, Iskra's spot: a bundle of eucalyptus branches bound with twine, fresh mint growing atop the recently turned earth. Below these, the others, all bearing some marker the boy and the girl had made of sticks and flotsam they had pulled from the river. Hiram's headstone nothing more than a single arrow driven into the dirt. Cora Crabtree's the same cedarwood marker from the Landing, bearing her name, her birth, her death. Miranda herself had dug up the grave and brought Cora's body here, to this place. The last of her old life set right.

A breeze tipped tin cans against one another in the boy's garden.

To Miranda, the sound was like the pleasant company of a new spirit. She wondered if any such magic lingered. Boards creaking in the still afternoons, laughter on a breeze that was soft and kind.

She had been inside the bathhouse once, after midnight, while the boy and girl slept on the floor of the unfinished cabin, the stars their blanket. She carried a lantern and sat on the bench. She did not light the fire or carry water. Instead, she sat and waited and listened. She heard only the boy snoring out on the pine planks. Long after she was gone, she supposed, the vine growing up the hill would cover everything here: the cabin, the boy's garden, the graves, this bathhouse. It would creep over the hill and the toolshed and climb the boy's tall tree and choke the canyon, too, and the mystery and magic of this place would be forgotten, consumed by the green, which of late had returned to its long, easy slumber, no giants in the trees, no whispers in the woods. The cicadas all expired, evidence of their passing the husks they left in bark and wall and leaf.

Forgetting, Miranda thought, *is a kind of protecting.*

The girl sat cross-legged against a length of root that curled around her, reading a comic book as she ate her sandwich.

Miranda knew that Littlefish had been pestering her to choose a name. She wondered what it would be.

The boy set his sandwich on his knee. He swept his arm to indicate the cabin, the girl, the hilltop, a fresh crop of toadflax blooming yellow where the fire had scorched. Clouds massing like great white frigates in the sky.

Beautiful, he signed.

I am not the boatman's daughter, she thought. *I am not the witch's child. I am not the leshii's slave. I am no one's but his and hers, and they are mine.*

Home, Miranda said.

ACKNOWLEDGMENTS

A number of books helped me write *The Boatman's Daughter*, among them W. F. Ryan's *The Bathhouse at Midnight*, Norbert Guterman's translation of *Russian Fairy Tales* by Aleksandr Afanas'ev, and *The Archer's Bible* by Fred Bear. Any dedicated student of Russian folklore will know that I've taken certain liberties with the term *leshii*, which is absolutely a masculine deity, but we call our gods and goddesses by the words that fit. Their true names are beyond language, beyond gender. I like to think that an old witch who's had her fill of crazy preachers conjures a certain power in "misusing" the word.

I'm forever grateful to the good people at MCD / Farrar, Straus and Giroux, who believed in the novel and helped to make it the best it could be. Thanks especially to my editor, Daphne Durham, and her assistant, Lydia Zoells. They're a crack team. To Sara Wood and Abby Kagan, for a truly beautiful book, and to Naomi Huffman, Chloe Texier-Rose, Jeff Seroy, Emily Bell, and Sean McDonald, as well as the scads of people I've yet to meet whose hard work and dedication have somehow touched this project: many, many thanks.

Of Elizabeth Copps, my agent, and the great team at Maria Carvainis, what can I say that I haven't already said? All writers should be so lucky.

ACKNOWLEDGMENTS

To the women who read early drafts of Miranda's story—Crystal, Genie, Kelly, and Dana—thank you for your wisdom, insight, and patience.

To Mom and Dad, who used to take me fishing when I was a kid, even though I mostly just sat in the car and read comic books: thank you. For so many reasons I can't even begin to list here, this book is dedicated to you, with all my love.

And finally, to Crystal, my first and best reader: every word's for you. I love you.